<u>Left in the Sand</u>

TRACY,
THANK YOU SO
MUCH + ENJOY!!
HAVE A HUNK-O-MANIA
READ FR ME

A book written by James McCusker
Front/back cover, inside images by Chris Pennestri

Edited by Kelly Eafrati and Eileen McCusker

It has been an incredible journey in exploring the many lands, skies and deep seas of love. To write about it and to fully indulge myself and others into an account that captivates, seduces, empathizes and bewails all in one emotion is awe-inspiring.

Thank you for the support, as always, to my family, friends, and those who are dear to me. A special thanks to the folks involved in this particular book. And of course to the adored, faithfully departed ones who are watching over us all. My heart is with you and this book is dedicated to your love and benevolence.

God bless.

-JCM III

Forewords

"When something precious is left in the sand...it can certainly drift to sea. But with enough time and patience, that treasure can eventually return ashore once again, tenfold its beauty."

Table of Contents

CHAPTER ONE – "Felt Like the First Time"   page 8

CHAPTER TWO – "Heatwave"   page 21

CHAPTER THREE – "A Dance to Remember"   page 38

CHAPTER FOUR – "Caviar for the Soul"   page 54

CHAPTER FIVE – "Euphoria"   page 67

CHAPTER SIX – "Gold of the Dawn, Dim of the Dusk"   page 88

CHAPTER SEVEN – "Philadelphia Nights"   page 104

CHAPTER EIGHT – "Chasing Ghosts"   page 118

CHAPTER NINE – "Catching Up"   page 128

CHAPTER TEN – "Old Friends, New Ventures"   page 138

CHAPTER ELEVEN – "Reunion of the Heart and Town"   page 148

CHAPTER TWELVE – "Ups and Downs"   page 155

CHAPTER THIRTEEN – "Resentment"   page 161

CHAPTER FOURTEEN – "Stay"   page 171

CHAPTER FIFTEEN – "Tides"   page 176

CHAPTER SIXTEEN – "Please...Just Stay"   page 186

CHAPTER SEVENTEEN – "Here Comes the Sun"   page 193

CHAPTER EIGHTEEN – "A Chance to Take"   page 211

CHAPTER NINETEEN – "Adore Me"   page 218

CHAPTER TWENTY – "My Reason to Live"   page 228

CHAPTER TWENTY-ONE – "New Year, New Tale"   page 243

CHAPTER TWENTY-TWO – "Hardening Losses"   page 249

CHAPTER TWENTY-THREE – "The Arrival"   page 257

CHAPTER TWENTY-FOUR – "Awakening Cries"   page 267

CHAPTER TWENTY-FIVE – "Junonia"   page 281

CHAPTER ONE

It felt like the first time being there when I was a kid, every time my family and I came down. Whether it was the rainbow of casino lights that lit up the city clouds or the exploding echoes of the sea crashing on the grainy sands that always put me in a state of glee, the recurring visits to AC only grew more special. This was the capstone to my entire year. Each daily beach stay, boardwalk run, and night on the old pier...it was those modest moments every summer for me, that were paradise.

Fortunately, for the majority of my early life, my grandma owned a sky-blue aluminum-shingled cottage on the beach corner of 36th Street and Ocean Avenue in Brigantine, New Jersey. It was a mere hop n' a skip away from America's Playground. She inherited the house from an old friend back when she was first married to my grandfather during the late days of Nucky Johnson's reign. It was an era where hustlers, hoodwinkers, and hoodlums ruled the shore towns of their bootlegging empires.

This notable domicile even had a tiny old basement with a narrow, manmade tunnel in the back leading towards the ocean. This was so when the "rum runners" brought in their contraband from the ships during the 1920's and 30's, they could do it in a stealth-like manner without hitting the streets. By the time I was born, the tunnel was almost completely caved in from the sand's corrosion, but it was still fascinating to see what was left. I always found it to be the coolest part of the entire house.

It was all very historic and I loved hearing its exciting tales and about old Atlantic City gangsters. We learned something new every summer…and never the same story twice. It's what made this town extraordinary to me.

Simply one floor, three bedrooms, and a closet-like bathroom, having our family of five down at this house including my grandma made it tight quarters. There was an outside shower in the back yard by the thick gasoline-smelling garage for rinsing off after those long and sandy beach trips. When all the cousins were down, we would race and battle to be the first one in, especially my sister and I. A small front lawn with hydrangeas overlooked the busiest avenue in the summer. Behind it, the sturdiest cement patio under a blue and white striped awning canopying the entrance.

Aside from the basement, the second coolest part of this place was the fact that my grandma made the attic a complete and fully-equipped bedroom once we started having all sorts of different company come down and in need of more space. I would stay up there by myself in the later days, from about eleven-years-old and on. I did a lot of thinking above those stairs. It was like a little getaway sometimes, a breakout from the madness on the first level.

I loved it all so much. The cottage was far from being a mansion but it seemed like the Kennedy estate to me at the time. You couldn't pay me to be anywhere else. After a long school year and what seemed like an eternity those 180 days in class of South Philadelphia Public, the itch to catch a piece of the action on the Jersey coast was exhilarating to the point where at times…I thought of nothing else. Summer was my ultimate escape.

Together, there was my mom, dad, older sister and myself consistently for the first sixteen years. We'd all stack into my dad's white Jeep Cherokee and make our way down the Atlantic City Expressway. It would always be that very night of the same day school lectured its final session. After packing the car to the gills with food and luggage, I was always the first one in and ready to rock without recourse. Geared up and set for the best vacation in America.

Inching down Route 42 South, traffic would barricade our voyage almost right away...but I never cared. I loved sitting in the back seat those warm nights with the windows down and June bugs whipping by outside at jumbo jet speed. I'd look jauntily at the sky and think of the good times to come. So much in store, so much ahead. We'd wait to move a few feet every five minutes and practically already smell the salt water...even if it was just all in my head.

Dad had The Police, Bruce Springsteen, The Eagles, and all the old classic rock legends' cassettes and CD's at his fingertips. He would blast their greatest songs on the radio the entire time so loud, you could still hear it on 10th and Wolf, back home. My favorite was when he would play Foreigner's "Feels Like the First Time" because coming down on this vacation, felt like simply that every year...*the first time*. No stay was ever the same as the one preceding. Those seasons in the late 80's and early 90's were grandeur.

It was all so innocent when I look back. Thinking about the next day...that inaugural session in the sand, body surfing the still-chilly ocean waves, and grabbing that sweet Kohr Brothers ice cream cone or a tasty chocolate delight at Steel's Fudge on the boardwalk.

Before those moments on day one would even begin, early arising, Grandma's initial pancake and bacon breakfast of the summer was the tastiest. She was always the first one up playing Old Franky Blue Eyes on the hi-fi, practically cooking immediately. I was next up after my parents, and of course...my sister Tina slept in as late as she could. She'd go til' high noon if the family let her.

She was five years ahead of me and a royal pain. By the time she was in high school, she grew aloof, moody and ignorant. She would miss breakfast and most of the day altogether following. I never minded though, it always meant more for me in the end. Food, good times, and all of what was in front of me. The hours in the sun and on Steel Pier always went hand in hand with a night at one of the casinos, running around while Mom and Dad gambled. Sometimes, we'd even have a trip to Ocean City, Wildwood or Cape May close by to explore different quarters.

The adventures were endless and I thought this would last forever. In my mind, this beat Disneyland, SeaWorld and Hershey Park combined. Although I never went to any of those places until I was much older anyway, at the time this was still everything I wanted...my summers at the shore. Heaven!

During the years my grandma owned this place, the first seventeen of my life, each summer seemed pristine and as if nothing went wrong.

There was never a bad day. Sure, we had the heat wave of '81, rain-out of '86, the unrest of '89 when the

Philly "racket boys" were getting in trouble with the Feds and spilling mayhem into the casinos, and that summer of '91 where my dad was sick...but somehow my family managed to show me a good time, no matter what. I never went back to school disappointed after those three months away.

It was all so wonderful until that undefeated streak broke before summer even started in 1994. One blue April night that year, a few weeks before my seventeenth birthday, we lost grandma. She passed away peacefully at 81-years-old. Needless to say, it wasn't an easy season ahead. Aside from saying a sad goodbye to her, we had a long road of work ahead of us at the shore clearing out her old stuff from the home.

She was my father's mother and he was an only child, so inevitably the property went to him. According to Dad, it was obligatory to maintain the place all year instead of renting it out. He couldn't imagine anyone else dwelling in it other than us.

However, it was going to be almost impossible to do given the fact we were miles away at a time from September to May and both of my parents were teachers.

The summer of '94 was a transitional stint. Things weren't the same. We didn't stay down all season, it was either scorching humid or pouring rain, and my sister was more a thorn in all our sides than ever. She would drive back home randomly. When she actually stayed down for longer than two days, it wasn't for the full weekend and she would complain the entire duration of her visit. Between bad break ups with boyfriends, money problems, and misdirection of life altogether, you could say she kept our ears ringing while she was here.

The worst part was that everything was weighing on my parents. It was affecting their relationship. Their endless nights of hand holding on the boardwalk and childish flirting turned into early bedtimes in separate corridors. They didn't deserve this headache. With them feeling down, it gave me a case of the blues as well.

Between the albatross of the house, my crazy sister, losing my grandmother, a topsy-turvy weather pattern, and constant nostalgic yet gloomy talk, it was the first go at this where we all collectively wished we weren't there. It was even sadder when we were happy the summer had finally ended.

Collectively, it was a depressing year, old '94. I knew that no matter what, I wasn't going to let that ever happen again. We went through a lot at that time, but I was a guy who always said "live til ya die" like Sinatra would. Things were going to change for me in Atlantic City, I guaranteed it to all. Because this town was either a make-you or break-you town, baby!!

So I stuck to my guns. I didn't want a repeat of that mess. I took matters into my own hands. The first season I came down without the family was the summer of '95, the very next year. I was now eighteen-years-old. Tina made the decision to move to Seattle permanently and my parents were set on a romantic season getaway in Whistler until

September when they'd go back to teaching. They wanted a change. The house became my complete responsibility.

Needless to say, that was the year I graduated high school and it was the start of a beautiful era. Notorious B.I.G. and Seal were flooding the Billboard charts. Die Hard with a Vengeance and Batman Forever lit up the silver screen and I remember being pumped to see both. This was all while we were all asking the same question around the country, "Did O.J. really do it?"

Other than that, I thoroughly recall caring about nothing else more than coming to the shore home after our commencement ceremony…but in a different kind of way this go around.

I drove down myself night one in my green Geo Tracker only to ear split the chart-topping tune "Big Poppa" over and over on its cassette player the entire way. I thought I was on top of the world. In the focus of altering my days spent at the shore from sandcastles and salt water taffies to short skirt grabbing and endless liquor drinking, you could say I felt like "the man" when I came into the second Vegas that June. I even picked up a job at the t-shirt shop mid-town on the boardwalk, right in the center of all the action. I was ecstatic. In my mind then, there was no stopping what the college years had ahead.

All of this occurred around the same period of time when I started having my two best buddies from back home come down to party on the weekends. We were a crew that enjoyed life and all it encompassed. Rarely did we have a bad moment. This was the time to shine.

The first of the two I will mention was one of the most feared guys in our high school. It wasn't just because of what he said or did…it was because of who he was connected to. When I say "connected", I'm referring to those "racket boys" I mentioned earlier, the "family" if you will.

He was the infamous Harry Mancini, but we called him "The Heat" because he was always hot as a pistol, on the run. Whether it was the principal at school, his family at home, or the police on the street, Heat was sprinting from some kind of trouble he started.

Harry didn't just earn this reputation over time, he inherited it. He was born into the life on the edges through a long reining tenure of wiseguys in his blood. His uncle was the reputed Georgie "The Griz" Mancini, a veteran captain in the Philadelphia Crime Family.

Our own families went way back. Not only did both of our last names begin with M, but we lived a few blocks away from each other down on 10th and Wolf Street since time immemorial. Everybody knew the comradery between the Mancinis and the Mulligans. They would ask me, "Brad, what keeps you hangin' around that Harry the Heat fella? Why are you friends with such a bad seed?" I would always reply, "He's not my friend…he's my brother," because it was true.

One of the most vital lessons I learned growing up was the importance of family and those closest to you. In a working-class Italian/Irish-Catholic upbringing, it was all that mattered. Harry was my brother and come hell or high water, I pledged that I'd do anything for him…because there was a never question if he would for me. He looked out for me like nobody else.

The only the other person with that kind of allegiance back home was Richard "Dickie" Valentine, another neighborhood guy and my second best friend. He was smooth and movin'…and always knew how to charm. You could have said he was a hybrid between my ladies' man facade and Heat's ways on the verge with the law. Taking everything into account, he was just a stellar dude.

Valentine was born in Brooklyn and spent most of his early life in different homes throughout New York and North Jersey. Once his family settled from their transient ways and ended up in South Philly, he was ten-years-old. Nobody ever knew what his family did, but they were somehow stable once we met them all.

Harry and I brought Dickie in to our circle right away at school where we all clicked almost instantaneously after a fight broke out.

I will never forget the day…it was the start of fifth grade. Harry teased Dickie in the hallway after he first saw him walking, calling him a "pussy" for wearing a giant blue Smurfs sweater. Keep in mind, he was a much fatter kid when he was younger than he was in his later years. Valentine replied quicker than we thought he would with, "that's not what your mother was saying when I had it on in her bed last night." Immediately after that first punch Heat threw at Dickie, the two ended up on the floor causing the biggest bloodshed our school halls had seen to date.

For some divine reason after the principal and teachers broke up the chaotic muddle, the two hugged it out and bonded on the spot. Harry realized at that moment, Dickie was a force to be reckoned with and took no nonsense from anyone, not even the great Heat himself. It was an admirable trait and one that went hand in hand with our manifesto on life at the time.

Valentine's voice of reason along with his appetite for destruction were his best qualities in a gainsaying way. They didn't make them like him. He was that kind of guy you could go to during any problem. There was always an answer.

Dickie, Heat, and I were together 24/7. Around town, they called us the "Three Caballeros" growing up. This was the best crew I could have had going into that summer of '95, purely because it was just the beginning at that time.

There was nothing like that first taste of the summer *squid* each season. When you're eighteen and your cock is nonstop hard as a missile, you don't miss one piece of tail that walks by the water's crest. Whether you're lounging in your beach chair or playing volleyball all the way by the dunes, your head is like a swivel. Those buns, those breasts, that hair, the waist…yum! It was all so enrapturing to us, the anatomy of a woman.

Myself especially, they even went ahead to nickname me "Braddy Big Poppa", not just because of my love for the Biggie song, but the way I got it "done" with the chicks. Nobody could touch my ways, not even my partners in crime. It was a gift that few others had in a lifetime.

I didn't have much money, especially working at a t-shirt shop and saving up for my time going into Temple University, but it didn't affect a thing. The females still adored me. All the while I cherished them tenfold, of course.

Not once did I care about nationality, age, or body structure...I truly loved all facets of real beauty. The scent of a woman, their kindhearted feel, the passion of an endless night, and the sensation of doing it all again was my ultimate pastime by all means. Each woman to me, was a mystery waiting to be solved. I was considered unique amongst the few of my strain for my versatility in the "game".

It was '95, that first year when we all realized we had the *party house* near the beach. Everybody knew us right away. The locals revered us, the shoobies cherished us, and the foreigner chicks down on their work visas worshipped us.

We knew we had to convince my parents every season to get away. It was going to be the only shot to make it ride. I negotiated...I paid them on a weekly basis to keep the place for my own and promised to take care of it while they went ahead to a different destination each time. I got Dickie and Harry jobs with me at the t-shirt shop, so we were all set.

Towards the end, the parents would show up to hang with us for a few days or so...it was good though, we always enjoyed their company for a *short* duration before they spit out the life lessons on us.

This kind of fun bled into the next four summers to come. We knew we owned the day, as well as the nights. There was no tomorrow. We took life as it came. To hit the ground runnin' and to never look back...it was the only way. Trust me when I tell you again, in the late nineties, us three made our mark on the Jersey shore.

I learned a lot those summers…and it wasn't just the curves and crannies upon every college hottie treading the beach. Although I must say, it was probably the best part…there were a few lessons in-between we all undoubtedly took heed to.

It made us more than a crew…we knew we were family going forward and would die for one another. Nothing and nobody would ever come between that. It's crazy how an old home in a seashore community can bring three wild city guys, already close as can be, even closer, summer after summer…but it did.

We never knew what to expect going into the year. Surrounded by water and sin…and in a town known for its life of gamble, flutter and chance, we enjoyed rolling the dice racing to the sand for all that it set the stage to.

Although, given as much as we left to the unknown, nothing could have been seen clearer as day than the preamble to the great summer of 1999.

A few weeks before my graduation at Temple, my parents announced to us three that the Brigantine house, which had been on the market that year, finally would be sold and was to be title-and-land-transferred at the end of the season to its new owners on Labor Day.

As much as I tried to talk them out of it prior, they were ardent on needing the money. I wanted to help them out and try to keep the place after wrapping up college early that May. However, I knew I wouldn't start my new sales job with J.R. Montague and Phillips, Inc., a software

19

company in Center City Philly until late September. Which by that time, the house would be gone.

Hearing this early on before the season, Heat, Valentine and I knew we had to do it right. This was going to be one for the books. It was going to be the finale of a hit show, the last episodes. Women galore, make money, tan like a desert dweller, drink our faces off, and take the minutes by the reins without recourse.

Whatever was going to occur, we knew we couldn't have any regrets. We couldn't end the year and say "we could have" or "we should have". This was it. School was out…no more lessons!

In the end, it changed me in many ways. To say it was like every other college summer in AC would have been a lie. It was the hottest season to date with record-breaking heat waves, but I was breezing through with cool times aplenty. It was when we all came together for that next step in our lives. I was twenty-two years old. It was when I met the world. It was the summer I first laid my eyes on the gorgeous Rachel Weston.

CHAPTER TWO

"What was she, Heat…like ninety years old?" asked Dickie that next day at our delicious breakfast atop the finest eatery on the Gardener's Basin Bay. It was right after the big '99 Fourth of July barbeque we put together outside the beach house, following an all-day n' night shindig on Brigantine's sand. I remember it as a real "banger", you know the kind of night where you *bang* your head a few times and don't realize you did til' the next day when you feel the jack hammers inside thrashing at your brain.

Furthermore, I explicitly recall being so hung over that morning, I thought grits at the renowned Gilchrist Diner would cure a bad stomach. However, it only led me to more trips running to the restroom, head in toilet. Round after round, the warm hours of that early morn were none too friendly leading into the sun's vivid peak.

I wouldn't trade a single moment of it though. It was more than obvious that the Caballeros were firing on all cylinders so far that season, only five weeks into it.

Yet this was definitely the summer of Harry chasing the grannies. He was on his race to conquer all the *cougars*. For whatever reason his keen particularity on this demographic fully suited him, God bless the young gangster-in-training…it was startling by all means at the same time, innovative. I never looked down on him for it. Braddy Big Poppa was the connoisseur of all types of women. It was always a pleasure to hear about the great victories amid the table of only the finest bros.

21

"Her pussy lips draped down like the curtains at a morgue but she rode me like a twenty-year-old cowgirl, lemme tell ya fellas," proclaimed the bold Heat, proud and grim as ever. Dickie, after spitting his Spanish omelet out all over the plate in front of him replied in laughter, "You're sick, boy…just fuckin' sick!" We were cracking up. This story was priceless.

Harry went on in that Italian accent he enhanced so well. "Skin like leather and a face, fifty-plus years of regret. You could tell she was bringing me back to a time in her life where she was swallowing more dick than Tracy, simply by the motion of her tongue and the way she gagged my balls. But once we got to fuckin', it was earthquakes and then milkshakes all over her stomach, boys…believe me when I tell you."

I cherished it. Anytime my friends got laid, I thought it was the best thing. The news was so great, it was always better than that of me hearing I was hired at my new sales job. Because when one of us got it in, it was like we all did. We were a family and this was a team effort, this journey into each night's great war. Every piece of the action was put on the table the very next day. There were no outsiders, and there was no spared words of illuminating the passion from the preceding evening.

After I threw up, round four, following Heat's tale of his time with one of the Golden Girls…I turned to old Valentine to see how he made out.

"She was stunning. Head to toe. Her tits so perky, the nipples popped out of her shirt when it was warm out on the beach. Ass so nice, you could eat it with a spoon. The moonlight shined upon her hair by the end of the night.

My eyes locked with hers…and…and…" rambled Dickie as he paused subtly while we all looked around the restaurant with the same expression of confusion.

I could tell what he wanted to explain was on the tip of his tongue but he chose to refrain. I went ahead and made it clear that his reluctance had to be nipped in the bud. "Go on?" I asked, brazenly. I couldn't wait anymore. Harry and I were on the edge of our seats, eager to hear the rest of this anecdote. The way Dickie's eyes lit up made it seem like he was with Pamela Anderson the night prior.

He retorted, "And then she threw her drink in my face." The diner grew quiet. Violent laughter then burst out so loud between us all, seconds later. It echoed so far, you could hear us from the front entrance. "STRIKE OUT!!" I couldn't help myself. Poor Dickie. "I can't wait to tell this one to Johnny Horsecock when he comes down. A legend like him will appreciate it much so," I went on.

Every night on the brink had to end and the days undoubtedly went on. While these two continued laughing, I decided to hark upon my own little relation. "Have you never met a woman who stimulates you to affection? To love and to grow. Every sense in you, every inch of your body is enamored by her beauty. You feel every breath she takes and you can almost taste every part of her being. You know that your soul has at last found its place. Your life…it begins with her, and without her it must surely end."

Digression into speaking upon great accounts was one of my strong suits. Avoiding it wasn't. However, I felt it necessary to voice the words of the heart whenever I had the chance. Especially when detailing about restless nights under the stars' gleam, speaking to it as if it were rare love.

There was nothing in this world like it. Even though the boys would rebuke me for it, I never let it stop me. I loved to elaborate. I felt like a poet sometimes.

"No," replied both my friends with that look of exhaustion. "Well she wasn't one of them but she fucked great! Pussy was like a vice grip on my cock, baby! Judges gave it a ten, a ten and another one-zero!"

Jovially, I came back in mindless rejoinder. Now, believe me this doozy was no Jennifer Love Hewitt at the time, but she certainly had the face of glamour and the body of a wonderland. The kind that would make you keel over after you fully hunger into its splendor.

"You're a writer, Big Poppa. You illustrate these women as if they're all dazzling beauties. Like they're all pieces of Picasso's great gamut. I saw what you were with, I don't know...she was okay...not a ten," the picky Dickie voiced as he smirked ever so haughtily. Heat couldn't control himself. I thought he'd fall out of his seat tittering.

Not that Valentine was wrong about my disposition, but he was merely being short sided, leaving himself the only one sincerely missing out. All women, to me, indeed had their exquisiteness. I tried to celebrate it all.

In my mind, it was what made them the magnificent creatures of God. By seeing beyond what the eyes were capable of. Not everybody could concur. I would hear things such as, "The nose of this one is too oddly shaped, that one...her hips were too wide, her arms were too flabby, the tits were too small."

But I saw these women for how they truly were...superb, radiant, spectacular, *seamless*. This was because I was never limited by my eyesight. These women would react to me the way that they did, because they sensed that I pursued the splendor that dwelled within until it overwhelmed all else. And then they could never evade their real desire, to release that beauty and encircle me in it.

"You didn't get a full glimpse of her ass, brotha. Once those pants left the scene, that thing manifested itself angelically," I told him. "Tight or was it cottage cheese?" questioned the obstinate Valentine, as if it mattered to me what this poor girl's ass texture was.

"It was big. It did the trick. Better than you made out, ya fuck!" We ended the breakfast in another session of laughter. "I'm tellin' ya this kid is an author," Harry had chimed in, pointing his fork at me. Even though I couldn't swallow one piece of my grits meal, I picked up the check and paid cash to the waitress before I left the guys for my next appointment that day.

"I'll see you two later...I gotta go chat with my pop in the city!" I walked out of the restaurant, still hung over and dizzy as hell, but feeling a little better knowing I was going to see my dad. It sucked, however, knowing I had to go all the way to Philly on the hottest day we had yet.

The old man wasn't being himself lately. The last evident memory of my grandmother was going to be gone soon. This was a very touchy thing. My dad grew up watching the shore house cultivate and become what it was at that point, which was lightyears ahead of its start sixty years prior when Grandma inherited it.

It was taking a toll on us all. My pop, my mom, me, my friends…even my sister called in from the west coast to express her concern although she never physically made it back to see the place.

The years we had there were doting to me and valued deep in my heart. Knowing all this, it felt heavy to me at times, but I knew this summer was just the accelerator to many other beginnings; my new job, life in Center City Philly at my sky-rise I'd begin renting, new people, new challenges and opportunities, new women.

Conversely, for my parents, this was everything. My father had to say goodbye to a sentimental piece of his life. I could see him inside, still teary eyed when I pulled up to the driveway back home on Wolf Street. He was sitting in his recliner by the street-facing window, looking at the funnies, awaiting my arrival.

I remember walking up sluggishly to the entrance, wishing I could've had more to offer coming through the door. I wanted to begin working immediately so I could hand him a stack of cash and say, "here you go, Dad…let's keep this thing another thirty years."

The thought even crossed my mind of going through Heat's Uncle Georgie and his crew, but I knew my parents would look down on me for it if they had found out. I didn't want to create an imposition.

"Happy Fourth of July, Big B!!" yelled my father when I came in, as he tried hiding his sorrows. He gave me a giant hug, which I always enjoyed no matter what. "Happy Fourth, pop!! You guys need an air conditioner though," I replied after feeling the sweat across his back.

"It's going to be in the hundreds just this week!! I survived through the summer of '81 by the skin of my nuts when it was hundreds almost every day!! You may not remember it. But they ain't breakin' me. I don't need one of those air device thingies!!" so proudly my father announced. I didn't even get off the stoop and into the living room before the whole neighborhood and anyone who was outside heard the old man honored to be melting away, Freon free in his brick layered townhome.

"Come on in," he greeted, adjusting his white tee shirt and taking his glasses off. He had such ceremonial grace even though I knew he was out of his element. "Dad, the place down in Brigantine is great. I have enjoyed watching over it again for yet another summer. Even though it's the last one, it's always special being there," I told him genuinely.

He couldn't help but smirk and riposte, "Yeah you and the cooz with the other two down there, eh?" We both shared a laugh because it was far from being false. He knew what the Caballeros were up to in AC, he was young once. Although, he'd be the first to admit...nobody was doing it like us. Not ever.

He went on. "Glad you are having fun, Brad. It's still so hard for me to go down and try to settle everything before the new buyers come and take over for Labor Day. I just can't bring myself to do it." He sat back down in his chair and looked out the window and at the kids playing on the street some more.

"Let me just say though...it's nice to be here," I countered, trying to make nice of the situation. My dad

27

would come back to say it was a pleasure having me and that I was allowed back any time, any day.

That's how it was with my family...I could be gone a thousand years and come back the following day, feeling like I was just there yesterday.

It was all so wonderful until my mom would come out and start talking crazy. "You mean you came up here and didn't bring a new girlfriend? Aren't you meeting new people all the time? What's the matter with you?" she'd investigate after kissing me hello.

"Let's not start, Mom!" I couldn't take it. She'd bring a nice time and turn it onto me. Questions, questions...but do you think I had the answers? This was a point in my life where I was having too much fun. I wasn't worried about settling down. For what reason?

"I'll tell you what, B. It's a fulfilling thing when you have the woman of your dreams appear right in front of your eyes," my dad chimed in. "Mom get to you too with this talk?" I asked, looking for a few chuckles. It wasn't working. They didn't get me. They didn't understand the magic that was going on down there, as much as I would try to illuminate them at times.

Both of my parents then went on into a chronicle for about five minutes on life and what true happiness really means. How it wasn't the quantity of partners, it was the quality. How every moment they had together was beautiful. How when they met, their only wish was that they had come across each other's path sooner.

"You're gonna have someone sweep you off your feet. You're not gonna know what hit ya, Brad...I'm telling you. You have the world to offer and someone specific and special to offer it to. I'm not saying it as your father, I'm saying it because it's true."

Okay…so I will tell you…I would think about those things *maybe* once in a while. However, I was having too much fun to care. Why worry about something that I'd merely leave to serendipity and a little effort later on?

I made a few more days out of my stay with the family back home considering they weren't coming down to the shore place like they used to. With the ostensible melancholy my father was having, my mother was busy trying to get ready for retirement.

I was excited to hear she was finally able to get out at the right time and was going to be able to enjoy life after working.

However, she seemed somber about the entire process after we shifted the discussion away from me. I wasn't sure if it was my dad's gloom, a collective grief about the shore house or the fact that she'd be leaving something so familiar…but it was starting to get contagious.

That is why by the end of my stay, I was ready to head back to the beach to keep the good times rolling. The clock was ticking and summer was getting hotter.

There was one other place in the world I considered an escape from reality besides the beach. It didn't give me the flavor of the ocean spray, but it gave the true taste of burning sweat, opulence and splendor. It was the local gym in little old Brig. They named it the Brigantine Fitness

Center but we called it "the B", "BFC" or most of the time: "glory" essentially because of the many champions it lodged over decades.

All the great *fitness gods*, *meat heads*, and *masters of the iron* would vastly convene at the B but it certainly wasn't limited to just the best. It was a place where the area of Greater Atlantic City and its intelligentsia would come to discuss literature, philosophy, music and other topics of merit...a place where wit and wisdom would bloom while sharpening one's mind, body, and soul. Many were welcome but few would go the distance and truly capture the crux of its daily revel.

Dickie V and I stuck to harking on personal weight press records, sports and pussy while we worked on perfecting the dream...but we were among the few of our strain. We came to set the tone, keep the pace and begin the days with nothing but the finest.

I met him there the day I came back to the shore after seeing the family to work on chest...or as we called them, "boom booms".

"Hey Brad...Uncle Georgie is down, he's seeing Harry at the house now...wants to say hi to you when we're done our workout," said Dickie as he piled two forty-five pound metal weights on one side of the bench while I racked the other.

"I will be there," I retorted. Now, this George Mancini was no wiseguy to be taken lightly. He was three away in the line to become boss of Philadelphia, and he could have gotten there already by this time with just the flick of a glock trigger if he wanted it.

They called him Georgie the Griz because when he came at you, he was like grizzly bear in the wild, tearing apart its prey limb from limb. When he hit, it hurt. He also had a distinguishing long beard most of the time, like Grizzly Adams did...yet groomed to perfection instead of disheveled.

Already being one of the most feared gangsters in the area since the Mafia crackdown of 1989, he was the last of the true golden era that ruled Philly and AC for the longest time during its heyday of its flourishing early casino empire.

Georgie only did a year for contempt in '89, but once he got out...he was kickin' ass and callin' names. He was an excellent guy to have on your side. He was everywhere, knew everybody and what they were doing...and he was Harry's father's brother.

Once I finished my set on the bench press, I leaned to my old friend for some advice. "Dickie, this summer is flying. Before we know it...it's gonna be your birthday, Labor Day weekend, and the house will be gone. We need to enjoy every moment for what it's worth and remember the good times," I was detailing.

Life was just too short not to savor the memories. There were plenty coming, I was just having a *moment* of my own that day. A different kind than usual.

"Isn't that what we've been doin, B? It seems like we don't let a minute slip," he replied with a bit of confusion, smiling before he put himself down on the bench to rep out.

I suppose he was right. For there wasn't a night where we didn't give it everything that we had. This was our Olympic year of partying. Which during all this time, it made me truly think what was next. How was it *actually* going to be after Labor Day? What about when the fiesta was truly over? Within all these new beginnings, what was justly going to be the next step once I'd be in Center City and selling for J.R. Montague? Was it really going to be as fun as I pictured it in my head? Would it continue to be so magnificent?

"You ever think there is more to life than booze and babes? I don't know...just thinking out loud," I rambled. Valentine got off the bench and couldn't help but chuckle. He took a sip from his water bottle and wiped the sweat off his head with a towel and looked at me with a blank stare. "Braddy Biggs...coming from you? You for real? The *guy* behind the *guy*? The man with the plan?" he asked me, shaking his head.

I was shocked myself. It was always 'live til ya die' with me. Yet, after that talk with my parents the week prior in Philly, I started thinking hard otherwise. Maybe for the first time in a long time.

I was hoping this feeling would simply pass. The analyses just kept rushing through my brain like a dam broken and the waters flowing, pounding down the river.

"There is nobody other than God who knows what the future holds, my friend," Dickie told me while I came over to lay on the bench. I kept talking as I worked out.

"It's just that I'm having the fuckin' time of my life ya know? More women than we can count, hotter days than being with Satan himself in hell, endless nights on the beach and fabulous mornings to follow. I just don't know what to do when it's all over. Center City and sales life is great…it's just, I worry this summer is the *coup de grace* know what I mean?" continued my inquisitorial self.

Perhaps I was off, perhaps I was just looking too much into things. I just remember specifically questioning it all for a brief stint.

"Like we've talked about before…it all works out, my friend. When hasn't it for us?" Dickie made some good points. This was such an obscure frame of mind for me considering I was historically someone who embraced life; one who wanted to be on a long journey with no particular plan or destination in mind. An adventurous man, open to the concept of living life in the minute you were in.

Everything came full circle. He was right. In our minds, it would always work out for the better, no matter what the conclusion would be. In the meantime, there was no other option than to indulge in the gaiety we were emanating so masterfully. I had to shake this minute of muddle somehow.

After getting done at the B, we arrived back to the *Seduction Lounge*. We had come to the realization that this was its appropriate marquee identity for reasons that were purely obvious to anyone who understood the magnificence of what the house was worth.

Soaked with sweat and sore around each muscle tissue, Valentine and I took our time exiting my old green Tracker to join the fun a few feet away. We knew we had a long night ahead of us, working at the t-shirt shop. It was time to make big money.

It was evident the glow scorching from the house at that moment. There he sat on our front porch. The boss, the man, the chief…Uncle Georgie. He was having some big words about the future of the family business with his only nephew, his potential heir to the throne. It looked important, these discussions…but it halted us none.

Now, Griz wasn't a burly bulging man like his name would imply but he sure made his presence known, wherever he was. You could see him from far afield in any crowd or setting. His sleek custom suits, black hair, handsome beard and sneaky smile…it was all so deadly to be in front of…like a sexy, Italian version of Chuck Norris. He was a guy who you *knew* could have you killed if he wanted.

Reputed for having over a hundred notches on his gun, both in the bed and on the street, Georgie's barrels only stayed the hottest. This wasn't a walyo you crossed. Like he had always said, "Stay the course with me, kid. If not, you might just fall into a ditch and probably die," and then wink at you.

But, I gave him a lot of admiration. He was a huge hand in getting me the job I was beginning that September. His connections were immense. I always valued his benevolence to my family. Often, we went to him when we needed him back in the day. Sometimes…I wished he was my uncle.

He always knew what I loved too. The Greatest Hits of Frank Sinatra CD playing on the porch, a De Nobili cigar prepped and ready along with a glass of 7-n-7 made to perfection. I could hear the two talking before Dickie and I approached the porch stairs.

"Gotta make it count, Heat. Especially with this job we're working on at the end of summer. Y2K kinda shit, know what I'm tellin' ya? This is your time to move up. You're gonna take this fuckin' family into the 21st century, boy."

Now, I knew the life that Georgie lived and the way Harry dipped into it. He was grooming him to take the reins and one day, to ascend up the throne. It was his mission. I never asked questions though.

"Boys, have a drink…a salu!!" the dapper Georgie announced to us all while going over to the ice and mixer. "Even after a workout?" I jokingly countered once I got close to where he was standing.

"Hey, don't be a fuckin' smart ass over here huh?" he said and smiled as he came to give me a hug and kiss on the cheek, a tradition in the old country. Dickie came over for the same.

"Sit down, sit down," he instructed. Georgie loved entertaining and making a show of the fact that he was down at the shore home with us. He had to though. A guy in his position was on the rise. He wanted everyone to know it so that when he was a boss one day, there wasn't anyone who was uncertain of his caliber.

"How's the tail been down here? Is it still out of control every fuckin' night or what? I saw three walk by since I've been here. Eyy." As he asked this, I responded with the words I favored often…'too good to be true, my friend.'

Things got serious once he handed me my drink. "Looking for you to pull through big in September. We got a lot of money going into that company, and we need the

35

potential buyers to buy up the product. It's gonna be a fuckin' nationwide thing, you heard me? This ain't no t-shirt shop operation."

"I know, I know," I told him. He went on, "This is gonna be the time, Braddy. Don't fuck it up. Start thinkin' big. Even now, eh." A lot of pressure coming down from The Griz, as it did often when I would see him. But, he was right. The company was on the rise and I had to make it count once I was there. Simply two months away from day one, I thought about it often. I didn't want to let anyone down and sought to excel in all they had to offer, especially for Georgie's sake. To be a star, you had to burn to shine.

"Out of the day's shadows and into the night I go," he concluded, winking at us all before he put his signature bowler hat. He then walked down the porch elegantly and slowly trotted down to his shiny black Cadillac de Ville that parked so gracefully in our driveway.

We watched Uncle Georgie steer away as we began talking more on the party we were having that night. Back at it again, yes. But why complain? Why question things? Why during an era like this?

It was an age that was going to go down as the *endless summer*. We were "closing so much ass", as we'd say, it wasn't even fair. Women were all over the place. The drinking, dancing, partying into the miniscule hours of dawn…it was almost like clockwork. It became routine. We were savages of the night.

At one point during these adventures, we imagined the moments would never end. Yet, deep down we realized this was the last season of its kind. But again, it was one that was unbeaten. Especially towards the end. The sun was sizzling but the nights were definitely cool. Those final weeks were most notable, the swan songs of '99.

You know, there are those events that truly exist outside of reality. It's almost as if they stand out like a dandelion in a dead patch of grass. It becomes more and more difficult to decipher one day from the next as time accelerates its gears, but here and there things pop out and make it easy to remember the finer moments. The way the sky looked, the way the moon dimmed, the reviving feeling of the crisp and chilly air…it helps enlighten us to a sheer minute all too familiar.

Life is funny that way. Ask me what I did last Wednesday and I'd have to check my notes and cross-reference all of my calendars. But ask me where I was on August 28th, 1999 and I can explain it as if it happened just seconds ago.

CHAPTER THREE

As the weeks progressed that season, we realized that Dickie's big birthday bash was coming up quicker than we all imagined. We had been longing for it the entire summer and it was now finally days away from happening. The numbered nights were winding down and the ultimate celebrations were upon us.

I mean, the kid was turning twenty-two years old and had a horrible twenty-first the year prior. So, as you could already guess, we were looking to go big. He had to make up for lost time.

The problem with last season was that Dickie started dating this broad early in the summer. It was the saddest thing ever. Rookie mistake number one: you don't get tied down after the Ides of March. Then to make matters worse, he let this girl change everything about what he had going on; his summer job at the shirt store, the way he acted and dressed...and most importantly, the time he spent with his best of friends. Not that we were the greatest of influences for a man in a relationship, but it was upsetting to see such a stallion like Valentine get sucked into this sorceress' ways.

She was cut from the cloth of the devil herself. Sexy as can be on the outside with her five-foot-five stature, caramel skin and brown eyed complexion...yet she was more than deceiving. A Sicilian and Puerto Rican mix, this venomous dame ruled with the iron pussy she held over the poor guy. She had our buddy drooling throughout the weeks, pending for her affection. So terrible.

Not only was he home by midnight on his 21st, but he was so far from being three sheets to the wind after we left the Beach Bar at Bally's, he drove back himself with his lady, sober as a judge. We were embarrassed on his behalf. Thankfully this romance had ended in those winter months that followed.

Fast forward to 1999. It was August 26th. Saturday the 28th was the big night. It was so darn close, we could taste it.

"I don't want to make it to Labor Day, boys. Valentine, I need your motherfuckin' birthday to be so historic that they bury me just to keep me from tearing this city down twice, baby," Heat assured, as the three of us were leaving a splendid workout at the B that day.

Dickie was cementing the fact that he was on board as he threw his gym bag in the back seat. "No vagina will get in my way this year, homies," he affirmed. I basked in the grin he put on my face as we jumped into my Tracker and let the radio spill the new Sugar Ray tune outside the speakers of my car.

Summer's wind blowing in nice and it felt even better with the top off of my car as we drove back to the Seduction Lounge. The sun was just setting. That ailing feeling I had back in July had since disappeared. Quickly, I learned what made me happy at the time…the lust of the night. I was getting more women in my bed in a week than some saw in a summer, maybe even two. It was insane.

"I want to find a chick so crazy and so delicious, I feel and taste her for weeks to come after this house goes."

I made it clear I was looking for something spectacular that weekend.

"Should've had what I broke apart last night. This fuckin' girl was suckin' my dick from the back and let me shoot it in her hair. Never had anything like it, "detailed Harry.

"That Australian broad I had last weekend had me *down under* like no other. I didn't mind one bit the way she was panting and groaning all night. She hadn't been that excited since her first pet kangaroo," Dickie chimed in.

Nonetheless, while we were on the topic of crazy, there awaiting our arrival at the Seduction Lounge was a babe so wild, she was already half naked standing at our porch. She was chewing bubble gum, coiling her hair and looking up at the sky while the birds flew around, chirping in their kernel.

Everyone in town had fucked her at that point, but it was never a piece you turned down…because it was always that good. A sultry little thing, 5'2 in height with a 32-25-32 frame. Blonde hair as white as the fire she spit and a tan as golden as her sexual talents.

We didn't know her real name but around our parts, she went by *Gemini*. This was mainly because you never knew what you were going to get. There was the ecstatic nutty side and then there was the somber needy side. Either way, she was our wacky neighbor who would linger around for days and then disappear for weeks at various and random times.

"Haven't seen you since the Lifeguard Run there, dolly. Where you been?" I yelled to this bantam flame as I pulled into my driveway. She had a bright red and yellow bikini on and began walking down our steps slowly, playing with her hair some more, twirling it in an erotic fashion.

"Lookin' good, Gemini. Why haven't we seen your pretty self around these ways lately?" asked Harry, taking his shirt off on purpose to show off his pecs and pipes that he had just perfected at the B.

She snickered as she looked down and up, going, "Nobody has fucked me hard in awhile. Since I went through all three of you, I was hoping to see some new talent."

"Whoa," and "ohhhh," we all shrieked after gasping at such prod. The derides from this pretty young thing were none too pleasant. The nerve she had to say such words...bold, however we figured it was all in good fun. I made it a point to give a hard jab back to Gemini, "New talent? You've already been through most of the tristate there, hunnie baby. I couldn't tell you what is left." Everyone started laughing as she kept her mouth wide open in shudder.

"That's okay, Johnny Horsecock is stopping by a little later. Maybe you want to wait and get a piece of the legend," went Harry, chiming in like he always did. "Oh, please. I had him pound me away years ago," the candid Gemini carried on. She was like one of the guys. We knew she was too slutty to date but certainly never too nice not to fuck over and over. There was always good times to be had with her.

"Aren't you simply the sweetest?" Dickie asked. "As a matter of fact, I was the first to have you. You were

41

so innocent when we met you as well. Funny how such a good girl can be so bad after all this time, ya know?"

Throughout all the ball-busting and stone-throwing at one another, the streets ricocheted with the sounds a hundred purring wolverines, breaking their quiet from afar ever so suddenly. There, in the same '76 Mustang he donned back in his prime, sat our master and commander of the night rolling up to our street in such fashion and elegance, the man, the lore...Johnny Horsecock.

Old school player and historically our mentor every summer, Horsecock was bound to make at least one appearance during the year...we just never knew when. He'd pop up out of nowhere like a bad STD after a good night. Thankfully, he was here for the grand finale.

He was barely fifty-years-old, but believe me when I tell you he felt younger than ever. His attire consisted of a white Kangol fugora on his head, a beige collared button-down with short sleeves made of silk, khakis and some fresh Reebok sandals proving to us all he was ready to party at any moment.

"I may be dressed for the LL Cool J concert, but it's a little more conservative than sweet Gemini here," he said as he approached the group at the porch. We were always so happy to see Johnny. He was a legend. Never a bad night with him. He was like our Sensei.

Gemini seductively strode over to the great Horsecock only to softly reply, "Maybe if you're lucky, I will have zero conservativeness later," as she winked at him walking away. Trouble was her middle name for sure.

"What the fuck is later? I came down here to play bingo tonight," sarcastically Johnny responded. He knew what the night entailed already even amid being coy. He just wanted to surprise us for sure.

Gemini then gave us all a kiss on the cheek, telling us that she was going to go get some more sun rays in on the beach before she got ready to join us for the big night,

"Dickie's twenty-second, Johnny…this is a huge one. We need to remind him that no bitch…no fuckin' piece of pussy is ever going to tell him to go early on a birthday night again unless we are dragging his ass out of the place ready to shove his cock in her for him!!" I proclaimed. We were on a mission for sure.

Johnny nodded and agreed it was going to be a good night. All of a sudden, he grew quiet. Dickie, Harry, and I couldn't help but wonder why he was wearing a moose on his face as he sat down on our porch. "What ails you?" I asked.

"I met somebody," he told us. It was is if the whole neighborhood grew quiet. Johnny Horsecock settling down was like Armageddon. It was truly the sign that this was the last summer of its kind. Nobody would believe it. They'd rather believe Santa was real.

This was a guy who had so many babes some summers, he had to sub-contract them out. Folklore has it, he had close to a thousand shots on his pistol of different dames, near and far. Women adored him not just for his massive shaft, but the way he used it.

Remind you, this was a guy who every summer we saw him was short in his stays. So imagine his stamina in a one-week stretch. Nobody ever like him.

"Could be the real deal I think," Horsecock continued. I was in shock. I asked him to elaborate more on who this goddess could have been to handicap such an all-star.

"That's not the important part. Nor is anything else except when I tell you...it happens to us all." I didn't like what he was alluding to, nor did the other two. However, we decided to pay regard to the life lesson he was about to give.

"You don't get tired of the random pussy...the pussy just tires you, boys. That's all I can say. You get to a point where you want a little more than just the crazy and various cooz."

This was self-evident of course, but it wasn't something any of us wanted to believe. It was bound to happen in life where we'd all take the next step and find that piece of yourself that completed you, there was just no telling when. Johnny was always the symbol in our faith that one could play on forever. Yet now, the story was different.

"Well it doesn't mean we can't have fun tonight, am I right Horsie?" Harry asked, patting him on the back. He reminded us all, "This is Dickie's weekend. Why do you think I came? To start things early. One final battle on the frontier before the cease of all fire!!!"

Our spirits rejuvenated. Now, we were ready. "HOORAY!" we collectively yelled as I went to get the Tequila bottle from inside and pour shots to start the weekend early. "Hey, maybe you'll even bag Gemini...ya know, for old time's sake," Dickie enlightened.

"What are you, fuckin' kiddin' me? If I wanted a willing dose of AIDS, I would just go over and suck on Braddy Big Poppa's cock!" he yelled, bursting into laughter as we all joined him. He was a firecracker, let me tell you…always breaking stones.

As the clock was ticking, we knew the great Johnny was going to show us all he had, all he was worth, and some of the greatest things about the Jersey shore and its women.

So, we assembled the crew early in the day Saturday the 28th to get ready for the evening's pending shenanigans. Harry, Johnny, Gemini, a few of her feisty n' foxy houseguests, and myself all triumphing convivially together to bring in the *double-two* for our one and only Valentine.

I was already feeling exhausted considering we had been drinking since Thursday night. But I knew it was necessary. Summer was ending and Dickie was going for the gold. I was planning to be there with him to make it to midnight, of course.

The Beach Bar was packed before the sun even thought of setting once we arrived. Atlantic City's nightscape vibrated all over the island from this party beating on the sand. Only in its second season of operation, Beach Bar had it going on for sure…the hottest spot to be at.

The long await of an entrance had security standing firm at the ropes, waiting for someone to get out of line. Dickie almost was a victim. He was stumbling in, swinging from one side to the next in the drunkest way he'd been out of the three days. Harry and Johnny held him up to keep him standing. As for the folks in this crowded area waiting with us, they gave thumbs up and pats on the back. "Successful birthday."

As we stepped past security and into the scene, I noticed the music playing in the background. The tunes sounded like that of my true youth; Def Leppard, Foreigner, Guns and Roses, AC/DC. It was amazing. I felt alive. I felt free.

The man-made wood-built ground that covered the massive area holding the bar, dancefloor and lounge chairs set the perfect festivity nature under the freshly given moon glow. It was finally completely dark.

I went over to order another round of drinks for the gang, even though Dickie didn't need much more. "Hey bro," Harry said, coming over to put his arm around my back. "How's it going? Are you likin' the night?"

I nodded. "You fuckin' know it. Glad to see Dickie do it right this year, ya know." Heat slapped me on the back. "He's something else lemme tell ya." He chuckled. "There's a nice crew of three that just walked in. Doesn't look like they're with any guys. Could be the targets for the night."

I shoved another Tequila shot in front of Heat's face as he continued talking. "Let us pace ourselves. Do you know how many fuckin' women come here a night?" We glanced around together at the myriad of babes that flooded the bar. There were so many.

"Just come take a look at these three. Give a quick gander, it can't hurt," he said. I smiled, took my cocktail, and started to drink. "The bartender is going to give you a tray to carry all these drinks over the crew. I gotta go to the bathroom. I will see you in a little while," I instructed.

I walked away to take a lap around the place, alone. There was beer pong, minor strip teases, dancing, and whatever else the crowd decided to do. There wasn't a piece of it I wanted to miss at all. This place was amazing by all means.

Bumping into Johnny, I saw him with his arm around Gemini coming out of the women's room while I left the men's. She was wiping her mouth. He smiled at me, walked up and gave me a high five. "FINAL FRONTIER, BRADDY!!" yelled the old man, zippering up his pants.

I loved it. We then put our arms around each other, walking around and leaving Gemini in the dust. "Fuckin' legend over here!!" I was telling people. "How was she?" I then asked him. "Better than when I had her in '96 but probably not as good as your run with her in '97," he told me. Always had me laughing. Reminiscing on our wild adventures with Gemini together was always amusing in a mischievous kind of way.

No one could have seen the dance floor. It was lit up, body to body while Horsecock and I were circling around it talking to every girl that we saw. Every beauty, and every not so pretty one. We were going off the cuff with a tale that he was my dad and we were down from Canada.

We even got away with telling a few we were brothers. It was all in good fun. They were eating it all up, kept getting us drinks and entertained our harsh anecdotes aplenty.

We got back over to the bar around 11:45 where Johnny began to sink into the seat he planted in. After eye-crawling the stools, looking for more women to meet, I reminded him it was almost midnight and we had to go and find Dickie to congratulate him for making it. Apparently this side had more underage girls getting sloshed than any other. Knowing sober wasn't his ally, Johnny spotted one down the way.

From her corner he watched, his neck goosing from side to side, his Adam's apple bobbing in his throat as he swallowed excessive spittle. He had to time it just right. She had to be drunk first.

She was a small red-head in a tight dress, not particularly developed but definitely female. Her older friend headed to the ladies room and the horse made his move, attempting to look casual. Johnny bumped right into her and then apologized, using his hands to wipe her front and offering to take her outside to help clean up.

His research suggested that a meeting that surprised the other person was more powerful than something subtle. This was his *last ride on the frontier* before he settled down, as he said. He had to make it count. I loved it for sure. But either way, I was set on looking for Dickie.

After twenty minutes of searching high and low, I finally spotted the sneaky Dickie and fast Harry talking with three pretty girls in-between the entrance and where the dance floor began.

I knew they were up to no good since I hadn't seen them in awhile. Per what Harry told me, I was certain they had some game biting the bait. Yet, I couldn't blame him. They were extremely gorgeous...but one in particular, I couldn't stop staring at. Brown hair, hazel eyes, tan skin...perfectly rounded shape, curvaceous. It was in those first thirty seconds, a picture I would forever and ever remember. I could not even move, the more I took a gander. I was in true reverence at what stood before me. She was a gasp of fresh air, a new kind of face you didn't see. So sweet, so young...so true.

"Rachel Weston," she introduced in the most beautiful southern accent I had ever heard. I don't remember uttering my name back so quickly because my loss of words were killing me. "This is my sister Lauren and my best friend Amanda. We are staying with my family this week at a cottage in the area."

I could see the other two girls were quite antiquated with Harry and Dickie, who at the time, I wasn't sure how they were still awake.

I inquired, "Where are you from?" She countered, "Mountain Park, Georgia. The sixth smallest town in the state. What about you?" As always, I boldly retorted in a proud tone, my hometown. "South Philly."

She smiled and nodded as we both looked around for a few seconds. I kept hesitating. This was not me at all. I didn't know what was going on. I was so nervous. It was then she began walking away towards the bar, all alone. All of a sudden, one of my all-time favorites by Foreigner was playing from the DJ speakers, "Feels Like the First Time".

"Where are you going?" I asked before I could stop myself. Her head cocked to the side, her eyes shifting from the ground to me. My heart stopped and I could barely breathe. All I could manage was a "Just wondering." What was wrong with me? I was never this nervous.

Before my heart completely stopped. "I'm guessing you need a dance partner?" Her voice was soft-spoken and mellow, sending a warm glow throughout my body. "How do you know?" "I saw your face."

She motioned me towards the dance floor and puts out her hands. "What's your name again?" she asked when we were on the dancefloor. "Brad." "Cute name." I smiled shyly once she said this.

"Not as cute as Rachel," I responded. Her big hazel eyes widened and a smile so bright emerged as she poked her head at mine. She looked like Mila Kunis, but hotter and much more beautifully built.

We circled each other, our gaze remained locked. Rachel placed her hand on my shoulder, my hand on her back, and our free hands finally met. Together, we danced to the music, our feet in perfect tick to the beating of my heart. The rhythm was telling me to escape in her.

Feels like the first time...
Feels like the very first time...
It feels like the firrrrsst time...
Feels like the very first time...

As the song progressed I felt relaxed, and allowed a small smile to form on my lips. She was perfect. She smelled fantastic, much like a spring rain. Her blue and white Abercrombie tank top matched my white button-up. Those tight dark blue cowgirl jeans, my finger kept getting a brush of as my hands remained adoring her smooth waist, tan and irresistible. One thing was for sure... I was one lucky guy to receive a partner like her on the dancefloor that night.

She turned gracefully, her body in tune with the music. Yet, there was a sort of arrogance to her, like she was someone who shouldn't be underestimated. She was not going to be another easy shoobie. I didn't quite care at the moment. Was it because I was falling for a girl I hardly knew? The warmth between us grew more powerful by the second. My heartbeat was growing steadily along with it. Our dance was flawless; everything from our breathing to how our feet moved stayed in sync. If, by the end of this dance my life was taken away, I would know the exact reason why.

Rachel guided me across the dance floor as if we were in a dream. She kept her eyes on me, yet still, she knew exactly where to take me. Every moment, every angle seemed to be planned in advanced. Nothing felt forced; I literally thought I was floating.

"Rachel," I whispered, "everyone is looking at us." She squeezed my hand slightly and smiled right as the song was ending. "Really," she chuckled softly and ruffling her nose, "I haven't noticed."

With that, I knew. She needed to say no more. My heart, my whole being was now hers and hers alone, even if just for the rest of the song. I allowed her to take me anywhere she pleased on the dance floor. She went right, I went right. She sped up, I sped up. We became one with the song, with the dance and with each other. We continue like that until we had to separate, though I was sad to be away from her warmth. "I'll let you go back to your friends there now," she said to me.

When the song ended the bar audiences' applause filled our ears. I couldn't help but beam. In that very minute I wondered why I waited to meet her, why I hesitated when Harry told me to come over and say hello to such a jewel.

"Believe me. We are past midnight and I fulfilled my friend Dickie's mission. The birthday boy has had three days of making up for missing out on much of last summer," I admitted, transparently. Amanda and Lauren were saying their goodbyes to Dickie and Harry during this time.

Continuing her laughter, she went on, "That's so sweet of you. Well we ought to go now. This is only our first night. We want to save our energy for the rest of the week. It was really nice meeting you, Brad...thanks for the dance."

I didn't want her to leave at all. "Let me buy you a drink!" I said. She shook her head no and implied again that they had to leave. Watching her walk away slowly after such a subtle handshake was killing me.

"Well, do you have a phone number at the place you're staying at? I would love to call you during the week," I went on. She turned back around, flipping her hair at me with a smile responding, "I don't know the number there."

I panicked as her and the girls continued walking. I didn't know what to do. "Well...well...well...when can I see you again?" I asked, hesitating to get every other word out. "Can you tell me where to meet some day this week?" I went on.

She kept laughing as her friends beside her were giggling much the same. I couldn't help but keep trying. Her leaving was piercing my heart.

"Maybe. We'll see. If you're lucky," she concluded, smirking, winking at me and then walking away. I stood there with my mouth wide open. Sassy little thing. I couldn't believe it. I wanted to end my night as well, right then and there. I was done.

CHAPTER FOUR

That Rachel. Boy, I just loved repeating her name over and over. She had awoken something deep inside my soul. Every moment, every breath...I felt it more. I couldn't focus on much else that next day. I had to see her again! There had to be a way...Atlantic City and its surrounding parts weren't *that* big.

The boys and I were enjoying a long walk back to the Seduction Lounge from Wawa after a "coffee run" that next day close to noon, still curious on how Dickie was able to function given he was falling down like a ton of bricks not even eight hours prior.

Harry even went ahead to say, "Leaning tower of Dickie over here all night...even still as he sways." Valentine was a mute with his big black shades on. He just shook his head sideways and went about his means on the walk with us. Mission complete.

However I had a bigger mission at hand now, an incredible one. I had to find this girl again. I wasn't going to let anything stop me in my search.

"How do you think you're even gonna go about trying to find her, Brad? The next piece of pussy you see you're gonna fall right for. You do this with all of them, ya know," said Harry as we all finally made it to the front porch. He sure thought he knew everything.

I reminded him vividly, "This one is different, Heat. I could sense it...purely in that one dance. I could sense it. I don't know...it just felt right. Usually I can't wait to see them walk away so I can start hitting on others. For the first time with a broad, it was like I got upset when she left."

We all sat and watched the early morning mist begin to clear, dew laden grass and cobwebs, the sky's casting of orange and pink onto a thin layer of cloud, birds singing, and animals stirring. There were many people walking Ocean Avenue already, heading towards the beach for the day.

"I just hope we run into them again...I don't know. It would be nice," I was telling them. "What the fuck, Brad? You gonna just do a little spell and a little hocus pocus and have them pop up on the yard here?" asked Dickie, still in his drunken state. Harry was laughing at my vertigo from this particular woman.

However, just as we thought Dickie was going to puke off the railing again, something incredible happened. To what my wandering eyes would appear...the *same three girls from the night prior* were right across our street!! Just like that! They were walking down the avenue together, multicolored bikinis and sun hats. They would have stopped any man in his tracks to take a peek. God must've been hearing me pray.

I didn't believe it at first but I recognized each one in their movements. "What are the odds?" I yelled from the porch. I could see them a bit confused at first, looking over to remember who we were. After a few glances, they came scurrying over to the house, smiling and all. They were stunned as well. "Oh my goodness, you're staying here in Brigantine too?" I heard one of them ask from afar. Those southern accents were so charming.

Oh, Rachel. So beautiful, so elegant. She took center stage of the three. She walked like someone who'd been in some armed service or other, there was a marching quality to it. Very dignified and real sexy all at the same time. Couldn't get enough of it. What a coincidence they were right on our street as we pulled up to the crib. I was flabbergasted.

Amanda was undoubtedly not as smart as she was sensual. Even though she was still smashed, she was walking unusually slowly...almost robotically, as if her brain was struggling to tell each foot to take the next step. It was as if she were in a stupor; like someone under hypnosis in one of those Scooby-Doo cartoons. "Hung overrrrrrr," she was slowly whispering to us all after every question or statement. I could tell Dickie liked it though. For some reason, this girl was making him wear the "twinkly eyes". It fully woke him from his unpretentious condition.

Rachel's sister, Lauren...certainly the lesser of the two sisters there. Thicker in frame and shoddier in face, she was what some of a lower mind would call an *ugly duckling*. I, however, respectfully went ahead to label her *second place*.

There she stood with a resting moody face on her. She had a way of walking that made her seem continuously in a hurry. Her steps weren't long but they were hasty. Like a speed-walker without that odd twisting motion they make. I thought she was rather weird. Still a nice girl though.

While these two went to chat with Dickie and Harry the Heat by the porch, Rachel pointed at me with her index finger then waving it towards her, signaling for me to come in her direction. Like a little puppy, I came trotting over to sidewalk where she stood.

"I was hoping to see you again, Ms. North Carolina," I told her. She scolded me in replying, "Mountain Park, Georgia, boy…get it right. How are you today? How are you feeling?" with that southern attitude.

"A lot better than Dickie, I will tell you that." I chuckled as I looked over quickly to my buddies chatting with hers. They were getting along really well. "And yourself?"

"Feeling like a million bucks," she assured. "Ready to see more of the area. This is our first time in New Jersey…we all really love it."

I genuinely averred I wanted to show her more. I didn't want her to disappear again. "So crazy you're staying here right in Brigantine out of all the shore towns near AC. What street?" I asked. She firmly told me, "Down on 9th."

"Not too far. Maybe we can have something at the house tonight…bring your crew. We will all be here," I had offered.

"Well…I don't know," she said, moving her head side to side, bopping it around in a confused childish manner.

With her hip jutted to one part, her right arm draped across her slender body, clasping the elbow opposite. Her head lolled down to one shoulder casting her bobbed hair onto her shoulders, absolutely the frontlines to her mystique. I kept getting turned on.

57

"What were you thinking then?" I asked. She remained quiet as I kept asking a few times with no answers given. She kept looking back at her friends, giggling and watching them converse with the others.

"What is it?" continuing the questioning. I wanted responses. "Do you not want to hang with me? I get it. I won't be offended."

"It is definitely not that at all," guaranteed Rachel. "You're going to think it is corny," she continued, looking down again. She then stared at me to figure out if she should have trusted me or not. I could see she was in deep ponder. "Not at all," I guaranteed.

It finally came out from her mouth. "Would you take a walk on the beach with me? I'd like to get to know you more?"

I was in shock. What else was I supposed to say? I mean, who could resist taking a saunter along the water's verge with this beauty?

There was much to be said for the appreciating of the liquid-and-sand allure that is the seashore...but even more when it's together with Rachel Weston.

"I wouldn't want to miss it for the world," I told her. "Great. Meet me here at your street at 7:30. Don't be late," she replied, winking and gesturing to her girls that it was time to leave.

I continued to stand in the same spot, still in awe...even after she ran away. By all means, I was still pretty amazed at the serendipity that manifested before us on our street.

They all left while I could hear Dickie and Harry chuckling at me yet still proud that I got a date with this girl. It was going to be an amazing night. I knew it.

Grocery shopping was our second favorite time after the weekend. Four o'clock every Sunday, we were in the Acme moving between the aisles, each pushing harder than the one before to stock up for the week.

The walkways were crowded and the Sunday sales were on, full fledge. Sacks of nuts and dried fruit, or meat roasting on roasting skewers. The bakers' biscuits being tossed out like hot potatoes. Powdered spices' aromas lodged deep into my nostrils as we glided past the cultural section.

Rich and unfamiliar scents cut through the smell of the fruit and veggie section, so heavy I could taste them in my mouth, like the air inside a fabrication green house. I wasn't sure if I was extremely hungry or if all of my senses were supernaturally enhanced…either way, I was on cloud nine for the day.

It was there we ran into Gemini and her pack of wolves. It was like a Victoria's Secret runway coming in our direction in aisle ten. Fantastic. Just as I was going to grab some Sun Chips from the snacks row, she came and picked up my hand.

"I had a great time last night," she detailed. She was smiling a little…a grin with a twist to it, like the smile of a child who is determined not to weep. I acknowledged that I did as well, one of the best nights of the summer. I certainly didn't ramble into my encounter with the great Rachel Weston...but I didn't need to. She continued, "Johnny came up to me later on, he saw you with that pretty girl on the dancefloor."

"Well, I think everyone saw that," responded my witty self with a snicker. She smirked along with my laugh, saying, "Johnny wanted me to tell you she is beautiful. If you let go of that one, you are absolutely fucking nuts. Verbatim."

Here I thought Johnny was out for the count once I left him at the bar attending to his young slimmies. But, he was watching me...as he always did.

I was delighted to hear...it reassured my endearing thoughts of Rachel and unquestionably made me even more excited about the walk that was yet to come that very evening.

I couldn't help myself. I was like a child. To learn more and break past her numinous magic was literally all my seconds encompassed that day. After all, like I've said, every woman is a mystery waiting to be solved. Rachel was top of the list.

Gemini and her babes went about their ways immediately after that as we tended back to the hustle and bustle, bumping into people, and toes trodden on.

The floor managers hollering out their special deals, customers haggling over prices, people gossiping in huddles, cacophony of sound, bulging bags swinging into people's legs. We fleeted out like a thief in the night to bring it all home.

It felt like waiting forever the rest of that day but it finally came time to meet Rachel on my 36th Street beach entrance. I was right on the money, seven thirty PM. Not a minute later.

The sounds that surrounded us that early eve and the polished talent of the light had a way of burgling into our hearts and certainly staying there long after we had left. It was like a caviar for the soul.

The slurpy cuffing of the sea was muted, a humble murmur. The waves were merely snoozing, sluggish and slumbering in their liquid robes. They dribbled up to the shoreline of the inimitable Atlantic lands, then shuddered and drizzled their spray onto its surface, whisking the sand before releasing. A current of cold electricity passed through the air. We shivered. The wind whipped up. The waters simmered.

"Gosh, this beats little old Mountain Park, Georgia any day!" she exclaimed, shuddering from the slight waft. I agreed after asking her if she needed a sweater, which she declined. Although I never saw much of the southern states, there was no other place in the world than the Jersey shore. I made that clear.

Also, there was no other girl than Rachel Weston. Shining like the sun that was setting before us, she radiated brilliantly. She was wearing a pink and white coral sundress that night. It was so light in fabric and tight to her skin, you could see every curve and crevice of her exquisite figure. To compliment it all, she had a cute beach hat...one that mastered her long brown hair in the wind, each strand simply glowing with every gust. I couldn't help but gawp at her every few seconds. But, I went on.

"It's hard for me to be anywhere else. I love to travel and see the world...but I grew up coming down here every summer. My grandma owned the cottage house my friends and I stay at. It went to my parents when she passed," I was detailing. I could see her face drop when she heard that my grandmother was no longer alive as she then asked for how long it had been. "Five years."

"I'm sorry," she told me, grabbing my hand ever so gently. It was nice to feel her tender touch. "Things definitely changed after losing her. She was great, a true gem in my life." I loved watching Rachel walk and seeing how she smiled. Hearing her voice was tranquil as well. "I'm sure she was lovely. As it definitely is here," assured this southern belle.

"Growing up in Philly, this was paradise to me when I was a kid. It still kind of is," I continued. "That must be exciting. The big city life and then coming down the beach year after year. Near me, it's all farms and horse," explained Rachel.

"Unfortunately, the house is being sold to new owners on Labor Day. After that, my mom is retiring and I'll be living in Center City Philly working in sales with a software company."

She grew sad, I could tell. So did I. "I can see you love that house. I am so sorry that it's being sold," Rachel sympathized. "Probably for the better, you know. It's been nothing but a nonstop party house these past five summers. I guess it's time for a change," I was saying. I couldn't believe the words that were coming out from my mouth, but I guess she brought it out of me.

"Is it just you and your sister or do you have other siblings?" I asked her, changing the subject. "Well, gosh…Amanda and I have known each other since first grade, so she is *like* a sister. But yes, just Lauren and I. We were born and raised in Mountain Park. For the longest time, it was all I knew," replied Rachel.

I nodded my head up and down as she asked me about my background. "My parents are still in the city. I got a sister somewhere out west, but Dickie and Harry are like my brothers. I'd do anything for them. We've been through it all together," I told her. She thought it was sweet.

"So you are in sales, huh?" asked Rachel. "I am," countered me, "what do you do?" She was telling me how she taught art and painting for a high school but had a dream of doing it abroad at a university somewhere, particularly Italy. I thought it was really cool.

"I would love for you to come sometime this week to the house, to meet my mom and dad. They will be having a barbecue Wednesday…them, some other family visiting, me, my sister Lauren, and my friend Amanda. Wil you come?" she asked me. Of course, I said I would be there with flying colors, eager to meet them all.

All of a sudden, Rachel stopped us in our tracks and gazed at the sand beneath her in awe. It was as if she saw a ghost swirling amidst the ground, right at her feet. It was then when she knelt down as her sun dress sketched for me, that immaculate rear-end covered with the bikini bottom she still had on from the daytime.

She picked up this unique shell…one I had never seen before. It was rather beautiful and a splendor to see.

The spindle-shaped remain appeared about four inches in length. The background was a cream color with a pattern that included spiral rows of mahogany- colored square dots all over it.

The radula, the tongue of the shell, was very small and short and had only one row of teeth. The initial coils were quite smooth, with the post-nuclear whorls being finely sculptured.

Its milky chamber left it to be an appealing vision, like a treasure of the sea. I wouldn't have seen it nor spotted it so quickly in a million years, but this girl noticed it all. Then again, I wasn't surprised.

"Do you know what this is?" she asked me, so giddily and free. Apparently she knew it all as well, so I asked her to tell me. "It's a Junonia...a deep-water marine mollusk, lives off the Atlantic Coast from North Carolina to Florida and along the Gulf. This is considered a fortune to any collector. A Junonia on the beach up this way is an extremely rare sight, making this a gosh-darn miracle."

"Much like yourself," I replied, winking and grabbing her hand again. She giggled so innocently and looked at me with that brightened smile, still holding this shell like it was a gem. I was very serious when I told her that. She was truly a rare sighting. "Do you know why it's called a Junonia?" she inquired in the cutest way possible. "I know you have the answer," I said. She lightly smacked me on my arm in a flirty way, still smiling, proceeding to detail, "

The shell is named after the ancient Roman goddess Juno. She was the Queen of the Gods and part of the Capitoline triad that also included Minerva and Jupiter."

"You just know everything in the world don't you?" I joked, yet still a bit serious. She kept going, laughing, "Annnddd she is very versatile. She was also the Goddess of marriage, pregnancy and childbirth. One of her titles was Lucino, meaning light, as she helped to bring children into the light of this world at birth. Each Roman woman was said to have her own Juno which represented her female spirit."

"Well, she sounded lovely. I'm sure this shell is pretty amazing with having such a deity tied to it," I responded. As I said this, she handed it over to me. "I want you to have it. Let it protect you," insisted Rachel.

I was taken away. Such an erratic and precious piece of the ocean unbeknownst to the Northeastern Atlantic, handed to me like it was a dead seahorse by this dashing darling. "I can't take it. It's obviously very special to you," I revealed. "So are you," she quickly responded, looking deep and long into my eyes for the first time all night.

She then handed me the shell as I held her gently, cupping her face with one hand. As she put her arms around me, I could feel Rachel's' body grow rigid with surprise as trembles shook her like rapid fire. Elated warmth blossomed within her. I put the shell into my pocket as I was gasping with delight. She then showered me with gentle waves of her delicate fingers along my back.

She gazed up at me. We were both thrilled beyond words to be the recipient of one another's affection. She drew back again and I spent a moment studying her face, up...down...and around.

My eyes softened with tenderness before sparking with something else. I skewed her head to the side and kissed her, all in, lips demanding. She felt a seething heat deep within her as my grip tightened. I slanted her head further, deepening the kiss.

That kiss obliterated every thought. It seemed like hours but it was only a few minutes. For the first time in forever, my mind was locked into the present. The worries of the day evaporated like a rain fall washing away a snowy wonderland. My usual mode of hurrying from one thing to the next was suspended. Rachel was absolutely spectacular. So were her juicy lips.

I had no request for the kiss to end. Drunk on endorphins, my only desire was to touch her, to move my hands under her smooth summer layers and feel her perfect softness.

In moments, the gentle caress had become more firm. I savored her lips and the quickening of her breath that matched my own. The sun was just now setting. A kiss like this was a beginning, a promise of much more to come. Simply amazing.

CHAPTER FIVE

I woke up that morning after one of the most peaceful sleeps I had gotten since the start of the season. I felt great...refreshed!

Even though summer was near its dusk, there was a light in my heart now flashing, one that was missing simply the day prior. A spark of hope, a ray of sunshine that I felt beaming through. Perhaps it was the optimism, the anticipation of good things to come. It was a feeling I hadn't had in so long that if felt as foreign as it was welcome.

By all means, I was confident it was the Sunday walk on the beach and the acceleration of the beautiful events unfolding right in front of me. I liked it way too much.

Rachel and I were grabbing a late morning coffee at the new *Casale di Java* joint in Brigantine before heading to her family's weekly rental on 9th Street. It was Wednesday, three days after our first kiss. We had spent every moment of the days together that I wasn't working since that night. I didn't let a minute slip Monday or Tuesday...and I certainly didn't plan on doing so this particular day either.

She'd hold out her hand for me to take. Every time, I complied. She'd bring my hand to her lips and place a gentle kiss upon it.

During these incredible split seconds, Rachel would tell me she felt her face flush warm and the hairs on her neck stand. Something fluttered in her stomach. She knew it was a feeling she adored just as much as I did.

There were times that she knew that if she spoke, her words would fumble and she wouldn't be able to make her usual witty remarks. Right there, I would be at a loss for everything as well; no words, no breath, no thoughts. The only thing that came out of my mouth at that moment was her name, and even then it came out shaky and quiet.

"I can't wait to meet your family but I have to admit, it's going to be very hard to keep my hands off of you," I told her once we purchased our beverages.

I exuded with nothing but grace as I caressed her arm with my fingers…and it had her enthralled. She was mesmerizing in every way. The glimmer of the day's shine illuminated her dark skin and eyes as deep as the heart of the ocean. And when those very ganders shifted and finally acknowledged my statement, my blood kept rushing. That splash of Creole in her, that horse-ridin', peach-growin', fun-lovin' harmonious way to her speech…it was just so perfect.

"I'm a good girl I told you, it ain't gonna be that easy. Especially in front of ma and pa," she revealed. Of course it wouldn't. That's all I heard the past few days about how good she was. It undoubtedly made me want her more.

"We're doing that house party tonight. You guys are all coming, right? You, Amanda, Lauren?" I asked her. She secured to me that she wouldn't miss it for the world, just as we got to her house where all of Rachel's family awaited.

The place even looked a southern plantation home with the long porch and big awning, so it fit the bill. I was impressed, never knowing this existed in Brigantine.

Out the front door came her effervescent mother. "It's a pleasure, Brad. So devilishly handsome with a heart of gold! I can see how you make all the girls swoon!" she told me with that completed *good old gal* tone. I could see Rachel flush red, smile and look at me while she nodded to her mom in a way as if she was embarrassing her in a cute way.

"Well, heavens Rae. You know around Georgia's way those boys are two-a-penny, but a man who loves you like this? And one this classy? Rarer than a pity party for Richard Nixon I reckon!!!" she went on. She was sweet. She reminded me of Dolly Parton in Steel Magnolias, just as pretty too. "I see beauty runs in the family," I told her, winking my one eye, which I always did so well.

Just as I said this and while Rachel and her mom kept laughing, blushing from my comment, out came her dad. Tall, gray hair and a horseshoe mustache.

He was fine and dandy as well. His cowboyish gait was one I expected from a dignified Georgia boy. There was a casualness to him that I liked. All that he was missing was the gun at his holster and ten gallon hat.

His handshake was manicured to perfection, the skin softer than a baby. His face was one of upmost confidence, whatever game this man played he wasn't accustomed to losing. I was just waiting him to say, "have at it there, hoss," but he wasn't talking much.

There was Cousin Earl, Aunt Betsie, Tammy Lynn, Jamie Lynn, Uncle Bob, and about fifteen people I barely remember at the time. They were all extremely nice nonetheless. Rachel and her family were very close, I could tell by all means. I was having a great day.

The moment I slid into my chair at the backyard picnic table, I was served an enormous platter of food by an aunt or cousin, or somebody. Man, I really liked this bunch. They were generous with this food.

Steak, piles of fried potatoes, pecan pie, and homemade wine. A casserole of fruit sat in ice to keep it chilled. The basket of rolls they set before me would keep me going for a week. There was an elegant glass of sweet tea resting nearby.

All of a sudden, Dickie and Harry showed up to grab a bite while I went to finish my dishes. It was great. Amanda lit up to see old Valentine, for sure. We all then spent the rest of the day at the beach together once we finished eating, the six of us.

A sun kissed afternoon was full of volleyball games and body surfing the peaking season's waves. The sky-rattin' birds wheeled overhead in the air, nonchalant until the fish jumped to the sea's surface.

The beach was more people than sand that day. They laid and sat on towels and chairs. It was a crazy array of color, every shade the world had to offer, all right there with no thought to coordination…all cultures, all kinds. I loved it.

By night's arrival, the gathering came quickly segwaying from sunbathing to drinking, dancing and eating. It seemed like all and their mothers arrived to the Seduction Lounge for the grand Wednesday night fiesta we were providing.

Folks from Brigantine, AC, Ventnor, Margate, and anywhere in the area were all in attendance. Horsecock the veteran, Gemini and her dames, various randoms from all the seasons came to give their appreciation to the night's doings and count down some of the final moments at the place.

We even catered the damn thing too. Huge platters and bowls stuffed with pungent fruit and nuts. Ocean creatures drizzled in sauces or begging to be dipped in spicy concoctions.

Countless cheeses, breads, vegetables, sweets, waterfalls of wine, and streams of spirits that flicker with flames illuminated the living room.

I had put out a bench dedicated to desserts; lemon tarts, rhubarb crème brûlée, orange blossom cakes, minted strawberries fresh from the garden, meringues so beautifully shaped it was a pity to eat them and apple strudels served with ice-cream. There were decadent chocolate bonbons that oozed rum cream on first bite. This was the way to make it happen.

The music I had playing filled the air without effort, like the waves filling holes in beach sand; the sound rushing in and around every person in the room. Some reacted to the beat, others continued in chatter, but as always…it speaks to them in some manner.

A lively tempo that lifted them, elevating the spirit. Before the notes filled the air every person was an island, with it they all feel the same tidal flows and the beginnings of togetherness feels warm.

The six of us gathered for a shot of whiskey in the kitchen early on before the madness began; me, Dickie, Harry, Rachel, Amanda and Lauren. "A la salu," I said. "To a great night mid-week."

The celebration went on into the night, everyone dancing like they'd forgotten how to stand still. Dickie was moving like his limbs were made of spaghetti and Amanda's face was an epic picture of pure excitement. I could see the two were finally getting comfy as I anticipated seeing some romance there.

Lauren was trying to clean up as the party went and Harry was making all sorts of drinks in the kitchen for everyone. I found this the most optimum time to ask Rachel, "Take a walk with me…on the beach?"

She quickly responded, "In this darkness? This late?" To her reluctance, I paused. I didn't want to say the wrong thing or make the wrong bodily gesture. This was time delicate and I had to strike while the iron was hot. Everyone was preoccupied and I wanted her more than words could have escribed.

Despite her hesitancy and my stillness, moments later, she took a deep breath and nodded her head in agreeance to peel away from the bunch. It was time, it was here!! My heart pounded in excitement as I would finally have her alone and out of the light. I could barely contain myself.

This was no normal sensation. She was not your average woman. The heat of this September night was upon us but I was chilly as can be, tingling all the way down to the bone. I wanted everything about her so badly, I was in actual amatorial pain...numb around every possible joint and fiber. I couldn't help myself. It was calling me from all over.

We made our ways over to a lifeguard hut quickly after getting through the soft sands of the dunes, not too far from 36th Street's entrance. I found this to be the perfect spot to indulge in nature's finest luxurious treasure: the sand and the water. Plus, she was the perfect kind of tipsy and I was the right kind of wrong that night.

My resistance succumbed. I knew in my mind, this female...this *beautiful* southern girl...I needed to fuck so bad and so hard, more than anything in the world. One solid look at those eyes, any man could cum. I was tired of playing games. It had been almost a full week of me dreaming about making her moan. The sheer thoughts were insanely intensifying inside my mind.

Time was of the essence, so I wasted none further. The docile placing of my hand at that moment, grazing upon her lean yet luscious outer thighs hastened my heart's beat faster than a freight train. It was pounding out of my chest. She continued to sit upright on my lap in the most innocent way thinkable. That belle-ish charm, that small-

73

town Georgia bliss…it only engulfed my loins more into the mightiest of flames. They were shining like the North Star.

Escalating a quick ride up the surface of those light blue cut-off jean short-shorts she was wearing, my fingers trembled overwhelmingly. I smoothed my touch around her curvaceous hips. At this instant, I was breathing heavy, now glancing seductively at these natural exquisite legs of hers. I had been ogling at them the past three days on the beach, already savoring their delicious flavor in my cock's fantasies.

I looked up at her face fleetingly and saw a grin emerge without effort as her flawless white teeth glistened from the moon glow like a thousand diamonds. I knew she was a good girl, she told me plenty of times. The question now was, how far could I go tonight? Was she gonna stop me? Did she want this? Or much like myself, did she *have* to HAVE it??

The show went on. I slid my perspiring palms once around that slender waist, full-circle. Her tan smooth skin, a perfect stomach you only see on a runway model…a stunning twenty-four inches, if I had to guess. It was all too unreal. However, I felt the mutual urge come alive between us. I knew if she was going to let me make any more hand gestures down her abdomen, throughout her impeccable arcs and over to that handful of an ass that exuded itself juicy as can be, I was at least going to have to come up and kiss her.

Once my eyes shifted from her stems to her smile, I curled my lips, getting ready to go all in. Before I even fully peeked back at her, she leaned her head to me and put her mouth to mine all the way until she could slant in no further. Right there, that memory…was one to last forever. I was able taste her, every elation of her being. God, she was so yummy…tastier than the other night when we walked the beach. I can still sense that first feeling all this time later when I think hard on it.

The summer wind kept blowing in while I felt the night's heart begin to beat…or perhaps, it was just my own ticker battering like a machine gun. I immediately took my other paw off around her waist and lightly placed it on the cheek of her face. Straightaway, she grabbed it with her own hand, in hunger for more of this imminent, perilous action. Eyes wide shut and locking me in more and more, softer and softer, I never saw anything quite as special before beneath the sky. I opened my eyes to behold quickly, the depiction of this candid ardor.

We continued kissing vigorously as I could finally hear her softly gasp. It was so arousing, I wanted to rip her shorts off right then and there. But I knew I had to wait. This one was too good to be true. I had to play it right.

Before I even thought of how to write the next chapter to this eve's saga, Rachel stood up from her guiltless lap-sit, turned around to face me, and squatted that bodacious bottom on top of my bulging hard on beneath my jeans. She began to straddle gently as she placed both legs on either side of me, one-to-one. My wretched old pants were screaming to escape my entity…and to take hers with them.

Now with her knees bent, the stance she took for a moment had left my face in the center of her perky breasts encased by that white tank top and enigmatic brassiere underneath. As she climbed on top in this motion, she pressed me up against the lifeguard hut, making sure I was planted up and could not go back any further.

I couldn't help but lend my lips to her fine-crafted chest. Keenly kissing her in-between this astounding bosom, I caressed every inch with my tongue up and away, past that delectable freckle on her neck. She was so breathtaking, I openly wondered how the good Lord made a beauty so untainted. Whatever enchanting fragrance she was wearing was making it harder to control myself. It was like walking through clean linens right before autumn's ingress, her sweetness was fuckin' killing me. "What the Hell already?" I kept pondering.

The ocean waves continued to fill the sounds of the night with their sonic booms while I kept kissing her neck. Strands of her striking curly dark hair didn't cease, coming down to brush my face. I didn't mind one bit. Its smell was just as sensually toxic as the rest of her.

Her mild wails, now increasing in sound, let me know I was doing something right. I made my tender pecks closer to her ear. That grand erogenous spot rested nigh by, there wasn't a doubt in my mind. However, I wanted to be precise with my coordinates when landing.

My journey through her nerve endings remained on course until I finally felt her body quiver. I was there. I knew she was defenseless. I was in, all in!!! There was no coming back. The home stretch was near. It was time to pump up the volume.

Just as I skimmed my hand down the back side of her shorts to grab firm, that revering rear-end I knew thousands of men adored, Rachel kissed my cheek twice.

Whereas I thought she'd linger with her groans for my hearing, it was then whispered in my ear with that alluring accent, "I told you I'm a good girl...I can't give it all up tonight."

My world shattered at that very instant. I couldn't believe she was teasing me like this. To say I saw this coming during our rein of lascivious lending would have been a fallacy. Hitherto, this halted me none. Ney, I was not a defeatist. Little Miss Innocent wasn't getting away this easily. Not with me. There was no shot. She was too irresistible and I was too full of white hot lust.

"I'd be lying if I told you that's not what tempts me more about you, doll," I retorted calmly, as I persisted to nibble on her earing-less lobes. Her genuine laugh was blameless by all means but it didn't leave me feeling guilty whatsoever. "You're trouble," she told me with her back straight, looking at me with that Peach State purity. I chuckled and jeered back cheekily, like the city slickster I thought I was, "So what? Even good girls get a little bad, baby." My beam was cheek to cheek.

Abruptly and without giving any warning, I grabbed the giant beach towel that rested to the right of me and threw it on the sand, a yard or two away. It spread perfectly flat somehow next to that hut without much mess getting on top. With all my power exerted and while every bit of my core was pressed down by the squat of this angel still resting on my lap, I managed to get my feet under my bottom and stand tall. This was all the while grabbing hold of Rachel's ravishing thighs, so soft and smooth lying in my hands. Her arms were around my head and her mouth was open in awe, looking directly at me.

77

I kept kissing her as I walked down the lifeguard hut stairs, praying not to fall and make an ass of myself as I carried her. She weighed next to nothing, it wasn't a question of my strength…but I was still nervous nonetheless. My knees were weak and I was dizzy as all hell from her aroma.

We made it to the rutted grains of the sands where my walk to the towel down yonder was a bit lumbering. Once I was given the opportunity, I gently positioned her on her back on top the towel where our kisses persisted. Her laments continued. "Brad, come on…please, not tonight," she crooned to me.

Was I taking advantage? Not even a little. I was taking a vantage on a voluptuous vixen…I could never consider that a crime. Like a conquistador exulting upon the seas, a lion on its prey in the savannas of the Serengeti…I was merely just trying to allow it all to come together so beautifully. This was my mission, a vocation if you will.

"You are the fulfillment. This you know. I want you more than I can handle. More than anyone has wanted anything in this lifetime. And I want you to feel the greatest sensation you've ever imagined," I retorted before I put my tongue in her ear. Her panting increased as she closed her eyes, put her arms back around my neck and surrendered to my lure with another kiss, this time she wasn't letting go. I could see her slight and slow pelvic thrusts in my peripherals. That was all the invitation I needed.

I couldn't let another second slip. At that point, I made my way back down to her bottom half where my hands clamped onto her jean shorts, gently as ever. I wanted her to feel my fingertips browse down those fantastic stalks slowly and seductively along with her shorts sliding away past every last centimeter of her erotic trail. Her tanga underwear rested so astutely around her pelvis. Although they were cute, white and pink, complementing her garnishing bra, I wanted them off her legs quicker than the rays of the stars firing down, bursting its light to shine.

Her mouth opened even wider as my teeth fastened heartily onto her garment's elastic band. Rachel went on, "This isn't fair...you are too sexy to resist." Little did she know how fair it was for me.

I released only for a second to let my tongue gaffe above her waist, right by her bellybutton. I could feel her nails already digging into my back, through my shirt and scrabbling me in passionate ecstasy.

So I rose up and ripped those panties off, once and for all. In the heat of the moment, I threw them behind me and didn't look back. After I made the toss, my shirt left the premises as well and into the sandy dunes. My severe temptation to shove my cock right inside her overwhelmed me so badly, I thought I was going to have a heart attack. It was all too welcoming. A hue like the blush of a rose, pink and pale, waiting to inveigled to open its pedals like the warmth of the sun.

Subsequently I took the deepest breath, I then soared down like an eagle and let my mouth do the initial work. She was already so soaked, it was coming onto the towel beneath her. It was amazing. "You are so beautiful, baby," I kept repeating in-between my thrashes of licking to the outer pussy lips. "Oh I love that...keep going…please don't stop, oh my God, baby!!" she wailed each time I got closer to the clit. Her legs were shuddering so bad, I thought she would be weeping by now to release.

Flicking my tongue back and forth downstairs, she was pulling my hair almost out of my head. Even if she had the strength to actually do so, I wouldn't have minded…like I said, I was still numb, top to bottom.

My lips went in an O-like, burning ring of fire fashion as I trekked up and took the clit into my mouth for the next thirty seconds. "Oh myyyy fucking Gah-gah-gah, ohhhhhh Brad you're the best. I'm going to cum!!!" Her volume was at an all-time high of a decibel, I knew she was adoring this. She was grabbing my arms and bracing my shoulders. Her thighs tightened around my face with every gasp that came out of her.

Following her going once, I came up to peck more on her stomach and right below her breasts while she was feeling me all over with her fingertips. Running her touch throughout my chest and abs before she came down and caught a grasp onto the belt of my pants, her moans didn't cease even a little.

Before she had the chance to unlock and see what I had in my treasure chest, I flipped her over powerfully to get another view of that charming bare bottom. With her tank top still on and only her legs revealed, there was nothing else perfect to see while I slid my hand down and entered my fingers inside of her. I kept smacking her ass cheeks to watch it wiggle a bit. The thing had just enough shake to be sexy as can be. "Oh, shit…that's how I like it. I want you to fuck me!"

Oh yes. That sweet innocence was lost, vanished and vaporized. I was loving it. "You like that ass? Yes, feel that pussy...it's so tight...it's just for you, baby!! Wet and ready!!!" With one more back hand smack to that derriere during this fingering interlude, I flipped her back over to look in her eyes again. It was now time for the tank top to go...except I didn't want to just take it off slowly. I ripped it down the middle with my punishing mauls and began biting on that damn bra once I got the chance. Shoving my fingers back inside her, I left little time for her to complain why I tore the shirt in half. She also didn't mind me trying to chew the lingerie off either.

My incredible beauty perched up so I could ultimately detach what was sheathing those tits of an angel, 36C sized and just the way they needed to be. Perky and pink were those nipples punching out, so perfect and small circle shaped. I couldn't help but nibble on them, massaging her breasts with my hands while she reached over and ripped off my belt. Once that was gone, she started pulling my pants down. Off they went, like dust in the wind. As did my sandals.

Already leaking myself, the MX missile I had in the center of my legs could be seen from outer space upon its revealing. As this darling thoroughbred stared at it, her body freezing and her head twisting, she wasted very little time before lending a mouthful just to get a taste for her own liking. It's beautiful what desire will make sweet belles do. I didn't fight it...she had the suck of a Dyson vacuum once she got on there. "That's it baby, suck that fuckin' dick," I panted, holding her head while she went back and forth on it.

She was almost too good.   Any more tongue gestures or five second intermezzos to come in and jerk it, I thought it was going to be lights out for me, like old faithful.   Considering I couldn't get anything else into my mind except the marvel that knelt before me, there was no chance of mental distraction.   Whatever was going down, I let nature take its course.   "Hang in there, Brad.   You can't go yet.   You can't look like a fuckin' idiot," I kept telling myself.   After promising the world, I knew I had to deliver.

The locomotive gesture of her silky smooth hands, her warm mouth and bold brown eyes open, looking up at me while each inch of me was above her tongue…it was dreamlike, I had to get inside her…there was no more waiting.   "You like that dick? You want in you, baby? Balls deep?" Live til' ya die, of course.   A detour was taken.   I gently relieved her of the finest felatio I've ever had before I began scrambling through my pants for the protection, which I knew I kept handy and dandy in my back pocket.

All of a sudden, there was a major problem.   I couldn't believe it.   The condom was nowhere to be found. High and low I searched, each pocket and around my sandals.   "What's the matter, baby? Don't you have a condom?" she wailed with a face more confusing than a lost child.   I halted.   For the first time all night, I had nothing to say.   Examining more around the perimeters we were at, my words became grunts and sounds.   "I…um. Well ya know…it was just….I had it.   I uh…yeah…um. Hmmmm."

Scurrying over to the hut where we first lit our fires earlier in the session, I took a few quick looks on the platform and steps leading to it in pure panic.   Real smooth,

Brad. Butt naked, running around the beach with every possible chance to get caught. Couldn't even remember protection. All I was thinking was, "You blew it dummy. You had the kill of a lifetime, the hottest girl you were every going to fuck and you couldn't even remember the God damn rubber."

The warm blood in my body rushing through me like a lava flow turned back into icicles. I felt fourteen-years-old again. I was back at step one. I looked ahead at the ocean waters and its whitecaps crashing more for answers, but only came up with impulse. It was usually my best contingency.

Figuring it was unsafe and unorthodox, especially for a daddy's girl type, I decided to throw a Hail Mary pass at this moment. So, I trotted back to my babe, knelt down in-between her laying down, admiring her once more and retorting, "We don't need one. Just lay back."

Her eyes widened quicker than a leer jet piercing through the clouds. "Oh gosh, I don't think so. What, do you want me to get pregnant? I don't know what kinds of diseases you may have there, crazy city boy. You better think of something else because that sure ain't happening tonight, sheesh." Luckily her accent was adorable, I was still turned on. Hoping she was too, I kept strategizing. My panic level was skyrocketing but I was trying to remain calm on the surface.

Often, I prayed to God for things other than this. After all, I was Catholic. And in those lovely moments, he was the only one who I could turn to. I needed salvation. I never had to plea for great romance but to walk away from this supernatural being without sealing the deal would have been a mortal sin and I would have had to live with it for the rest of my life. I begged for his mercy and cried for justice.

Just as I sighed, picking up the towel in defeat, the good Lord gave me the response I needed. As she lifted her right buttocks from the one side of the towel, to what my wondering eyes would appear…what I should have had in my back pocket. Somehow the thick Trojan made it onto my beach towel before I put it in my pants. We both saw this simultaneously and kicked back into fifth gear, revving our engines full throttle.

Couldn't keep wasting time. I let her slowly and intimately slip the rubber onto my shaft once I opened it up out of its seal. There was a stimulating feeling for both of us during this.

I knew she was a classy girl so I wanted to make sure the move was to her liking. Always a solid exchange in my book.

I passed the ball into her court. Before I could even lean over to kiss her once the condom was on, she slipped me right in her, smoother than a highway ride after midnight. Let me tell you…it was paradise. Trying to illuminate to you about those first few seconds is the ultimate challenge. Euphoric would be an understatement.

Her mouth remained open while I went up and down as slow as I could. Even the thickest of protection couldn't decelerate this explosion that was pending, ready to burst out of me like an atom bomb. I had to extend this bridge from start to finish. I couldn't end it now that I was finally inside of her, deep as could be…it was just too sweet to cease fire so soon.

Escaping away from the quaint rapture that was her body, I bit my lip extremely hard to contain the energy. That delicious waist, that perfect skin. The more I kept focusing on it, the more difficult this became. Yet nothing else could have distracted my mind, the more and more I tried. Again, this was not your ordinary girl.

So, I took a two second intermission before I told her pretty little self that she had to get on top and ride me like a cowgirl. This always helped my situation because I wasn't the one steering of the boat amid the mighty seas. It was great to be co-captain sometimes and the let the ship sail in another direction by a different controller. It allowed me to get myself under control for a little while.

Then again, she was amazing at doing what she did as well. I realized this almost instantaneously once I let her take over. Her hair blew in the gentle wind as she leaned back and let her pelvis do the work. "You act so innocent but you ride like a bad ass," I panted to her while she was dangerously thrusting those thighs, squeezing her pussy on my cock. Her moans were once again escalating. She couldn't stop herself. It was just too great for us both.

Watching her move up and down like a see-saw made it harder to contain myself while feeling this tight grip clasping onto me, snugger than I've ever felt. Even in her gentler of movements that she began after a few minutes, the mission remained the hardest to complete in the attempt to keep my release.

All of a sudden, we saw a police SUV down by the water's edge riding in our direction, a few streets down from where we were. The headlights were bright enough that if they were near us, we would be exposed to all who were within that block's radius.

She hopped off me in a flash. I feared not. "Don't worry about a thing," I reminded her. Subtly I could see the fear in her eyes. She was worried about the car coming our way. She didn't want to be seen in such a manner. I murmured, "they would have been here already, baby." The poor thing was scared as all hell.

While I watched the vehicle continue its trot down the sea line, I knew we were safe. Continuing this beautiful time, I turned her around and put her on all fours. That ass was right in my peripherals. That delicious, bodacious and perfectly curved rear end was directly at my disposal, ready for whatever I was going to bring to it and around it.

I knelt down behind her and slowly made my way back inside. Her mouth opened up wide, right at insertion. She felt safe again as I grabbed her hips, feeling the friction come alive. She knew I was in control of the situation once more.

Soaked. I could feel how wet she was down there. I kept slipping in and out. The end was near. Unfortunately. So close, such little time. It was all just too grandeur to keep myself from discharging. Sweat was dripping down my head and onto her body. She loved it.

At this point, it wouldn't have mattered who came by. I didn't care. It would take an army to stop me from doing what I was doing to this gorgeous heaven-sent.

I was now a hundred miles an hour with my speed, pounding away like a rabbit would. While I was grabbing her long dazzling brown hair and pulling on it vigorously, Rachel kept thrusting while I was, simultaneously to get one more cum in. She didn't want me to end this. She wanted it all night long. As did I. "Fuck me, Braddy. Oh my God. Ah ah ah!!!!"

Just as I pulled out, I realized in less than a second that the condom wasn't on anymore. It had fallen off and was resting on the towel beneath us. My warm explosion went all over her back and ass, ten times the amount of my usual load. However, I don't think she was upset about it one bit. Euphoric put this experience best. I was in heaven.

"Messy boy," she whispered looking back at me with a bright smile, running her fingers through the mess. It turned her on. I remained completely frozen, still kneeling behind her. There was nothing else I could continue to do but admire her zeal and allure. Not for a single moment did I want to get up from where I rested. Nor did she.

CHAPTER SIX

Night's darkness is surely a bag that bursts with the gold of the dawn. In its course, Rachel and I both watched the sun creep up above the ocean after awaking from a long rest in the sand.

The seagulls were arcing and swerving between the magic of the morning light. An occasional scream would echo from the wind, eerie and hollow. The immense vista leading to the horizon was jaw dropping, as always…yet so was the fact that my darling was sitting up against me while we watched it together, harmoniously with the sounds of the shore.

However, we knew we had to be up and at it…getting back to our respective homes and planned days ahead. "Last night was incredible," she leaned back and told me, kissing me on my cheek.

Incredible wasn't the only word. I mentioned euphoric, but even that was barely enough for me to fully describe the essence of our coaxing, caressing, and climaxing the night prior.

Before we got up and left, I murmured that I had a gift to give her. "Top of the mornin' to you, pretty girl," I uttered in her ear as I pulled out from my pocket, a necklace I had crafted with the junonia shell she gave me.

Creating it two nights before, it had a lot of meaning to us. I left the shell just enough a size hole at the top to put a brown rope around it and tie it in the back. "I made this…because it is just as gorgeous as you are. All must see it on you." I then put it around her neck, securing it on her, gently.

She loved it. She couldn't believe I made it for her. The symbol of our first night. The first kiss. The first walk. The first chance. "Brad, you are amazing." Her eyes struck like a lightning bolt.

"You're more amazing than I could ever be," I responded. "Please be there Friday?" she asked. It was the final shindig of the summer, legitimately. Her family was having a weekend-long jamboree for Labor Day, celebrating good times profusely.

"Have I let you down yet?" I asked her, winking my left eye. She smiled cheek to cheek and came over to kiss me, holding her precious new necklace beneath her face, finally telling me, "I love you," candidly without any question.

"I love you too, Rachel," I had responded in a flash. I meant it, every predicate of the word in the sentence. The week was just too short. After this weekend, she would be returning to Georgia. I didn't know what I was going to do. It put knots in my stomach just thinking about it.

She went on, "I keep falling in love with you and each day, falling harder than the one before it. Every moment the feeling gets deeper, more complete, more bewitching. There isn't a thing I wouldn't do to make this work. I don't wanna go back to Georgia, I don't!!"

"We will figure something out, babe…we won't let anything come in our way," I told her. She made me promise.

"Cross my heart, hope to die," I reacted, going in for another kiss. I didn't want any of this to end. I didn't want her to leave either. We both had our lives in different parts of the country. She had her career, I had mine. I had to make something happen though, one way or another. I kept guaranteeing it.

It killed me even more leaving her Thursday night and into Friday day. I was visiting my family and going over the finer details of the house closing with my dad. We scattered through the paperwork and were preparing for the big day that was coming late Monday.

All of a sudden, my mom came over to me with the house telephone in her hand, jumbled. "It's for you," she said, quietly with a puzzling look on her face.

I took the phone from her, walked over into the kitchen and put it to my ear with the other hand covering my open one. When I said hello, what I heard was, "Braddy...it's George, what are you doin'?" very fast and stressed out. Much noise in the background as well, cars honking and police sirens going off.

Uncle Griz sounded pretty flustered but I figured I'd still exude my vivacious self, especially considering the great mood I was in. "Yo Unc, what do you say? What do you hear?" He didn't laugh nor did he acknowledge my glee-like disposition. "I've been calling you all day. I thought you were in AC," responded Georgie. It was rare he came to me with such strain. I then detailed him on how I was seeing my parents before the last weekend at the shore. The house was to be gone Monday night.

"Meet me at 9th and Passyunk Avenue right now! It's important," he instructed, hanging up the phone immediately. This was not good. I never knew Uncle Griz to be this way with me, short and nervous.

Nonetheless, I always told him I'd be there for him...as he was with me. He was family...both him and Harry. I loved them. For there was no friend like this man in calm or stormy weather; to cheer one on the tedious way, to fetch one if one goes astray, to lift one if one totters down, to strengthen whilst one stands.

So, I made it happen. There I mounted myself outside both steak shops, waiting on the man. It was hot as ever as it was in the city, especially that season...but I let the sweat drip as I lingered.

I stood, listening to the hums of the city, to the sounds of the people I loved. Everyone was speaking my language. Philly does that with its native tongue of the street.

Screeching past an alleyway nearby and appearing abruptly next to the fire hydrant I remained by, the great black Cadillac de Mancini revealed itself before my eyes. Out of it came Griz, fixing his suit and combing his hair as he steadily approached me, almost face to face immediately.

"Feds. They're doing another crackdown, just like they did ten years ago. Word on the street is Harry is in the indictment, but not me. He has to go on a lam until Monday." I didn't ask how or why this happened, as always. Yet I couldn't believe how far Heat was now into the game. But, again he was being groomed by his uncle to take the reins quickly…so I shouldn't have been surprised. I just always thought there was a chance of him getting out.

"Jesus Christ…are you serious, Griz?" I asked. "What the fuck, that's terrible. Where is he now?" I didn't know what to do and I wasn't sure where Georgie was going with this particular meeting with me.

"He's at my place downtown. We gotta get him out of here. And I need it to be with you. They're handing out subpoenas by tonight, we have seven guys we're moving out of the city for the weekend…I cannot have Heat go away before the big job this month. We gotta cover all facets here," detailed Georgie the Griz, drama a plus.

He was trying to get me involved. I wanted no parts in what they had going on. So, I responded in the most panicky way I could. "I haven't even talked to him. I figured he'd be back at some point over the weekend. I can't do this, Griz."

He kept shaking his head at me in disappointment. I knew he was acting quickly with what was going on…however, this just didn't make sense to me. Why did he want me involved? "Brad, you're the only one I want with him. I need you to take Heat tonight, right now to the safe house down in Maryland…just for a few days, that's all. I will give you an address and plenty of cash," he said.

A few days wasn't going to work. I had to get back to the beach for the prettiest girl right away. Nothing was going to stop that. I responded, "Uncle Georgie, I can't…I have the thing with Rachel and her family tonight."

It wasn't making sense how huge this upcoming weekend was to me and how badly I did not want to do this assignment. Yet, I shouldn't have been shocked by his lack of care…bigger things were happening in his world. "Brad, you gotta do this for me. There's no other way…I need you with him until Monday," insisted Georgie. There was no way I could wait until then. It would be the end of Labor Day weekend, Rachel would be leaving, the house would be out of our hands, and summer would be officially over.

Even though I was throwing our other friend under the bus, I thought of him right away as a consolation. "Georgie, c'mon…what about Dickie? What about anyone else in the family? I just can't do it."

"It can't be Dickie, Brad. He can't be trusted like you, nobody in the family can. What are you fuckin' kiddin' me? You can't miss one fuckin' weekend for me? One piece of pussy? After all I've done for you and your parents? When do I ever ask for anything??"

There came the guilt. The man was always dear to me and I was certainly grateful to him for it. This was the last thing I wanted as a favor repaid though. I would have rather gone on a killing spree with him when the weekend was over. To disappoint Rachel at the time…I couldn't stomach it. "It's not that. God…I mean…Georgie…I love you and I am humble to your graciousness. But I just don't know if I wanna get involved with this particular thing. This makes me a fugitive on the run," I said.

Crossing the line between right and wrong was not my deal, not the Mancini life. Here, aiding and abetting a potential felon…even though I loved the man, I was shocked Georgie wanted me in on this. He kept going, "Knock it the fuck off. It does not make you a fugitive, believe me. It makes you nothing but my dear friend,

Harry's friend, loyal...you boys are like sons to me. Now you owe me. You wouldn't be at J.R. Montague if it weren't for me, kid. I keep you protected and I will continue to help you the rest of your life, you know that."

I was speechless. He had me by the balls. I was going to have let Rachel down, miss our last weekend at the shore, and pass that threshold to the dark side...all for the great George Mancini.

"You do this for me and I will make sure your future is as bright as can be with J.R. Montague. You will never have any problem EVER!!" he continued. I was selling my soul to the devil. It had a lot of perks...but one caveat I just couldn't accept at the time.

"Let me just call...," I requested before Griz interrupted me immediately. "Can't call anyone. Not your million women, not your family, nobody!! They're tapping phones everywhere as we speak. You got it?? I had to put a block on every time I tried to call you today...it was a pain in the ass! *Maddon' a mia*! Call nobody."

It was over. She was going to kill me for missing this weekend. She was going to hate me so bad, she'd probably never talk to me again. I couldn't believe what was happening. I felt like I was thirteen and being grounded.

"Come with me now...I have cash, a car and an address for you. But I repeat...don't you fucking call anybody while you're away. No payphones, no nothing. It makes you easy to track. The Feds are moving quickly, like NOW!" instructed Griz as we jumped into his Cadi and into the city.

He was giving me instructions on the ride over to his place. All I could think about was Rachel. I could barely pay attention to him. I was livid. "You'll get one phone call at the safe house. It will be from me. It will be when I tell you leave. Until that point…you remain where you are…got it?"

I was thankful for having a man that was there for me like a father. He'd been there from the time I was a child to even now with my family helping in any way. It was worth more than words could ever describe. That was one of the ways I was able to stay grounded. But this just seemed like too much.

Handing me a duffle bag before I left his car, Georgie then said, "There's five large for you in there…five G's for you to keep. The rest is for emergencies. You did good, kid. Take care of *that mezza morte*, Harry the fuckface for me eh? When you get back, we're gonna celebrate."

I smiled, took the bag and got out of the car right as I heard, "Love you, son," from Georgie. He then sped away as his crew along with Heat waited for me, preparing for the *Lam*-or day weekend.

Everything was happening so fast at first, yet most of that time away was a blur. I felt alone, hiding with Harry in a cabin outside of Assateague, Maryland…the last place on earth I wanted to be at. I still couldn't believe what was going on.

It was depressing. The darkness swirled around this cryptic border town, tendrils of inkling bleak reminders of our solitude. The silence echoing in my ears was the constant white noise that never shut up.

Harry, nervous as ever, was a mute the entire time. Loneliness eats you alive, swallowing every ounce of hope you had yet to spare. It feasts upon any happiness you have left, leaving behind empty carcass; full of desolation tenfold. It takes your heart into its claws, squeezing out every bit of life you had circulating throughout your opaque veins. It craves for you to suffer a life without any warm hands embracing you, or any shoulders to go cry upon. God, I was pissed off.

I could barely get through night one. Trapped. No way out. One hundred percent awful sure summed the experience up.

Harry started to liven up by Saturday night but I still wanted to escape so badly. We played poker and had some great talks late into the evening…but I was sick to my stomach, missing where I really belonged.

In the half-light of Monday morning, the street was eerie. It wasn't just that it was a still day; the air simply didn't move. The leafy avenue was bereft of noise, as if every mutter and rustle was stolen away in the night. The sky was empty, not just of birds, but of clouds also. There was no weather at all; even the sunlight felt cold.

Early as I could on that final day, I got Harry up and the car ready. Enough was enough. It was time to get back to reality.

Revving the engines and making a four hour trip into three, I knew I'd be hitting a little traffic considering the weather reports were none too friendly for Labor Day. It didn't matter to me. I let nothing stop my steaming path of destruction to drop Harry off in Philly and then make it back to the shore with my baby.

Once I approached Georgie's house in record timing from driving to let Harry go on his way, Griz came up to the car thanking me again with a handshake and a kiss on the cheek. He handed me another envelope but I didn't look inside quite yet. "This meant the world, kid. Here is a little extra," he told me.

"You got to get to your mom and dad's. Dickie has been calling everywhere looking for you. I don't know...he sounded upset. Something happened but I do not know what...but I did let them know what was going on just so they all stopped worrying."

Right away, I made ways to the parents. I hope Dickie was okay. Was it him? Maybe he got in trouble. I wasn't quite sure. It didn't seem good per the grim look on Griz's face when I was there.

Nor did the expressions on both of my parents' mugs help when I got to their place either. "I can't believe you have been gone this long, Brad. Call Dickie," they instructed without any further ado. I wanted to know what was going on.

Time manifested itself. I didn't even need to go and dial. Dickie was already calling my parents' house with the news. I picked up the phone, knowing it was him. "Brad, I had to tell Rachel what was going on. Your parents made me aware. Listen...there has been an accident," he said. "What? What do you mean?" Is it Rachel?" I panicked in asking. I never caught him so down.

I could hear him taking a deep breath and countering, "No. Rachel wasn't a part of it. Friday night though. Lauren and Amanda. They spent the day in Ocean City. They were coming off of the AC Expressway to get back over to Brigantine and the car spun out of control after they were hit by a tractor trailer switching lanes so suddenly."

I urged him to go on and to spare the preamble. "Amanda is critically injured. She's up here at Jefferson Hospital in the city. Lauren didn't make it...she is dead," he told me. My mouth widened and my jaw dropped to the floor. I almost let the phone slip from my sweating palm. I was shaking.

My heart skipped a few beats. I couldn't believe what I was hearing. Dead? Her sister, dead? And Amanda in a coma? This was awful. And I was away for it all. 'God, Rachel must have been a mess' were my thoughts. I had to see her immediately.

"I'll be right over," I told him. "Which building of the hospital?" But it wasn't going to be that easy. Dickie stopped me before I could hang up the phone. "That's also why I wanted to call you."

More news? What else could he possibly detail me on? How much did I truly miss while I was away for those few days?

"Rachel...she's livid. I don't know. She had tried calling the house numerous times and contacting us all. I didn't know what to tell her until today when I talked to your mom. I had no idea what happened to you until this morning. But, now she's distant. Very aloof. She doesn't want to see you nor does she want you at the hospital. She even told the front desk not let you up."

Dumbfounded I was. I must have destroyed this girl. For her to not want to see me? Her heart must have been shattered. Dickie probably could have covered a little better but I wouldn't berate him during a crisis time like this, he sure wasn't the one to blame. He was a good friend.

So, I hung up the phone slowly. I adhered to Dickie's message and walked out of my parents' house slowly, not saying a word, dreary as could be as I got back into my car. It was time to say goodbye to the shore house. That night, it would be out of our ownership for good.

Brigantine was desolate when I returned that evening. A squally wind from the screaming ocean brought a chill to the block before the beach.

The pending rain bulletin cleared out anymore summer bodies earlier than the usual Labor Day departure while I was alone to face the storm…more than one, I was sure. Especially with when I'd see Rachel….if she would even come my way.

I felt so terrible for what had happened, I wasn't sure where I would start once I'd potentially see her. I couldn't fathom her aching.

As I parked my car in the driveway and prepared to say goodbye to the place I adored with all my heart, my childhood, my early innocence and later years' onus…I anticipated the worst in all ways.

Death - you never know how it feels, or what happens, or why. Most of the time you are too busy to think about it. The rest - you are either too scared to think or you believe that you still have a lot of time.

What if today is your last day? Would you still not think about it? I guess you wouldn't. That's why when it happens around us, especially in a blindsiding way, it's almost too much to bear. My poor Rachel. Her sister was significant to her. An amazing friend.

Finally and to a somewhat shock, there she pulled up right as I approached the house's staircase for the last time. Curiosity was gone and pandemonium struck. Alas, I wasn't certain how she'd react.

The tears flowed unchecked down her cheeks and dripped from her chin as she exited the car and came towards me.

She was too sad to cry out or wail, she just stood there as still as a statue while the magnitude of her loss swept over her. She would forever be tormented by a terrible damage that could not be undone.

I stumbled down my sidewalk and rushed over to her. "Baby, my God. I am so so sorry...are you okay?" I idiotically blurted as I got closer to her. She was clearly NOT okay. Rachel raised her hand and wiped the tears pouring from her eyes away from her cheeks.

As they continued to fall, I attempted to help dab them with my own hand. She wanted no parts. She looked at me like I was the devil himself.

After she began slapping away my hands when I tried to help her, I questioned her subtly. "I needed you, Brad!! I FUCKING NEEDED YOU!!! One of the worst nights of my life and you were nowhere to be found," she said.

As much as I tried explaining myself, there was no justifying it. "And come to find your scumbag gangster friend has a warrant out and you guys go missing for three days straight! No warning to me at all? Nice. Real fucking nice!!!"

I assured her that was not completely the case. She never cursed like this, not in angry way. I was terrified. As soon as she had cleared her tears away, a fresh torrent bust forth. Her body was wracked with great sobs and she shook like a leaf.

I pulled her to my chest where she stayed until her crying subsided. When she finally looked at me, her beautiful brown eyes were swollen and sore, she said, "I came to say goodbye and to let you know that it is over between you and I."

"Rachel...baby...you have no idea..." I tried to say until she immediately interrupted me. "NO! You have no idea. First, you leave me high and dry Friday for dinner...then my friend gets injured in a car accident and MY SISTER IS FUCKING DEAD!! AND YOU HAVE NO DECENCY TO LET ME KNOW WHAT'S GOING ON AT ALL!!"

"It's not that simple," I attempted to say. "Goodbye, Brad. I came here to tell you it's over. Do not contact me, do not find me. We are done! You broke our promise!" she yelled as she threw the Junonia shell necklace I made for her at my chest, turning around and walking away.

She then got in her car and sped out of the neighborhood quicker than a bolt of lightning. Out of my sights…out of my life.

Just as she drove away, it began drizzling out. The raindrops certainly reminded me that it was all over. This was it. This was rock bottom for me. I had never felt so alone, so lost…so incapable of even wanting to walk over and say goodbye to the old house before I departed. And this was only the start…the beginning of the pain, the suffering and the endless line of emotions that were in store for me.

I bent over to pick up the shell necklace she threw at me just as the rains were intensifying. I looked around for a quick minute, gasping in the isolation. At this moment, I simply wanted the water to melt me into the ground beneath me. I was so guilty, hopeless, and didn't even want to look at myself in the shadow.

I finally stood to slug over to the sand. Walking towards the ocean one more time, the last for the season…I took a few looks around at how dead the beach was. It was a ghost town, a forbidden ground for sure.

The sadness flowed through my veins and deadened my mind. It was a poison to my spirit, dulling me and killing off any other emotion I had. I let her down so badly.

The black mist settled upon me and I refused to shift. No matter how bright the day would get in the future, I would feel no sun and hear no bird sing. The world was lost. I knew of nothing that would bring it back into focus other than Rachel. Looking at the shell necklace one more time and then glancing quickly at the sea, I stepped back like a baseball pitcher and launched it as far from my hand and into the Atlantic as I could.

If Rachel were gone, so should the necklace be as well. I didn't want to think of her...I let her down terribly during the worst moment of her life. I would wear that albatross around my neck for a very long time.

CHAPTER SEVEN

Shining fiercely in the heart of the city, a pulse reverberates with the constant rush of its night life. Words fill the air as Philadelphians begin to let themselves out. A myriad of voices echo. Cars fighting to get through on the street, folks walking in different directions, chasing various dreams on the pavements toward the future. A picturesque scene of Brotherly Love at dusk paints out before our eyes. I certainly loved living in it, if you couldn't tell.

The New Year 2015 began just like the past sixteen did, rooftop partying under the city sky with J.R. Montague, Inc. in high hopes and toasts of topping the revenue goal we exceeded from the year previous.

At the time, I was making an incredible amount of doe. To be honest, I rarely looked at my bank statements. I had spent more money on spilled liquor in bars from one side of this world to the other, than some folks I knew made. I had the initial-engraved Rolex, the company Cadillac…you name it!!

Hitherto, I was top salesman in the office for a few years straight, inching for that partner spot soon with my boss and direct contact in the company, Steve Smith, President and C.E.O.

My days were spent working like a mad man, chasing the number, putting in twelve hour shifts…and of course, the nights were celebrated and entranced in the renowned and exclusive *Liberty Club* in Center City, the newest and hottest place for anyone to be at.

The bar was hundreds of conversations told in loud voices, all of them competing with the music that dominated the atmosphere. The melodies of tunes featuring DJ Snake consumed the ears of all who were listening. The crowd...full of life, twenty-somethings, students and grads from the Main Line colleges for the most part along with a few young professionals from the area.

My taste of the night...Gabriella DiAmonte. Twenty-two, fresh out of LaSalle University, and looking to make her mark in the world...far and away from her roots up in Long Island, New York.

We met a few weeks prior at the holiday party. I had my eye on her then. We were indulging in much more dialogue this night, we were speaking in body language. She was best friends with one of the new secretaries. "You're a sexy little thing, you know that?" I whispered, right after we closed up 2014 together. She smiled luminously and told me in reply, "I could use a drink inside," with that sly come-hither stare. Long blonde hair, thin waist and an ass that was the fruit of her squatting labors at her weekly gym sessions.

We made our way off the roof, past my well-oiled co-workers, free-loading guests, and the enriching chill of darkness to venture off into the nightclub with the many crazies that it ceiled. After all, it was the first of January and this poor little thing was shivering head to toe.

In the club, smooth vibes flowed like a virus...but a good one. There was love and lust in the air, all hyped up and ready to give us a great time. Harry and Dickie were inside somewhere also...but they were up to no good, much like myself. Gabriella held my hand as we walked quickly over to the bar. When we got there, she leaned far in-between many who were already waiting, her blonde locks lying over one shoulder of her sequined dress. I knew they would serve her quicker than they would me.

She lolled her head to one side, pushing out her red lips just a little. She wasn't drunk yet but she liked to give the impression that she was. The bartender was there to take her order in a flash, his eyes dropping only momentarily to her low-cut neckline. She twiddled her hair in a seemingly absent-minded way and giggled girlishly before ordering a Malibu Bay Breeze.

She'd practiced acting and drinking sexily from home in front of the mirror, you could tell. "Tell him seven-and-seven for me," I yelled, handing her my debit card. Within seconds, we both had what we were sipping on, able to go off and find somewhere to relax.

Things were good. I mean, as good as they could have gotten at the time. I thought back on the last sixteen years often, but rarely during particular moments like these.

However, I knew with turning thirty-eight years old in May, this was going to be a unique year. How good or how bad, I wasn't quite sure yet at the time. I just knew something was in store.

This was the age I always figured had a fork. People took either one path or the other. One to further maturity, an outward facing mentality geared to help others. The other is a path to narcissism, selfishness, an inward facing mentality that puts the self first and others a distant second.

I had been at this yield sign awhile, more or less drifting towards the second road. Yet in the midst of it all,

I was having the time of my life. Still pulling in women almost half my age was something that didn't go unnoticed. Not to anybody who knew my merit.

So, I took the beaten path and decided this young college hottie needed to come home with me to ring in the New Year correctly, seeing that it was practically almost two in the morning at this point. There was something about Gabriella that evening that made me feel so young inside, but not in a childish way.

She woke the devilish side of me, the best side. The facet of myself that only required smooth words, silky charm, and a sixty minute session no dame could ever forget, even if they tried.

I probably could have settled for a coat closet or the girl's bathroom while she did the line of cocaine she had been searching for, off my cock…but I figured taking her to my sky-rise was the best move. I wanted to enjoy destroying her vagina.

She was already wet by the time I got her into the cab. I wasn't sure if I was that handsome or if she was that drunk. It was a fun ride back home though, nonetheless, while she fondled me everywhere and anywhere.

My jokes got funnier to her. I became a comedian of epic proportions and in any way that I flirted, she melted her mouth on mine.

I noticed her pull her dress a little lower and push her chest out a tad further. She rumpled my hand through her hair frequently to draw attention to it. She knew I liked the blondish curls.

I'm barely through the door of my apartment when we get back before she starts stripping me down to nothing.

My clothes were scattered amid the entrance. She wasted no time herself with her own.

Her lacy bra became exposed above the low-cut line of her dress, which appeared to have Malibu rum spilt down the front now that I was seeing it in a good light. She was a mess, but I liked it

When I took a step forward so did she, staggering around as we swayed over and about to my bedroom before we both blacked out and enraptured into each other's pathways to passion.

Those jackhammers to the brain came battering at me when I woke up hours later, practically close to noon time. My mouth was very dry. I was dying to get something to eat and something quenching to drink. I looked over as I rose up from my slumber at the girl next to me on my bed. She was bare naked with her hair looking like electricity passed through it all over my pillows. I was embarrassed at the time, I had forgotten her name.

Oh well. Another one down in the scrapbook. 'Twas time to start the day. She was sexy, young, and cool…but not one I planned on calling again. I'm sure she felt the same way.

I wobbled over to my bathroom to splash cold water on my face just to feel something refreshing and instantly wishing I could wash my head free of the toxins too. The mirror showed my eyes, a lattice of pink over the white. It was definitely time to tell *what's-her-toosh*, "hit the road, babes." I had a big breakfast to get to with Dickie and Harry.

Grabbing the first cab I saw when I came downstairs from my apartment building, I was finally off and away to eat as this mistress vanished into the day.

The fellas and I convened at Maria's Diner, a few blocks over from the Liberty Club in Center City. It was always a delight. The place was always packed and was a great locale to meet and catch up. We did this often.

I walked in and the two were waiting for me by our usual booth by the window. They were smiling as I quavered over in my hung-over fashion, eager to get fuel into my body and kickstart the day.

At this point, Dickie had become an entertainment lawyer, working primarily in Philadelphia, New York City, and Baltimore with television stars and producers. He ended up going into law school the year after the shore home sold.

Once he earned his degree, entertainment edict became appealing to him. His true dream was to get out to Los Angeles and represent movie stars, but that came with time and experience.

Harry on the other hand, kept on the opposite side of the law…with that of his uncle and the good old boys. As many expected, he had become a *made guy* in Griz's crew and was doing a lot of big jobs recently for the family. I never questioned what he did, but I knew it was big.

He even had a position in my company somehow, placed by Georgie. I wasn't sure why he was there, however I figured there was an inimitable reason. Perhaps I'd find out one day…who knew?

I still loved them both and we spent a lot of time together, of course. There was much to draw level to with the night before being yet another success.

"You gonna get that big deal this week?" Harry opened as I sat down at the table, referring to a sales lead I had gotten end of the year, teed up for 2015. "Looking to close them up in the few days to come. Should be a hell of a way to hit a nice number early and focus on crushing the year," I went on. I signaled to the waitress for orange juice, coffee, and French toast.

"Work has been fuckin' chaotic," said Dickie. "They have me goin' all over the coast for a producer putting out a bunch of new Netflix shows. They better get off the ground and runnin' soon so I can get paid big. Sometimes I'm not home for days, it's wild. My main chick can't stand it. At least she was out for New Year's."

We then got into talking about the night prior. How great it was and how many people were in attendance at Liberty. Full house for sure. And of course, how everyone *made out.*

"Ah yes, the mermaid lookin' piece…right, Dick?" Harry asked. Valentine replied, "Yes. I call her Ariel. I get lost in her ocean eyes, every time…she casts me away. That purple hair and her seashore glisten…it's paradise. Except when she opens her mouth…then it's all hell. I'm just like *shut the fuck up already.* She just needs to have the kids I want with me and be done with it."

"That's good for you, I suppose," Heat went on. "I will stick with my Eastern Europeans. My Bulgarian and I…we're great together. She may not understand English

110

and I have no clue what she is saying…but that's okay, we speak the language of love, brother."

The tales of sweet yet short steaming passion always had a ring to it, even the rough ones. With these two, you never knew what to expect hearing as always. With me, of course, you had only the syrupiest accounts of desire.

"Nice work with you there, Brad…she was a doozy, that one ya took home there," chimed in Harry, referring to girl of whom I had forgotten her name. Confused at first as to how he saw the chick, considering I didn't see him or Dick, I questioned immediately where he spotted her before I got into the nitty gritty details. I thought I crept out in enough stealth-mode to divert.

"I had just heard from around the office. I think everyone there went through her…much like old Gemini down the shore." We all couldn't help but burst out in laughter, loud enough for the entire diner to hear and head-turn. Harking on the old days, thinking back to those summers in AC and Brigantine.

"Speaking of the shore, Brad…we were just talking about an AC reunion this summer before you got in. Us three…what do you think? Maybe give Johnny a call? See what's up," Dickie detailed.

As enthralling as this had all sounded, I remained quiet and looked around for a few. In the past sixteen years, I'd been everywhere. I traveled as much as I could have and attempted to see the world as quickly as possible. There was so much to it. Hawaii, Puerto Rico, San Juan, Santa Monica, all the tropics…Europe, Asia, South

America, wherever…I loved it all. I'd have even gone to the moon if I could have.

In the past sixteen years, I'd seen most of the Jersey shore as well. From the Atlantic Highlands to Cape May…yet, mark my words, I kid you not…I hadn't been to Brigantine or Atlantic City since that somber September day in 1999. I refused. I just couldn't do it.

"I'll get back to ya," I told them. As they persisted in telling me how fun it would be, I grew even more silent. It wasn't striking me as any type of alluring. I just wanted to get to my breakfast and continue on with my day at that point.

Being reminded of it down there when I spoke with these two sometimes distraught me as great as most the memories were. When I really dug deep in reflecting on that final day, I couldn't help but become sad.

One of the finer things that gave me pleasure at this time was my interest in writing. It elated me. For the past year prior to this, I had begun penning a story about my childhood at the shore, my college years, and my adult life in the city. I wrote of the best of times and certainly the worst, as gloomy as it was to think on. My memoirs.

This hobby gave me more happiness than anything. Coming home after a long day, unwinding…sitting down with a smile, relaxing in my comfy office seat with wheels, and popping open the laptop was truthfully an escape from the madness of the day, selling and swindling til' I was blue in the face, dusk to dawn.

112

Sometimes, an idea for a chapter would just pop into my thoughts. Writing in sequence when suddenly, I would envision, hearing the words for a chapter farther along in the novel than where I was. GO THERE NOW! If a word fairy would give me a gift, I'd step out of my flow. I figured I could always edit it later when it came time. Adjustments are the massage therapists of the creative mind.

Just as I got into a nice flow, my cell phone went off. Odd that it was around dinner hour but I expected anything these days. I looked at the screen and it was Uncle Griz. Now that he was underboss in the Philly family, it was almost taboo to not pick up his call.

"Hey, Uncle Georgie...what's what?

"Have you gotten some rest since New Year's, kid? All that cooz still drainin' ya, huh?"

"HA! Just a little rest, Griz...can't let the mind get too idle...back at it workin' now, ya know?"

"You're not young anymore. Don't let the pussy kill you, boy. Slow it down a little."

"It's just so much fun. Still as easy as it was in my twenties...maybe even easier at times."

Georgie always called once a week or so to check up on me...and of course, what was going on in the company. He was a man who wanted to know everything at any time.

"I hear ya. You did fuckin' good. 2014 was your year, biggest one of your career...Steve has been talking about it, the whole company has. Him and I had dinner at the Ritz the other night, he can't stop tellin' me he has high hopes for you this year. This could be your transition to partner, Brad....I'm tellin' ya 2015 is it. Stay the course and keep fuckin' killin' it."

"Of course. Eyes on the prize, Georgie...you know that. I don't do it any other way."

"I expect only the best. You need anything, you let Harry or me know."

I always felt like I could go to Uncle Georgie for anything. Although, these days...I'd go to him less than ever. Not that I specifically resented him for what happened back in the day, but it stayed on my mind for sure. It was hard to let it not.

"Thanks Georgie, I know that. I love ya."

"Love you too, kid."

I hung up the phone and went back to my writing, immediately. I thought of nothing else. It truly did relax me. I loved putting these stories together for my memoirs, seeing what I could come up with. There was so much to tell.

The threads of words, weaving them into a pattern that could fill another person's mind with beauty, or the choice of words may be patterned to create a wide array of responses and emotions.

Continuing to type on the laptop, I started to want to take notes on the side. Scattering through my drawers of my desk for a yellow legal notepad, I came across a treasure I looked at here and there...often enough I recognized it blatantly every time I saw it, keeping it nearby.

It was the only known picture of Rachel and I from that summer of 1999. I had a disposable camera that week, taking pictures randomly...and this one, this particular photo had all the reason and all the memory. I'd even look at it sometimes and shed a tear.

She drew me in with a sweetness I'd never found before, something so strong that I still felt it all that time later. But those periods where I looked back so heatedly, it broke me in ways unimaginable.

While I reminisced, I heard a knock at my door. "Come on in," I yelled. I hated anything interrupting my writing or looking at this picture, but I was curious as to who it could have been. Low and behold, my old man came by to drop off some of his homemade wine.

"Long time, no see, Dad," I said as I stood up, going over to give him a hug. "It's a good aged wine this one, Brad. I'm tellin' ya it's my best batch yet. Your mother hates my hobby but I said, oh well."

It was great to see my Dad whenever I could. He had been off and on sick the past few years with cancer, off and on. He would beat it, it would come back, he'd get real sick, he'd feel good again...it was a viscous cycle that nobody in family or circle of friends enjoyed dealing with. It was a terrible thing.

So, I figured it was important to savor every moment with a man who had more wisdom than anybody I knew...a man I loved and adored.

"How's the job going?" he asked me. "Better than ever, Dad. Had the best 2014 and looking to do amazing this year." We continued talking as we walked over to my desk where I offered him a seat. He moved slow, one foot in the other at molasses speed...but I knew he was exhausted these days. He'd lose his breath quickly and I'd see his face white as a ghost sometimes.

115

As I began to tell him about my recent work on my memoirs, he stopped me in my tracks when he saw the picture of Rachel on my desk that I hadn't put away yet.

"Brad, you gotta let go. It has been sixteen years, buddy. You've emailed her, wrote to her, sent Facebook friend requests and messages to her, tried getting Dickie to contact her friend for you...none of it's gonna work, pal. She blocked you completely."

"I just wish I acted sooner on it, Dad. The day I last saw her when she threw the necklace at me. I let her walk away, right then and there and didn't contact her for years."

"Now listen, you're still a young guy with the world by the balls. She was great, I'm sure...but that one week existed long ago when you were a different man. She's a different girl now than what you remember. You need to move on."

What my father was saying had ration, but he didn't understand what went on in my head. "You know, you told me once...I was meant for a specific girl. One that was the fulfillment, one that would sweep me off my feet, Dad. Well, this is the one...if it ain't Rachel...it ain't nobody."

He couldn't help but chuckle. "I wish I got to meet her, son. I hear nothing but great things from all you boys...and about her sister too, God rest. But I said it and I still mean it today...you will find someone else, I guarantee it. I think it's crazy you still think of Rachel...but I understand. Just quit beatin' yourself up about it."

Of course, sixteen years later, I still thought of her. It made me miserable. I had tried to throw her out of my head. But her memory kept coming back every night. I didn't know if I should have really called it a nightmare. I

116

always woke up before I got to see the part where she threw the necklace at me, walking out of my life and into the world without me.

Maybe I couldn't have gotten rid of it, or maybe I didn't want to. It was the only part of her I could hold on to. And every time I'd see her in my sleep, I'd revise through all the other options I had…to skip the job I was assigned, to call her in spite of the instructions I was given, to have tried harder to reconcile immediately after. But I had done none of them, and what's done was done. I couldn't have ever changed that. I let it haunt me every night as I looked at that one throw-away camera photo we had, so I could still have had part of her and hope that one day she'd forgive me.

CHAPTER EIGHT

Dickie was already sending me links to my email that brought me to various summer rental websites on the shore within the first few weeks they had spun out the idea of a reunion. Those two may have been excited for such a merriment...I however, was quite the contraire. It wasn't top of my agenda.

"Let's look at Ocean City, Maryland instead...or one of the Caribbean Islands for a reunion," I kept consistently replying in the email threads.

While I entertained his messages briefly at work, I quickly went back to doing what I did best at the time: selling top tier software.

Business was business. There was money to be made everywhere. My company and I traded all over the world at this point: London, Paris, Rome, Istanbul, Tokyo, Singapore, Hong Kong...this thing befitted global.

Without a doubt, I enjoyed becoming wealthier over time. It was the life I always imagined growing up. Champagne for breakfast and caviar at happy hour amid the finest eateries in the city. I went from struggling that first year with J.R. to free of having to show up to work. It was like being handed the keys to the greatest castle.

The apartment grew classier, meals more opulent; nights out became whenever we wanted them, money no object. My suave hair became so pretty with weekly visits to the salon, nails and clothing too.

I upgraded everything: car, appliances, whatever I needed to. It was all for the taking and my friends and I indulged in the greatest of splendors wherever and whenever.

Harry, Dickie, and I even got the "Goodfellas" treatment one night at a club in South Philly where the owner met us in the back and walked us through the kitchen over to our table to avoid the crowded lines out front. Between all of our successes and connections to Heat and Georgie, we had a free pass to anything.

Meanwhile, that same day, sitting in my office…I get buzzed by my secretary that the boss wanted to see me. It was urgent.

So, I got up from what I was doing and made my way to my floor's lobby. I came off the elevator that opened directly into my boss' private office, a huge room occupying the corner of the building with floor-to-ceiling windows giving views of the city from all directions. The two remaining walls contained a door, a low bookshelf, a fireplace, a mini bar, and a single elegant oil painting - a vase of flowers by Vincent van Gogh.

Steve Smith was different to the other "funny guys." He used his wit for satire, his comments were clever and insightful. Even the subject of the ridicule often joined in the joke, he always presented it in such a way that they were free to laugh at themselves and become the star of the situation rather than himself.

Being the subject of one of his remarks made you feel like part of the group, if Steve thought you were worth an observation you were one of the gang.

He was never cruel, never aimed to injure or cause distress. I did appreciate him as a boss, and in due time…he became a friend.

"Mr. Smith…how are you this lovely day? Thanks for calling me up," I came in, welcoming. "Brad, I've told you for years…call me Steve. Mr. Smith is no way to address a friend," he replied.

He went over to his mini bar by the big desk, offering me a Mimosa. All of a sudden, he jotted back over to his speakerphone, "Brenda, I need more oranges STAT!!" "Right away, Mr. Smith."

I was always flabbergasted when he would raise his voice. He then looked at me and smiled, "It's okay, she likes when I yell. Especially when she is blowing me in the office here." I held my chest and couldn't help but crackle. Steve knew how to be the right kind of insulting.

He did it with such *joire de vive*…the only person I knew who could get away with such things. It wasn't only because he was the boss…he was also very likeable in his role by many.

"What can I do you for, Steve?"

"You can do yourself…a favor, and take care of a little business for me."

"Tell me more."

"The software trade show coming up in February…biggest event for the United States numbers we bring in. Historically, it went to Larry…but you know he has since retired after being us for thirty years after much merge and acquisition. All the leads come from there…I'm giving it to you and your unit."

"Steve...oh my God...I don't know what to say. This is fuckin' incredible."

"You have well-deserved it, buddy."

The trade show was always a great experience. There would be plenty of people to meet and it was a three day getaway that made it worth it.

Historically, it had moved around to different spots in the Northeast: Boston, New York, Baltimore, sometimes Philly itself.

"Where is it going to be this year, Steve?"

"They're hosting it in Atlantic City."

I couldn't believe it. I even asked him to repeat himself just in case I misheard him or hoped he had said somewhere else.

Go figure. The one place I hadn't been to in almost half a lifetime is hosting one of the biggest events of the year.

"Convention center, Brad...right by the Sheraton. I want you to go alone. Nobody with you. This is all yours...all for the taking. You'll love it...great food nearby, do a little gambling at night. Everything is paid for, all expenses."

Looked like my reunion was coming quicker than I thought. I had to listen to the man, I couldn't argue it. This was a big opportunity. Yet out of all the places in all the states this was held...this had to be the year of AC, right? Crazy when I kept thinking about it. I had to still give acknowledgement, Steve was giving me a big thing.

"Thank you again, Steve...this means the world."

"Just get us some big clients, that's all. Have fun but make us money…but what am I saying? Ha, you always do."

We both took a look at the city view from his lovely windows one more time before I exited his office and went back to work.

It was bittersweet to me. Yes, this was a great mission to endure…at the same time, it would have been a time warp. The memories, the nostalgia. It was going to consume me. I had no idea what I would be driving on down to.

I called the boys to let them know I was getting a sneak peek into the old lands in just a couple short weeks. I packed my bags early and started the ignition for a ride into the past.

The most drastic changes I noticed when I got into town that February were a direct result of Superstorm Sandy…even two and a half years after its hit. Houses were raised, some demolished. So many changes in such a small area. It was honestly a sight to see. A new landscape on an old frontier.

On the other hand, it was bizarre, being here again after so long. Like a time warp. I even had "Boys of Summer" by Don Henley playing in the car as constant reminder of nostalgia.

Despite the amount of years I'd been away, I still remembered everything about the place as I arrived to its entrance; the blue hydrangeas planted in the front yard, the soft tinkling of the wind chimes that reminded me of summer afternoons. The sky colored paint on the old shingles had faded since I had last seen it, but I still recognized it without a doubt.

It looked like the color before a bad storm. I walked up to the door and raised my hand to knock, but I stopped. Contemplating going back in my car, I kept looking back and then immediately towards the house again.

I took a deep breath, and forced myself to hit the doorbell I noticed, something that wasn't there in my years dwelling here. I heard the "ding-dong" sound coming from inside, but nobody scurrying over to the door.

I peeked inside the windows, seeing nothing inside but what remained years ago. It was almost as if the folks who bought the place from us never moved in.

I looked all around the property. The old house seemed to have collapsed inwardly on itself somewhat over time, like a loaf of bread taken out of the oven too soon. The roof sagged and the shingles stuck up in places like wonky teeth.

The windows' glass had yellowed and they seemed not to be quite rectangular anymore. They were a bit askew now, perhaps from all the great winds.

The lean-to garage in the back hung downwards as if the fight had left it and it could no longer bring itself to stand up against any weather.

In the high winds of another potential heightened hurricane season, the place I'm sure would crumble like a deck of cards with the right gust.

When I came out front, I looked for any other clues that would solve the mystery of this abandoned enigma. It was then I saw something I should've noticed when I arrived; a for sale sign right on the front lawn. "Go figure," I said to myself.

I walked away a bit disappointed. It was hard enough leaving the house many years ago…but to come back almost sixteen years later and see it unkempt and not taken care of hurt a little more. The lack of care was too much to try and fathom.

Whoever the buyers were that summer and whatever followed it must've had a sad tale…because I was slowly developing a sadder one myself the more I looked around at the wintry no man's land that the disheveled old cottage was centerpiece to.

So, I got out as quickly as I could and shot over to the madness of the trade show immediately after seeing the place. Time was money.

It was insanity all day. Software wasn't the only hot topic of the week…there were various other conventions happening simultaneously in the same building.

The crowd had a life of its own, the vibrant folks who shined like vibrant light and those who moved like enchanting shoals of fish. You had it all.

Each person in the crowd moves as if unseeing hands drag them this way and that, pulling their eyes to one thing and then another.

There was chatter between sellers and buyers, old friends catching up, new friends made. It was busy for sure, but the hustle and bustle brings a life to this job I wouldn't want to be without. I was making some great connections in one day.

Yet, I had to escape for second and get to the bathroom. For a brief moment, I thought I would pee my pants given I was standing and talking so long. And to people I figured I'd never see again either.

Making it outside, the fresh February breeze from the entrance doors of the center didn't feel too bad creeping in escaping the heat of inside the show. It was relieving.

However, I couldn't get to the bathroom once I tried. My walks got harder. Something was slowing me down to a turtle-like speed. It was probably the last thing imaginable.

I was completely aghast. I couldn't move. There I stood as if the wind was taken out of me, a shot to the stomach. I couldn't believe it. My face fell faster than if it had cement boots. In that instant my skin became greyed, my mouth hung with lips slightly parted and my eyes were as wide as they could stretch. It almost seemed surreal.

All of this was because right before me, right at the Convention Center in Atlantic City...low and behold, fifteen yards away...Rachel Weston stood by the water fountains. Of all places in all of the world, here she was. By fate? By chance? By coincidence? I wasn't sure. It probably would have been less shocking to see a ghost.

God, she didn't age a bit. She was a year younger than me but I still saw her like she was twenty-one. The same exquisite body I could see through her long ivory-colored dress, the same long brown hair curling down in soft twists, dark skin, and the smile that beamed like light

125

on polished stone containing a wealth of mystique beyond any other covert.

And her eyes... the brilliant hazel I remember so well. As jovial as she was…they were warm, lively, and sparkled with mirth. The smooth green on the edge contrasted stunningly with the amber color in the middle, capturing this heart of mine every time I saw them.

Amazement didn't quite cover this feeling. It was like someone just took my spark of wonder and poured on kerosene, igniting it into wildfires.

The smile I showed on the outside couldn't adequately have reflected what I felt inside; every neuron of my brain was trying to fire in both directions at once - the best kind of paralysis.

I wanted to run up on her, say hello and see how she was doing…where she'd been and what she'd seen these past sixteen years. However, for the first time in my life, I didn't know how to.

I feel lost and confused, but happy and certain to see her face. I was a ball of tangled yarn. The parts that were untangled were available, useable; the rest was a complete mess. That mess felt endless and unyielding.

Relinquishing my fears was a must, I couldn't let this opportunity pass. Perhaps it was once in a lifetime. There was a feeling pushing inside me, demanding me to be brave and strong. I never had these kind of butterflies before.

There I went. I put it all behind me. Fury drained and nothing but focus. I took several deep breaths and counted to three, cracking my neck and knuckles before I approached her premises. Any bit of courage I had left washed into me like a perfect surfer's wave and allowed me to ride on.

After a few hard steps, I stopped in my tracks, face to face with her. I couldn't believe it. I could finally inhale her. She smelled so wonderful, like the fresh cotton scent I recall.

We locked eyes for the first time in sixteen years. "Hello," I said, softly. She was speechless, eyes wide open, smile gone. For a moment, I could swear, she was immobile as well...maybe even more than I was.

CHAPTER NINE

Out of my dreams and into my life. Although, I still felt like I was in a trance as I drove over to Maria's Diner back in Philly. It was a day after the convention ended and I couldn't wait to tell the boys about who I had seen during my travels.

They would have never believed me. Paranormal activity seemed more likely. And I knew at the time, I was going to catch a ton of shit for bringing this one up. It was to be expected.

Yet, both Harry and Dickie heard me out…as much as they didn't want to. They knew this wasn't an everyday occurrence. No matter what the result had been of that short period of time I saw her, it was certain this was out of the blue like no other.

"It's like she hadn't changed at all. Looks even more gorgeous than she did back in the day," I was detailing. I could tell right away the fellas weren't interested in this tale. It was all over their faces. Dickie was the first to give his words.

"Brad, I love you…and I'm glad you saw her. But, I just don't want you to get your hopes up here. It was a battle with that one, long after that dreary old day in September '99."

"I know, I know," I replied. A lot had went down after that occurrence. Like I said before, it changed me. I did some out of the ordinary things.

Dickie continued. "Even after I lost touch with Amanda, you still wanted to contact Rachel. I'm sure she'd want to put a restraining order on you if it ever went down again."

Amanda Jones, Rachel's best friend stayed in touch with Dickie for a long while after that summer. She was critically injured from the infamous car accident but survived miraculously.

I wasn't a hundred percent sure if she had any permanent damages but she was fortunate enough to be alive for sure.

I was never quite sure what the romance between Dickie and Amanda detailed. He didn't talk about that one much. I knew it was something mutual, something that had come into fruition that summer...but what that exactly meant was always a mystery.

And yes, I got a little crazy for awhile. I never got into stalker mode, but I sure gave my full efforts to win her back about a year or two after the summer of '99. I couldn't help myself.

Harry leaned in and said, "Brad, if you try going for this broad again...you're a sucker. I mean, she blocked all your numbers, blocked us all from Facebook, and won't let us see anything that's going on. You've wrote to her, tried channeling through Amanda, tried her family, and sent her everything except practically a smoke signal with an S.O.S. attached to it. It's just not worth it, brother. It's long over."

What Heat was detailing me had reason, but he wasn't the one who saw her just prior to that day. It was like I was reliving a fantasy, on cloud nine and just couldn't jump off.

The colors of a thousand different types of skies swirled in my mind like a waterfall. As they billowed and spun in the breeze they left hues behind, until all that was left was a beautifully painted picture of Rachel Weston.

I kept envisioning her holding out her arms wide and awaiting to fall into mine. I simply couldn't help any of it. It continued coming into my thoughts, fresh.

"I don't care what you guys say, I am pretty excited," I responded. "She gave me her business card." I pulled it out of pocket, proud as ever to put on the table and show them.

Rachel Weston, Education of the Arts – Department Chair, Stockton University

"Hu-oooo...what the fuck? Stockton? You mean she is living in South Jersey now?" asked Dickie, holding the card as if it were a crime scene clue, boggling his mind like a riddle.

"About twenty minutes outside the city," I assured. They then went ahead with a million questions, the both of them. Now they wanted to hear everything. "She's not in Georgia anymore?" asked Dickie. "Apparently not."

"So, what are you gonna do then? You gonna try and make a move here?" inquired Harry with a bit of aggression. "I have no idea yet. I know nothing about her life other than she is in the area. Our encounter was brief, but she left it open," I retorted.

It was then we heard noises from the front. Out of the blue, we saw from the entrance, Uncle Georgie walk

130

into the diner, saying hello to everyone he encountered before he came to our table.

He was shaking hands and kissing babies on the way as if he were running for president.

"Uncle Griz!" we all welcomed. "Hu-ooooooo," he replied. "Either I have three handsome ladies' men hunks in the midst of my presence or three *finooyks* that love to fuck each otha!!"

Always the kind word. Georgie sat with us and ordered some last minute food to go, just as we were wrapping things up to leave. I knew he was there to break some kind of balls given the way he came in.

"Brad, what are you doin'? You gonna waste your time again with that *putanna* I hear? She couldn't be away from ya for two fuckin' days way back when...it's been too long brother, let it go," said Griz.

I was beginning to resent the man. He had too high of expectations. Everything had to be to his liking. If it weren't of his approval, he made it known...even if the thing had nothing to do with him at all.

It was starting wear on me, finally. As a matter of fact, any time he came around anymore...I tried to scurry away before we could chat.

"Yeah, Brad...let it go," chimed in Harry, echoing his uncle's advice. We all stood up as the waitress came out to give Georgie's food for him, to go. He signaled to his nephew that they needed to speak business.

We all stood up at the same time. Right away, Dickie stopped in his tracks and turned around to have me in private, away from the other two. He knew where I was at, mentally.

"Listen…you do what you gotta do with Rachel. Don't let us tell you," he assured. I smiled and hugged him, thanking him for his kind words. It was much appreciated at the time.

The next day, back at the office, I sat in my chair and looked at Rachel's business card, over and over. It was so elegant, blue and white colored with an image of a daisy in the top left corner. Her name was in cursive-like font and done so beautifully.

I had just gotten off the phone, informing my parents of my sightings that week. They couldn't believe it. They were happy to hear, my mom especially. With my dad getting sicker, it was hard for him to feel joy about anything. Yet, I knew deep down what he would tell me… "Do you, pal…do what makes you happy."

Steve Smith entered my office around noon to discuss the trade show. He could tell I was distant, very little in detail and not excited about the subject at all. "It was good, ya know."

I remained diligent in front of him, focusing on various other tasks as he continued to try and talk. It was like I was in an organized state of massive clutter before me. He kept going and going, asking away. I remained coy and brief.

Yet my stillness was somehow comforting and spoke for itself. It was peaceful in a way where he could feel that no matter what was happening, I was doing my job and was still loyal to him.

He walked out after a few minutes and left me to it.

Little did anyone at the office know, I was feeling optimistic this day. I knew what I could do…take whatever I wanted, whoever I wanted, and however. "I'm Brad Mulligan," I told myself. There wasn't any reason to doubt my strengths.

Hope beaded my skin like dew on spring grass. I feel it radiating in to soothe my blood. If formed such perfect spheres, each one like a tiny world of its own. It was time to go for another win.

So, I called her. Right then and there.

"Hello?"

"Rachel…it's Brad. You know…Brad Mulligan, how are you?"

"Oh, hi…how's it going, Brad?"

"Pretty well, how was the rest of your trade show?"

"Fantastic."

I didn't want to leave too much of an awkward silence between parts of the conversation. I was working with very little time here. I wanted to ask her out, so bad…right away.

"Sooo…listen. I was thinking. It has been a really long time."

"Haha, oh gosh…it really has."

"I wanted to see if you wanted to grab dinner with me tonight. Nothing crazy, real casual…you can pick the spot near you if you like. Just looking to catch up with you."

Who said silence was golden? How could it be? When I need to hear her speak right away. Say my name, Rae. Even just a whisper. Speak to me…if only for a moment. I can never be content in your silence. If I could just hear a response, I would be fine.

I was going crazy. I could hear her contemplating. This was sudden. Her "I don't knows" and my "come on's" were getting draining. Finally, she gave me a solid answer.

"Meet me at Tony's Baltimore Grille on Iowa Avenue in Atlantic City. Let's shoot for 5:30."

"One of my favorite places. I'll see you there."

I hung up. I was back in the game. This was it! My time to shine, for sure. That night was going to perfect, a return to our love once and for all.

I had been so lost in constructing scenarios for the evening ahead, I was starting to sound crazy. I had to just let it all take its course. Tony's Grille was in sight. There was nothing slick about it...no fancy fonts, crazy neon signs, or white etching upon the glass.

You could pick the whole thing up and send it back thirty years and it wouldn't look out of place. There weren't elegant doors with illustrious designs, just the uneven pavements that bared the cracks of age.

Despite the early hour, the jazz music was moving and grooving as I entered. A live Miles Davis tribute band was performing. I'm sure they were going to be there all night. However, I knew her and I wouldn't be sitting at the bar, chatting until the wee hours. She seemed like a business girl with a bedtime per our talk a few days prior.

134

Rachel was already be inside the restaurant, waiting. Suddenly all my preparations fled my mind like scared children. My brain felt full of static like an old television set losing the signal. I stopped. Part of me was screaming to turn around, but I knew my possible future was ahead of me.

"You look dashing," I opened, hugging her gently. She certainly did. There wasn't a question she was the belle of the ball that evening at Tony's. Not that it was hard amid the stragglers, hustlers and street gals that hung around the place, but Rachel would light up even the brightest of establishments.

"Ain't so bad yourself, boy," she replied. We couldn't stop laughing immediately. It felt so good. The vibes were like old times. Things were off to a great start.

The hostess signaled for us to sit wherever we pleased. I always preferred a booth. It was in the corner, innocuous, and in sights of everything ahead.

As Rachel's bright eyes kept looking up and at me, I continued to remind her that the food was a neighborhood classic.

The whole place, in fact, was a classic. The old waitresses with their red shirts were diligently running around the restaurant, earning every buck they could. The same pasty-haired manager with those thick glasses seemed like he was standing in the same spot in the kitchen for the past thirty years, keeping a close watch on each pizza pie.

By every red-checkered table-clothed sit-down was a miniature jukebox on the wall, compounded with great tunes, old and new. Yet tonight, we had the band.

"So, catch me up on the last sixteen years," I requested. She giggled. It was almost like she didn't know where to begin.

"Well, I left Georgia about four years ago and got out of teaching high school. I found a job near here that paid really well as a college professor. Given how much I loved being near the beach, I took it. Still chasing my dream to get to Italy, but right now there is an opportunity in Spain. We shall see."

The time I last saw her, I wanted to take her by the hand and lead away. I wanted to walk with her, talk with her, and show her how sorry I was. Now, she was close…once again. It was like I was given a second chance here to do all that.

"That is fantastic, Rae. Sounds exciting. I think you should certainly pursue that dream and get to Spain or Italy, or wherever it may be. Fulfill that part of yourself."

"Of course I will. It's going to be a lot of work and effort, but I feel good about it. What's going on with you?"

"Just stayin' busy."

"Oh, gosh…that sounds cryptic."

"Hah! Just doin' the big city. Still with J.R. Montague now…looking for partner this year! It's stressful as ever over there but I can't complain because I am doing well, better than ever."

"Oh wow, that's so great. Congrats and good luck."

I didn't want to tell her about my memoirs. A lot of it consumed my years at the shore. There was a huge part of the book that highlighted our time together. Perhaps the next date, I'd bring it up. I wasn't ready. Tonight was strictly about her.

I wanted to hear it all. "Tell me more," I instructed. There was nothing I expected her to leave out. If our hearts were going to be open books this night, there wasn't a detail I didn't want to catch. She then continued.

"So…I'm engaged. Have been for about a year now. The wedding is this fall. We're having it in Barcelona, right near where I may live soon," she said, plain and simple. I choked up, drinking my water. My eyes were wide open.

I immediately regretted asking her to tell me more. It was a moment where you wish what you had just heard was a mistake. My light immediately faded to black. The new dream I was living had just become a nightmare all over again. Devastating.

Although it was obvious she was a gorgeous woman, I should not have been surprised she was with somebody else…yet it was still extremely depressing to hear. I thought there may have been a chance.

I tried not to let it break me. I continued to smile and converse with her, yet I could barely focus and made out very little of what she was saying after that statement.

CHAPTER TEN

I was at a loss. A true feeling of failure. A flood of fluster ran through my system at lightning speed. As I exited the restaurant, disturbed, I began thinking that the whole night was a waste…a complete defeat.

As shocking it was hearing she was engaged, it was something I should have expected. Yet still, I wasn't sure how to comprehend it all quite yet. Knowing she was in another man's arms was ruthless to torture my thoughts with.

While I was devastated to hear about Rachel's new life and how she had completely moved on, her best friend Amanda was excited beyond belief to discuss the wedding plans with her on a daily basis.

She was another character nobody had heard from in a dog's age. Yet, from what I gathered during Rachel and I's discussion at dinner, Amanda had settled, living in the area recently as well. She was a nurse at one of the hospitals on the shore. She did great. Always a smart and attractive girl herself, we knew she'd be a success somewhere.

The two were chatting at Rachel's house that same week in Galloway, New Jersey, talking about the upcoming marriage in the fall, taking place in Barcelona, Spain. Amanda was to be her maid of honor, a duty she held with high prestige.

"The azaleas are perfect. I think our bridesmaids' dresses are going to compliment them really well, Rae.

Totally what we need to have. Oh my gosh, this is going to be a magical day for you and Edward."

"Oh yes, just beautiful…I cannot wait. I just can't decide on a flavor of wedding cake though. We are going to be in Spain, so I wasn't sure if we should do a Flan-like dessert…what are your thoughts?"

"Ixnay on the Lan-Flay, Rae!"

Their faces became beat-red with laughter. Rachel was giggling so hard, her stomach was in pain. They always had fun, these two. Planning a wedding was one of the things they looked forward to since their youth, being the life-long friends that they were.

While topics of flowers, deserts, and wedding-wear consumed their days, things took a turn when Rachel hit her with the news. She held it in as long as she could have. She had to tell her of her recent encounter with yours truly before she burst, holding it in.

"So, I didn't tell you yet…but…I ran into Brad at the Atlantic City convention the other day."

"Get the heck out of here!! No way!!"

"Not just that, but we kind of met up for dinner as well…it wasn't that bad."

Amanda paused from working on the laptop, searching for *save the date* templates to send out to guests. She gave a blank stare to Rachel as if she just stole money from her purse. She began to scold like never before.

"You can't be serious. Why would you do that?"

"I don't know. It seemed innocent. He wasn't being crazy or anything."

"Rae, he *is* crazy. You know it, I know it…your family knows it. What made you think that was okay?"

Amanda was not my number one fan, this was evident. She felt strongly against us ever talking again after the infamous incident that occurred in the summer of '99 and my association with unsavory friends like Harry and Georgie. I felt she was a key factor in our mass separation given all her hostility.

"It's just...I don't know, Amanda. I mean...as hurtful as he was years ago, he's still so sweet. Very caring, very all about *me*...you know?"

"No...I *don't* know. He's a player, same as Dickie. Those guys care about nothing except finding girls and getting into their pants. It' ridiculous, if you ask me. Disgusting."

Rachel disagreed. She knew I had my fun...but when I was with her, it was all about her. There was no question about that.

"Now, Amanda...I know that's not why you stopped talking to Dickie. You guys had a lot of fun too, don't deny it."

"We did have fun. But, all good things come to an end. Just like you and Brad. We all move on, that's just simply life."

There was a bitter way to Amanda about love that nobody could quite understand. She always spoke of it in an unpleasant, uninviting way and certainly at speed that was brash.

All of sudden, Rachel's mom came into the room, catching the conversation mid-way. She wasn't a supporter of mine either. What I did that weekend would never be forgotten, not by anybody who was there for duration of the tragedy.

"Rachel, stay away from that boy. He's a gangster. He's bad, trouble with a capital T. What would your father say?"

"I don't care, mother. It's not like I am leaving my fiancé for the guy, it was one darn dinner. Everyone has their panties in a bunch!"

From the way it looked in the room, it was as if her mother's trot over to her was one that intended she was going to slap Rachel in the face.

"You are marrying Edward in September, Rachel...the love of your life. We are all going to be spending a week in Spain, it is going to be so beautiful and the family is very excited!!! It was good you saw Brad but we all know it's time to let it go! He was no good for you, darling!!"

It was clear where her friends and family stood. I was the enemy, banned from existence in their world, like an exiled prisoner.

"I just think it's a bit harsh to see it all that way. I don't want to keep resenting and holding a lifetime grudge over somebody who, at one point...meant the world to me," she told them.

It was depressing that they were against me. What happened was terrible, all around. But I was humble in the years to come and gave a thousand apologies to her and her own.

As long as Rachel still cared, which it seemed she did based on our dinner that night...it was all that mattered to me at the time.

I had a feeling there was a tiny flicker still alive on our once fiery-lit candle. I didn't want to cease my fight just yet.

I tried calling Harry that night to chat about stuff, but I forgot he was meeting Uncle Georgie at Liberty to touch base.

In the presence of various mixed drinks, a cocaine buffet, and random young women galore in their VIP booth, The Griz was giving Heat a big talk that night about his duties in his role at my company, whatever that entailed. At this point in time, I still had no idea what the kid was doing there at J.R...but he showed up every day, on time too.

On the same token, Griz was reminding him about his rising prominence in the crime family. Harry was ascending quickly since our early days. Knowing he had an eye for the fast and furious things in life, Georgie made it his responsibility to put his nephew under his wing as his street protégé.

"I'm honored, Uncle Georgie...I am, believe it. Not a day goes by where I don't appreciate being a part of the tradition that the family entails," said Harry, bold and confident as ever. Griz knew Harry was all in...he just needed to keep it top of mind sometimes.

"I have gone on a record with you in front of all the skippers, you better not fuck it up. These are people I've known before you were born...people your father and your grandfather knew for *years*," said Griz, with force.

You could see his face illuminating and his hands gong a mile a second as he spoke. He wanted to make it a point to Harry that this *thing of theirs* was something that was to not be taken lightly. Heat assured him that he wouldn't let him down at this point in his life and that he was clear as crystal with what the family's legacy truly entailed.

"You're moving up very fast; don't let it go to your head. You are my nephew and the future boss of this family...but it ain't gonna be easy," said Griz. "I know, I know," responded Harry.

Georgie pinched him on the cheek and told him he was a good boy. "Make sure that what you're doing at the office is 100% done right. We have a lot of money comin' out of there, into this family's pockets. We're talking a quarter billion dollar operation over time. This is huge. You're administering this thing. Now, I know you're doing a good job, you just need to keep doin' it. Don't ever think you can slow down. This is a fast-pace thing we are working on here."

Harry told him, "I hear ya, Unc. Believe me...I am there every day making sure what's done is done. You'd be proud if you were next to me for it all to watch, first hand."

"I want to stay proud of you, Harry. I love you so much. It's the age of a dynasty, kid...you're livin' in it. Keep your head," concluded Georgie, kissing him on the cheek as Harry leaned over for some white powder to inhale into his system.

Griz was stealing Harry from us a piece at a time. Every week he pushed him slightly further until not only did he have no morals, he thought that the organization's way of thinking was a desirable freedom.

His friends, we who truly loved him, became his enemy in the eyes of Griz. He looked at us like we were vile to him.

With all the efforts of trying to convert Dickie and I to their world, the exhaustion became an indifference. He didn't feel the same way about us.

It was rare I ever saw him in a moment of remorse. After that last summer of '99, he sunk lower each year into his criminal ways. He sunk so low, nobody got close unless they were bringing news of the next family order. It wasn't the same kind of Harry we knew.

I was unable to reflect rationally or clearly, sitting on my couch in my living room, looking at the city skyline that night. I kept reaching for a magazine on my coffee table to distract myself, but it wasn't quite working. I was all alone, just my iPhone and I.

More importantly, I had gone astray with my thoughts. Biting my lip and tapping on my chin…I knew one thing above everything else I was contemplating, I wanted to talk to her again…badly.

So many reasons against it, yet I didn't care. Even with the disheartening news, speaking to Rachel was still vitally important to me.

I felt like we bumped into each other in AC for a reason. Whatever that meant, I was still unsure. I just knew she was back in my path now…it had been half a lifetime since I was able to say that.

The obscurity of what would happen after I reached out to her remained evident. My head was spinning and I couldn't stop it.

I stood up quickly and walked around for a few minutes, holding my iPhone in my hand with her number out, a ring away with just the simple touch of my index finger.

I felt like every fiber of my being was vibrating with anticipation. Adrenaline was coursing through my veins. My hands trembled and my eyes were wide. "This is what a cat must feel like waiting to pounce on a mouse," I thought.

Instead of wasting more precious time, I went for the kill. This had to be done. So, I took a deep breath, put the phone to my ear and saw the call go through.

It rang twice on the other end…and immediately went to voicemail. "Dammit!" I yelled. I was very upset but I gave the situation the benefit of the doubt. There was more to be done.

"Perhaps I should just text her," I concluded. I kept it simple. "Hello…just wanted to say thank you for joining me for dinner the other night. I had a great time" I delivered it.

All of a sudden, the alert popped up, "Message failed to send," leaving the words in green and nothing to her screen. I tried a few more times, but to no avail. It was useless.

Did she block me? Was there no signal? How could I have been so dumb? What had seemed so good of an idea was only to be full of flaws by the end of my tries.

Everything was starting to catch up to me. I couldn't contact her. It was painful. I threw the phone at my couch and sat back down.

Who was I kidding at the time? What made me think I even had a chance? I already blew it years ago, big time.

I was miserable. I wasn't happy with my life…I was just hiding all my shallowness and depression every day in the shadows of work, women, and partying. There was no real joy acquired from these things.

It was all a façade to my buried cave of dark emotions, a growing one. The money and success meant nothing without love.

Loneliness is what you get out of the absence of love; it makes your life miserable, and breaks your heart into thousand pieces. And still, each broken part of your heart misses that one girl that got away like your heart missed her as whole.

It keeps you obsessed with her, missing her face, her eyes, her smile, her scent…all the time, knowing that you are never going to get her again. She is happy elsewhere.

Life becomes vulnerable as you are enslaved by her thoughts. You try to be normal but you just can't. Each and every thing seems meaningless. Starting everything looks extraordinary and ecstatic but at the end you are left with nothing except agony and emptiness.

I couldn't let this continue to eat me alive, withering me away at thirty-eight. I had to do something…and it had to be big. I had to make my mark again, whether it was going to win Rachel back or not. Redemption was near.

CHAPTER ELEVEN

This was a huge decision I was making. It was an all-day affair but I got around to it once I had the chance to contact the homeowner of the old place on 36th Street and Ocean Avenue in Brigantine that same week in February.

I knew what I needed to do. The house was for sale and ready for me to buy. It was time to construct the ultimate negotiation. Wheeling and dealing was my forte. I didn't want to let this one slip. The window of opportunity was too small. It had to be mine again.

To my relief, there was no severe storm damage from Hurricane Sandy and all the opportunity for me to make it a masterpiece of a home.

Cash wasn't a problem, neither was time. Weekends were going to be my escape…I would spend each one turning this place into what I'd once again call *mine*, the way I always envisioned it during my years that I grew up in it. The ideas of renovation were already spinning.

Stones would engulf the flower and shrub beds, both front and back. Instead of the weed-covered lawn where grass should have grown the past decade and a half, I'd have only the greatest and most fertilized greensward that could bloom. The exterior would be shielded in blue vinyl siding instead of the old aluminum. Windows needed replacing, the gutters needed tending, and the roof was in need of a makeover.

My biggest plan for this house was adding a second story. Throughout my tenure dwelling there, especially during my intense thinking sessions in the attic I adored, I always dreamt of having a direct ocean view from a patio through the back. This was a vision. It was finally coming alive.

I was so excited about it, I told the boys as soon as I had the chance. They needed to know that this "reunion" of theirs had just been turned up a notch. The dawn of a new era was ahead. The boys would be back in town, soon enough.

"What is this, Brad? Is this to win Rachel back?" asked Harry, jittery as ever when I brought him and Dickie to the closing. I didn't like his attitude. It seemed a bit hostile. However, I gave the benefit of the doubt in giving him the answer he would rather have heard.

I grinned, replying, "No. This one is for me. I've let go of that for now." I had a feeling neither one believed me. I certainly had a hard time thinking I was telling the truth myself. But, I wanted to bury my love into the house and not Rachel. I even wrote about it in my memoirs:

My old shore home is rooms and walls like any other...beds, tables and chairs, yet it is only the love I have for it here that matters. The walls are the colors of the ocean and sand, the secrets of nature that I adulate. The ceilings are smiles and cheekiness, the eyes in the sky witnessing the memories of the people who hold my heart. While I dwell here this home is so much more than the sum of its parts and for that I have the past to thank, the glue of my existence.

Perhaps I was going off the cuff, a bit too impulsive. But to me...spontaneity was what made life interesting. Each day held surprise.

I wasn't necessarily afraid to receive those surprises, whether it came to me as sorrow or as joy. I never wanted to live in fear.

It kept me open and allowed new places in my heart, places where I could welcome new friends, new experiences, and celebrate more fully...a true quality of good life.

However, there was one surprise I still could've lived without experiencing. As much as I told the boys it didn't bother me, there was a pain I continued to feel...perpetual and punishing.

Seeing how Rachel had moved on in life, it threw my emotions into a loop. While I tried to hide it in the process of buying my old home, it was still treacherous. Her relationship with her fiancée Edward seemed too good to be true.

He was an elegant man, this Edward Bowson....a handsome one too. His athletic lifestyle was as active as an Olympics participant. His face told of a lean body beneath his wintry garb and his expression was always serious, but not unkind. He had that salt-and-pepper look to his hair, against his still youthful skin.

The wealth I had was pennies compared to his. I guess you could truly call it "old money versus new". I had a Cadi while he donned a Bentley. I strived to reconfigure a shore home where he could have purchased the entire community if he wanted to.

He was also a painter in every sense of the word, a real master of his craft. He created many different types of modern art. Some thought he was the next coming in a new era of skill. Very intelligent.

Rachel and he had been together for four years before he proposed. The way they met...even more enchanting. More like...unusual.

Edward tweeted that he was moving to the east coast from California and had a bunch of old paintings he was looking to give away that were based on the Renaissance era, a Botticelli-like collection.

At the time, the two didn't follow each other on Twitter, so a mutual friend responded to his tweet and included her in on it.

Rachel, being a fan of the Renaissance period, agreed to pick up these paintings from his front porch while he wasn't home. For some reason, she wasn't worried. I suppose she felt safe given his gay manner.

They then tweeted back and forth about the paintings, and he asked her out for a drink over Twitter to 'interview' her for a book on art, admitting he was not only a collector but a painter himself. His next mission was fulfilling becoming an author, writing a book. I always figured, how *unique*.

She met him in person and he proceeded to ask all sorts of questions about her career and took notes the whole time. At the end of the meeting he then asked what he'd like to do for their first real date. She had to laugh! She truly thought he really wanted to interview her and that was going to be it.

After several months of dating, she asked him when he planned on writing this book and he admitted, "There was no book. You were all the story I needed to read for my true *chef-d'oeuvre*."

He then pulled out a sketch he did of her face during the interview...the "notes" he pretended to take. She fell in his arms and it had been true love ever since! I mean...hey, it's not like pickin' up a chick in the bar and dancing with her, but it's still sweet.

Now, they were living in Galloway, New Jersey, a point somewhere in-between Philadelphia and Atlantic City. Edward worked particularly with high-paying collectors to seek new talent in Philly, appraising work that was upcoming to be valuable, at the same time selling his own art.

Nonetheless, in the midst of planning for their wedding, Rachel was asking for thoughts from Edward one night about the job she applied for in Spain that she was still pending to hear from.

"I certainly hope I get this shot at the job in Europe," she implied, on their bed and painting her toenails. Edward had just come in, taking off his watch and tie from a long day's work. He replied, "They would be crazy not to accept you, my dear."

At the same time, there was another issue at hand. Edward was given a job opportunity in Chicago to be at the counsel of a very wealthy amasser.

The job wasn't to start for another month. He was still in the interview phase but it was looking promising. Again, he was a man on the rise.

"What if you get your thing in Chicago?"

"What do you mean?"

"You know what I mean, Edward."

"Ha ha! Rachel...tell me what is on your mind there, dear."

"Well...you still haven't heard back from the collector who wanted to work out there with him. What would you do?"

As Edward paced around the room, he scratched his chin while he smiled. In preparing himself for bed, he assured that everything was going to be fine and reminded Rachel not to worry about what would happen. "We shall see," he simply put.

As much as she was smitten with him, it was a response that was quite ambiguous for her to hear. Whether he meant he'd be taking the job in Chicago or ultimately following her to her dream in Europe was still an uncertainty.

"Either way...we will make it all work, my dear." He gave her a wink, kissed her on the forehead and left the bedroom to wash up before sleeping.

For as vague as it sounded, Rachel believed him and that it would in fact, work out...somehow and some way. He was hard to decipher. It was very tough to determine what direction he was coming from sometimes....or where he was going.

But one thing was for certain…he was always there for her, thick and thin. He supported her, took care of her…and was unquestionably loyal in all aspects.

There was no denying that. This was much more than I could ever say I did for her up until this point. Edward was in the lead. And of course…to the victor, goes the spoils.

CHAPTER TWELVE

Dickie and I had just finished up our time at a strip mall near the city where I received beautifully drawn blueprints from the architect who was working on my new home. I had to admit, the plans were better than I envisioned in my head, superior to what I described to the man and to all I told of this recent plot. I couldn't wait to demonstrate to everybody…the masterpiece I planned on creating.

"We're gonna relive the old days…and then some, brotha. Lemme tell ya!" I exclaimed to Valentine. In my mind, 1999 was going to be merely a fragment of the good times that were ahead.

I was super excited to see this place come alive. "Let's go visit my parents. My dad is going to love this," I told him, smiling and continuing to look up at the sun shining down. We scurried along quickly, rushing past the crowd around us.

Just as we got to my car, it was as surreal as things could have gotten. We weren't sure who saw it first…but we were quite certain that anyone who did would have been in awe.

From a distance, in our direction…Edward, Rachel, and Amanda were walking out of a cake shop at the strip mall. I should have known when I saw a dress store and a florist on either side of my architect, this place was "wedding central". I just didn't think everybody else that I knew went there.

"Hello!" I yelled as the three came closer. This was the first time Dickie had seen Amanda in as far back as either of us could remember. They were just as shocked to come across one another's path as anyone else was. It was awkward, but nice for them to reconnect. I know, for sure…there was nothing she wanted to do with me whatsoever. I avoided her at all costs.

"How have you been?" asked Amanda, walking closer to Dickie. "Not too bad. Long time," he responded. He smiled and proceeded to ask her a million questions. She was very short and tried avoiding certain ones.

Nostalgia was thick with the two, harking on their favorite parts of the past. It was sad that a good thing they had dwindled. Yet, the old phrase *keep in touch* never really sunk in with either for however many years they had been distant with one another. It was a paradise lost, much like Rachel and I.

Nonetheless, they agreed they would enjoy the moment they were in. They'd learn more about each other's lives, maybe even in more detail in the days to come. He told her he was a lawyer, she mentioned her nursing career. They kept it casual and exchanged phone numbers at the end.

Edward introduced himself formally to me. I was vague with my actions and unyielding with my attitude towards him. I didn't want to make it seem like we'd ever be any type of friends.

I wanted to leave an impression on him as if he could hear me saying, "I don't just want to kill you, I want to put you in a pit and add the shovels of dirt slowly until your God damn mouth is full of muck. I want to hear your cries as the rocks rain down on you thicker than a hail storm, you motherless cocksuckin' mothafucka!"

For he was with the woman of my dreams. I was jealous, as much as I was angry. I smiled at Rachel as her and the other two kept walking after we said our goodbyes. What made it sadder to watch her fleet away was seeing how she was with Edward.

The looks she gave him, it reminded me of the way her and I used to be. It was the kind of way she used to stare at me. Those breathless seconds where a kiss felt like a lifetime...yeah, we had that once. That precious feeling of your heart melting with the other's. Now, it was all his. His for the taking.

She bit her lip as she watched him move. You could tell their love was burning bright. It made me hotter than a white flame, pissed...ready to destroy all that surrounded me like a wildfire.

Dickie and I were en route to my parents' place. I was driving. Out of curiosity and in hopes of taking my mind off the thought of Rachel for the moment, I inquired about what happened between him and Amanda.

"What the fuck went down with you two? You never told me." Dickie scrunched his face and hesitated to digress into the account. I kept asking while he tried avoiding answering.

"It just kind of died on the vine, B. Ya know? We grew apart, that's all. She stopped talking to me after awhile. It was rather weird but she was never truly upfront with me about anything. We always played this cat and mouse game that never really went anywhere."

These were the same kind of answers Valentine would always give me. Whether he truly knew what happened with her or not, I never was sure…but he always seemed sad when I brought it up.

"As much as I tried reaching out, she resisted. So I gave up. I never knew what was the matter with her." I nodded my head and let him tell me more. It seemed like seeing her truly bothered him.

However, I hoped for the best. Now that they had one another's number, I longed for a better outcome between the two and that they would communicate effectively.

Once we got to Philly, the skies grew grey. I knew everything was wrong by the feeling I had when I got to the stoop of my parents' house…and my sister was there to greet Dickie and me.

It was like seeing a ghost. Tina hadn't stepped on grounds of the eastern part of the country in more than a decade for a planned visit. Certainly never unannounced. In my mind, I kept repeating, "This can't be right. What has happened?"

"What are you doing here, sis?" I asked. She simply smiled and came over to give me a great, big hug…and we never ever hugged. Our affection was always as cold as a snowman's hand.

Even though she tried being nice as pie when I came inside, I couldn't shake the feeling of transgression around me.

Everything had already been perfect with this scene, and I mean too perfect. It was like awakening in some 1950's television show where somebody is overjoyed to be alive.

It wasn't until I saw family members inside, ones I hadn't seen in half my life, when I became terrified. The room was eerie and quiet...growing more unnerving by the second.

It was the kind of silence that falls right before you get knifed in the back. It sent a shiver down my spine and I felt the blood chill in my veins.

I saw an aunt I hadn't seen since I was a kid...my father's cousin. She looked at me like she was unsure. I knew she was there for a reason. I could sense the discern searing from her like heat off a radiator.

Looking back, I begged my sister to tell me what was going on as she let me in. This was becoming a maze, impossible for me to try and complete.

"Dad passed away this afternoon," Tina whispered to me. My eyes widened as I fell to my knees. I became dizzy from the descent.

The blueprints in my hand spilled out to the ground and I was an emotional wreck after that. I froze...crying, shaking, looking all around me to see if this was a nightmare or not.

Dickie came to pick the papers up and to try and come to my aid...but it was no use. I had no feeling of gravity whatsoever.

There was nothing scarier than not knowing what to do, what to say, or how to react to such news. Everyone around me tried to make me feel better...but there was no use. I was already distant from everything once I got the news.

My poor mother…she sat on her old chair in the living room, wailing away into puddles of tears around her while many came over to comfort her in this time of madness.

To see my father dead was to die herself. There was no her without him, no life after his love. No willpower once the absence of his strength and presence manifested.

He had been her all, her raison d'être…and existing when he no longer did cracked her mind in a way that would never heal. I certainly didn't know what to say to her.

I knew he was sick for some time…I just didn't know how badly. I certainly didn't anticipate this during my visit. It was the ultimate blow to a moment I was so happy about only minutes prior.

In that moment of loss…my world collapsed - where there was light became shadows, the pain coming and going like waves on frigid sand. He was gone. My father, my best friend…taken from me with no warning.

CHAPTER THIRTEEN

Grief. I was full of it. It felt like an empty pit inside of me, a shear of nothingness that somehow took over and held me tight, threatening to kill me entirely. It gave me this heavy feeling…like the weight of the world was resting on my shoulders and there was nothing I could have done to get out from under.

My father was my hero, my one true role model. I always enjoyed our talks, our hangouts, our memories…and looked forward to so much more that was to potentially come.

The golden years, grandchildren, my plans of renovating the old home, aging gracefully. It was terrible to see him go before he had a chance to experience any of that. I wasn't quite sure of who I would go to for advice at this point.

And my mother…what was she going to do now? All these years of retirement were spent with him. What was in store for her ahead?

I could see the tale of deep pain down inside of her as I watched each tear run down her face, slowly and sore with every fall.

After the funeral, I spent a few days at her house. I didn't want her to be alone. Then again, I didn't want to be alone myself.

All around the walls were pictures of Dad, scenes from the beach and the days growing up by Brigantine and Atlantic City. The whole family altogether.

I closed my eyes, letting my mind fill with his voice. I could hear him talking to me as if he were just feet away. I went through journeys in time from my youth to as far as the very last day we spoke. My memories filled with his witty retorts, his delightful stories, and his priceless guidance.

I wanted to call him softly to see if he could step out of one of the dusty frames...but I was no immortal, no wizard nor a time traveler. Things were what they were. We could not have changed them.

It was an extremely long week. We had a lot of visitors...some familiar and ones I had never seen before in my life. All to pay tribute to my dad's life and to give their condolences to me and my family. I had one visitor at the end of my stay, who took me aside from the madness for a short while, close to the end of everything...good old Uncle Georgie.

It had already been a few weeks since we talked last. I could tell he had a lot to chat about but didn't want to engulf me too much on a day like this about many other things. Yet, I never truly knew.

We went into my backyard to get away from all the hub bub. "I'm sorry about your old man," led Griz, patting me on the back.

As gracious as he sounded, he had a different agenda to delegate with me. He kept smiling. All while this time, I was silent and grim to him.

"You know I'm here for you, kid...always."

"I know, Georgie...you always were."

"I love ya."

"Love you too."

I could see in his face, he had more to tell me. I was hoping our conversation didn't change directions and that he continued to be kind. I was in no mood for any of his meaningless lectures or his usual berating anymore.

"Just keep your damn head at work. I don't wanna hear from Steve that the sales numbers are low. You have done so well over there and are so close to becoming partner, I can't see you fuck up! Because when you fuck up, everything else fucks up!" he exclaimed, looking at me with a cold stare.

There it was. I shook my head sideways. It was probably the last thing I wanted to hear in the entire world. Work meant nothing to me compared to what was going on. I felt like I was going to explode on him. I didn't care anymore.

The emotional pain had unpleasant warmth to it, eating at my stomach. The nausea too, just enough to make me hold onto the outside table on my mom's back patio for support. I was breathing slowly. I had often prized myself in ignoring pain and just rocking on regardless, but it wasn't possible at this moment. The melancholy owned me, dominated every thought, and controlled every action.

Once Georgie walked away in his own disgust, I felt a little better. Seeing him made my insides curdle like milk with lemon anymore. He revolted me. I never wanted to look on him again. I was done.

Dickie, Harry, and even Johnny Horsecock came over to give more reassuring and positive comfort. I knew I could count on them, as always.

Although as much as they were uplifting, nothing came close to giving me a better release than getting started

163

on the revitalization of the shore home. It was the ultimate bliss, a true getaway…my new hobby.

I thought of myself as the true carpenter, even though I had an architect construct the plans and a professional crew during the week down there to work on the major parts of the renovation.

Each day I went down, I hammered at least one nail, placed one board, or erected one wall. I built wisely. I always looked at any development in life as a do-it-yourself project.

By the end of March, the place was already looking beautiful. My greatest pleasure was seeing the second floor go up so quickly. My study and the patio in the back were going up quicker than I ever imagined. I must have hired the right team. I still had wished my father were alive a little longer to see it.

My home was all I thought about while I sat at work, bleak and mild, attempting to write more on my memoirs when I should have been picking up the phones and sending emails, attempting to make sales. With it already being a rough morning, there was no guess as to what the outcome was going to be for anything.

This was when I got the best text I could have gotten during this entire mess. It was Rachel. I couldn't believe it.

"I'm so sorry about what happened with your dad. I wish I had gotten to meet him. If you want to talk…I'm at

4355 Pitney Road in Galloway. Let me know before you come. Or just call me."

Take me away, my sweet escape. Oh, how I would have died just to land there so she could fall into my arms that very moment. It was all I needed. The retreat of a lifetime it seemed.

All of a sudden, I heard a boom from my office door. In walked Steve Smith. He was in no mood to toy around, especially given the recent vibe I was giving him…even before my father passed.

Here was a man who told my entire life story to Georgie, a fuckin' crook. They both were. They robbed anything and anyone they could've. Disgraceful.

A man I busted my hump for year after year…and from whom I never felt appreciated. All the success I brought him for sixteen years…and for what? No appreciation.

"Listen, Brad…again, I am sorry about your old man. I know it hasn't been easy for you lately given all you've had to deal with."

"Thanks."

I could feel it coming. I knew he didn't come in just to feel sorry for me. He wanted to tear me to pieces and light me on fire. "But these sales numbers are despicable. The first quarter of this year has been nothing but shit. I feel as if you are distracted," he told me, throwing papers onto my desk of charts and graphs I could care less about looking at.

Enraged, I stood up from my desk and stopped what I was doing. I dropped my pen on my desk and pointed my finger directly at him.

"Jesus, Steve...you've got to be fuckin' kiddin' me. First from Georgie, now you? I don't need this shit!!! My dad passed away this month, does that not mean anything to you?"

My hatred for this guy colored my soul. It spread throughout my entire system, shutting down all other feelings for him, and becoming central to the life and the intent.

"Hey, kid...if you're looking to make partner here, this isn't the way to do it." I didn't even respond to him. There was nothing to say.

I walked out of my office and out of the building. I truly didn't want to come back.

I made it a drunken afternoon, plain and simple. My lunch was whiskey with a rum chaser. I was slurring my words by 2:30 and practically passed out at the nearest bar down the street from my office building.

What little food I ate was in the form of chips and cold pickles I asked for. I didn't leave until they kicked me out of the joint. I even paid the bartender keep it open another hour longer...just to sit there.

By 5:00, I stumbled outside. I stood in the doorway as the smoke from inside billowed out into the bitter wintry air. It swirled in the momentary light that streamed out until the door swung shut.

I toppled down the step onto the cobbled street as the sights of the city swayed like they were part of a fun house mirror illusion. After only six staggering paces I

166

doubled over, vomit splashing on the concrete and spraying my new jeans.

I was certainly in no condition to drive my car…but I went for it anyway, picking it up and heading to one spot. It was the only place I cared about going since I discovered where it was.

4355 Pitney Road in Galloway. I had to see her. It was as irresponsible as it could have gotten but I made the drive from Philadelphia all the way to her place, unable to see the road clearly in front of me. I didn't want to be deterred by anything.

After the never ending lights of the city, I underestimated the utter blackness of nighttime in the woods.

In my mind the trees would be black trunks against a bluish charcoal sky, the path would become deepest brown and the moonlight would bleach the stones within it. But that wasn't the case…especially in a drunken state.

I pulled up to her house where I noticed a few more cars in the driveway. They were ones I hadn't noticed before.

I prayed she was alone…but there was certainly company, more than just her better half. What was the occasion? What possibly could have been this night's celebration?

I crept out of the car and slowly jogged to the back of her house where I saw light beaming onto the grass. "RACHEL!!!!" I yelled from her back porch as I tumbled up the stairs.

Inside, it was more than just a few random people…it was her family. The same family that hated my guts. They were all eating dinner, watching me jump around like a moron on her porch.

"RACHEL!!! FUCK YOUR FIANCE!!! I LOVE YOU!!! I NEVER STOPPED LOVING YOU!!!! COME BACK TO ME!!!!! COME BACK TO MEEEE!!!!"

Oh, what a fool I was. For this was by far, a setup for disaster. One that my appetite for destruction would never crave...not even what I thought was in my worst of drunken states. However, once again, I proved myself wrong.

Rachel approached the sliding glass door that led to her back porch. I smiled, screaming her name a few times more. It was then I saw Edward behind her, with a face...one to die for.

"Brad, c'mon...you can't show up like this!" he yelled, coming over and trying to consult me. "Don'tyouuuu try and fuckinnnnn' help me, cocksucka!!! She is mine!!!!! Alllllllllllllllll minee!!!!"

"Brad, come on. Let's get you out of here."

"Noooooo...you faggot ass pieeeeeeeeeeeeece ofshitttttttttt."

"Brad, you need to relax."

"FUCK YOU!! FUCK YOU FUCKER!!!"

He then punched me in my drunken face. My head bounced to the left as it tumbled on down with my body, slamming into the cold, unsympathetic wood of her back porch. What I thought were tears falling down...turned out to be blood.

Everybody stood around in awe, hands on their mouths, gasping. They were frightened. Nobody wanted to come near us.

Edward began immediately apologizing as he walked away from me, telling me he was done. "H-h-h-heeeeey! Wheeeere d'ya think yeeeeer goin'?" I slurred, jabbing a finger into Edward's chest as I stood up from the fall. He wasn't provoking me, he was just trying to keep the peace.

However, I didn't want to hear any of it. He socked me hard and I fell face first like a loser in front of Rachel and her entire family.

"Iamsickofyourshit," I yelled, my words tumbling from my mouth in a rush of barely distinguishable syllables. It kept getting more embarrassing as the moments continued.

Edward came and over tried to lead me out of the house. "Let's get you a cab," he insisted, putting his arm around me, attempting to keep me from tripping over my own feet.

"Gerroff me!" I screamed, fussing and fidgeting to escape his grasp. "I'm ash sober ash 'm gonna git. And nuffink I - wait wait wait - nuffink *you* can do 'boutit." And I ambled back to my car without so much as hiccup in my direction.

Everybody watched from inside the house as I slowly made my trot down the driveway. The wind seemed to echo annoyingly in my ear. And the blood...the blood dripping down my nose, thanks to Edward, didn't help the situation at all.

"Shitttttt!" I said, wiping it away. I momentarily looked around the woods in front of her home. The trees' leaves swayed from side to side and I heard the soft chirping of the distant ravens. In my stupor, this helped me regain my determination, my strength, my anger.

Killing Edward wasn't my mission or assignment anymore: it became my destiny at this stage in my drunkness. I looked behind me once more at everybody before I got into the car and sped away.

CHAPTER FOURTEEN

Amanda was working late at the hospital one night. Dickie had been trying to contact her for some time but it was to no avail. Knowing Valentine, he didn't want to waste anther second waiting to see if she'd respond.

So, he showed up during her break. The hospital corridor is stuffy and the air has an undertone of bleach. The walls are magnolia and are scraped in places from the hundreds of trolleys that have bumped into them. The pictures on the walls are cheap benign prints of uplifting scenes and above the double doors are large blue plastic signs with the areas of the hospital that lie ahead.

"Dickie, hello. How are you? What are you doing here?" asked Amanda once he entered her path. He chuclked, replying, "Just wanted to say hi."

"Hi."

If this was the Dickie she knew, he wasn't there to stalk. There was an important matter at hand he needed to address, whatever it may have been.

"Listen…I would love to get together with you in the future. But, I think more importantly, I need you to talk to Rachel."

"About what?"

"About Brad."

All of sudden, she began walking away from him as if she kindly wanted him to leave the hospital without saying goodbye to her.

"I want nothing to do with that man. He is your friend and your problem," she responded.

Valentine replied, "Let me tell you this. Not only is my friend, he is my brother. And I would die for him. It's not that I think that he and Rachel are the perfect couple...it's merely that it's obvious they were destined to be together!"

"He showed up to her house drunk and cursed out her fiancé in front of the family. He then got punched in the face for it," told Amanda.

Dickie was well aware. "And rightfully so. Believe me, he deserved every bit of that." "But I just don't think Edward is right for Rachel," he told her.

"Why? He is elegant, charming, is sweet to her...not to mention wealthy."

"Yes, but does he know her as a young girl? Was he the one who met her that magical summer? The same summer I met you? The one who gave everything to her and fell in love in less than a week?"

Amanda smiled, inching her was closer to Dickie. It was turning her on the way he spoke. "Are we still talking about Brad and Rachel?" She gave him a wink wand was practically face to face with him.

He smiled, took her hand and asked, ""Does this guy really have Rachel's best interest at heart? Would he die for her? Because I know for certain...Brad would. He wouldn't question it."

Amanda looked around without an answer. What Dickie was saying had reason...she just didn't want to admit it quit yet. He continued.

172

"Now the past is the past. My friend certainly fucked up in more ways than one. But he is willing to keep trying and to keep proving to her that nothing else matters in the world other than her."

She nodded her head up and down. Valentine then drew himself closer to her. "This comes from a man who I've seen with every type of woman possible...but I've never seen him like this." He held her hand as she giggled.

"You know what they had was spectacular. It was love like nobody has ever seen, Amanda." "I know," she replied.

"A love I wish to have in my life, something I would love to experience," concluded Dickie. She then leaned in to kiss him.

The next thing he knew, she had slammed his lips to hers and nearly knocked all wind from his lungs. Valentine hardly had a moment to react before she pressed her tongue to the seam of his lips and, at his grant of access, delved inside his mouth.

His arms reached down and tangled around her thick, strong waist. "I'll see what I can do. I'll try talking to her," she told him.

My black-and-blue eye was getting better during that week, beginning of April. My mom kept yelling at me when she came to see the place at the shore and all the work that had been done to it. "Stop getting into trouble," she said. "Especially over that girl again."

But, I knew she didn't mean it. She wanted the world for me, whatever it took. If it meant me pursuing Rachel, she would support it. I inherited the sense of great love from my mom, of course. Her and my dad had something golden together while he was alive. Nobody could deny that.

"The place looks beautiful, Brad. Your father would have loved it." She was admiring the renovation. It was like she had returned home.

It was like a tortoise retracting into her shell. The troubles of the world evaporating. To anyone else this is a house like all the others exactly like it on this street, but to us it is sanctuary, it is cocoon, it is rest.

While we were looking around the place together, we had another visitor. Low and behold, Rachel stood at the entrance. This was the first time she had met my mother.

It was amazing. After all this time, they finally were able to grace one another with their respective presence. "Very nice meeting you," she said to my mom. Flattered.

However, the tides turned once my mom left. Rachel became a different person. She wasn't there to have a good conversation.

"What the Hell was that about the other night?" she asked. I didn't want to talk about it. I tried walking away from her and attempted to tend back to working on my house.

"Just needed to release a little. Sorry…but it's not like your family didn't already hate me anyway!" I replied.

"What is your problem, Brad?"

174

"What's yours?"

"I just don't get why now…all of a sudden, you care. I mean, you took an entire year to contact me after my sister died. Is this how you operate? Wrong place, wrong time?"

She knew how to press my buttons. "I guess it's never the right time for you at all," I responded. I didn't even want her to be there anymore.

"I'm sorry I waited so long. I was afraid. I didn't know what to say at first. But I never intended to make you feel bad. Not then, not now."

"You could've said anything, Brad…it wouldn't have mattered. You just weren't there when I needed you."

The regret would come to me in quiet moments, such as when I was going to sleep or stopped to take a lunch break.

It would seep to the foreground of my mind and demand to be reexamined again. But I was tired of thinking about it, no amount of analysis was going to turn back the clock. We both had to get on with the here and now, make better choices next time around.

"Well, now it's too late I guess, huh?"

"We can still be friends."

"Yeah…right…"

She then walked away. Neither of us were going to agree on each other's points. It was like beating a dead horse on both ends. I tried to be sympathetic.

"Alright, alright…listen, I am sorry, okay? I had no right to come to your house drunk." She stopped to listen. "If it helps, I yelled at Edward for punching you." I got her to chuckle. "I mean…I deserved that too."

175

She smiled at me and said, "I'll talk to you soon." But I didn't want her to leave. Just as I had her there, it felt like everything was complete...my happiness awoken. I knew if she didn't stay, my dark days would continue.

"Why can't ya just stay? Stay here with me? Why can't we build on what we used to have?"

"That's just never going to happen, Brad. I'm sorry."

CHAPTER FIFTEEN

Considering it was getting a bit nicer out, I took a walk on the beach one Saturday...alone. I needed some time to clear my head about what had been going on.

I forgot how much I appreciated its serenity and why I considered the beach my go-to place. I sucked in the fresh air like it was an elixir. It tasted like one thing: home. The lifeguard huts were ahead, no bigger than a garden shed. For miles, seeing even one person was foreign for this time of the year. Above, the sun was bright, but as always in early April, it had no real heat...only the power to render the ocean a glittering green-blue like the iridescent algae it would lodge in its depth.

The spray splattered seaweed, scattered along the shoreline. The salty water on their surface made their emerald color sparkle when the sun shone down on them

After so much bleaching, the various types of driftwood were almost as pale as the sand. The ocean had taken care of the softest wood, gently carving it as only water can do. The eyes that had once sat in the wood were raised arching curves that reflected the swirling of the water so close by.

The seashells were radiance among the beach and her out-stretched palm. Most of them, semi-translucent white. Although they weren't big, each one was like a perfect horn of a unicorn, spiraling from the tip to the opening at the base.

I always wondered what type of creature had made them. I figured that they all once belonged to tiny sea-snails of some sort. I knew if Rachel was near me, she'd have the answer.

Inside the seashells were lustrous, marvelous with the colors of the ocean. Reds swirled with yellows and excelled prettily in the early morn.

I slowed my walks down just as I looked at an irregular cluster of conches, noticing something fascinating…something so rare, it made me assure the faith and that higher power was true in its every way. I thought it was a dream. However, it was a sign…for sure.

I couldn't believe it. There it was…the *junonia shell*. It was the *exact* same one from the summer of 1999, the *exact* same string in the same hole I punched on the top of it. My eyes and mouth were frozen, wide open in an expression of stunned surprise. I was aghast…at the same time, astonished.

There was no doubt that day sixteen years prior I had pitched this thing to the other side of the Atlantic. However, I seemed as if I didn't do it far enough. Here it was, right before my eyes, shimmering with its coated salty splash.

Motionless for a moment, I dozed off while harking on that day. It was as if the impact of the memory had knocked every wisp of air from my lungs, much like the feeling I had that very day. Trying to remember how to breathe, unable to speak, totally stunned as a million emotions bounced around inside my skull.

I had quit wasting time. Reminiscing was for chasing ghosts. I had done enough of that the past four months. I was here to take onto reins of the future, not dwell on the past.

I grabbed the *junonia*, stared at it some more and placed it in my pocket. This was by far, the last thing I expected to see during my walk. Rachel needed to know I found this.

At last, I had something to prove that our love still existed in the heart of the sea, drifting its beats to the sandy shore.

Just as I began my text to her, Rachel had been greeted by Amanda at her house in Galloway. They planned on getting breakfast nearby before kick starting a promising Saturday. It was one of their weekly customs. They rarely missed a date.

Girl time was important. However, Amanda had a different kind of quandary...one that she needed Rachel to advise her on strongly. It was something she wasn't used to dealing with.

With the recent reconnection that Dickie and Amanda had, it almost seemed too natural to fight. It seemed like a great pair to me...or to anyone who saw them together before. I never knew my best friend to say a bad word about the girl. And for as much as she disliked me, I still endorsed her...for I knew she was always kind to my friend.

Yet, she was so reluctant about the linking, it almost seemed like there was something she had been hiding. Deep down. "Why would you talk to him if you're so adamant on not starting anything with him again?" Rachel asked her, coming in.

"Shouldn't I ask you the same about you and Brad?" countered Amanda, quickly and hastily. She was a bit on the defense and didn't want to enlighten as to why. It was more than obvious there was something wrong.

"That's different! I didn't kiss him at my work!" Rachel replied, laughing.

"That's because he showed up to your house drunk when your fiancé and family were there!"

Rachel shook her head sideways, unable to answer her. It was never as simple as putting it into a mere paragraph before breakfast. What we had built upon required a novel.

They then both became silent as church mice. The room was all gentle creeks and subtle noises...nobody spoke for a few minutes. There was a tension that had to have been released, it was burning into their peaceful talks. Amanda knew she had to let go. Those bitter spirits inside of her were changing the way she thought and the way she was with everyone around her.

"It's not just this feeling I have of uncertainty between Dickie and I, Rae. When I saw him last, he asked me to talk to you specifically. What happened after that...just happened," said Amanda.

. At this point, Rachel was all ears while she noticed her friend's disposition change completely, and so quick...it was like she flipped a switch inside of her at that very moment.

She knew Dickie only had one thing in mind when it came to inquiring of her through Amanda. She asked her to go on.

"He made a lot of good points. My hostility about you and Brad all these years…it's not my fight. I know you're engaged to Edward…and I would never tell you to leave him for another man. But, you do what you do gotta do. Brad isn't the worst thing going."

It was the last thing she ever expected to hear from her best friend. "Are you feeling okay?" she asked. Amanda assured she was, smiling like never before.

With her hands in her pockets, Rachel walked back and forth around her kitchen. She was confused. Her mind was still a surging perplexity. Her thoughts her tangled up like a ball of yarn, unable to find where the jumble began.

"I don't resent him. I never did," continued Amanda. "Neither should you anymore. I guess I was just worried about you. A lot of different emotions in those yeas clouded my judgement."

Just as she was about to utter the fact of how important both Edward and I were to her, she felt her phone vibrate. She pulled it out to see the message, blinking bright from yours truly. "I need to see you. I found something!" I exclaimed through iMessage.

It was as if I could almost feel the excitement through the feel of the phone. Perhaps I was overthinking, but her smile came alive in the emoji she replied with.

"Go see him," instructed Amanda as she looked at Rachel gluing her eyes to the words I typed. She kept smiling in her friend's direction.

"But this thing with you and Dickie…I need you to tell me more first. I cut you off," responded Rachel. She didn't want to go without lending her ear as well.

"Another time," she replied, winking one eye and grabbing her coat before she left. As perplexed as Rachel was, she knew she had to see me. Something magical was about to come alive.

She scurried over to my house in Brigantine like the dawn through the night, shining like the sun. I couldn't wait to show her what I found.

For I was holding an extortionate prize of deep, lustrous gold and silken silver coruscated in the glimmering lighting provided, shooting beams of pure wealth into every corner. She was going to love it, I just knew.

I had been landscaping all day, outside with my shirt off. I was going for the greenest grass and the tallest shrubs that season. It all started with an early spring dethatch and fertilization…certainly the key to success.

Certainly, it was a plus having my shirt off for Rachel to see. I knew she noticed it the other day…but I wasn't sure on how much attention she paid to it. The dirt on my face, the shovel in my hand, and the sweat pouring from every part of me exuded a hard day's work to anyone who took notice.

However, I wasn't all about seducing this time. Even though she was stunning head to toe, as always. She was so hot, my sunglasses were fogging up looking at her. Her tight jeans, blue track jacket, and rich ebony hair. It flowed in waves to adorn her glowing, porcelain-like skin. Her eyes, framed by long lashes, still pumped the hazel hue I adored. Straight nose, full lips...she was the picture of perfection.

All while I was rubbernecking in her direction, I still remembered that I needed to show her the shell. There it rested on the porch like a trophy for all to see. "Look what I found!" I yelled as she slowly strutted to my entrance.

She smirked and squinted, looking at it and me every other second. "You can't be serious!" she replied, just as loud as I was in my tone. "You had to have been holding it this whole time, Brad!!"

Oh, how little did she know. For this was as rare as it could have been...like finding the same extraterrestrial in the same desert two decades apart.

"I found it just this morning, I swear to God." I then saw the surprise in her face...however I knew it was forced, like a Thursday lunch with a distant cousin you barely know. "That's amazing," she said...but not nearly genuine. Not the reaction I wanted.

It wasn't the enthralling scene I had in my mind. For I knew this was a pretty supernatural occurrence, Rachel seemed as if I was showing her just an ordinary shell...and not the gift we gave each other several moons since.

How had something so fun and exciting come to this? The sound of her voice and the look in her eye used to warm me, the scent of her perfume had made my heart race and the touch of her hand would sent tingles down my spine. This reaction though...it was cold and prickly.

"What's wrong with you? This is fate…Rachel, it's a sign. I threw this thing in the water years ago. For me to find it left in the sand…I mean, what are the odds?"

Annoyed, Rachel took a deep breath and responded, "I just don't know what you want from me." There was no traffic or bird song, just awkward silence as I tossed the shell lightly to the ground nearby us. I didn't know how to react. Her nerves were blasting and my disappointment was overwhelming me.

So, I stopped beating around the bush. I put it the way I felt. "Listen…I rue the day it ended with us. Because every moment after that has killed me softly. There's nothing I wouldn't do to make it work again." She stood with her head bent, unable to look at me in the eye. A million things for her to reply with…she picked that of the worst.

"Brad…I'm sorry. For the love I have for you always was and still is, a burning flame inside of me that will always be lit. I just can't leave Edward. He's the one I am marrying. He's the one I am with now."

My mouth was set in a semi-pout. I kicked a stone along the sidewalk with the side of my mud-splattered boot as I replayed this as one the worst moments of my life.

"We will always be friends. Nothing more. I've told you. I am sorry." My tides continued to roar as she spoke these awful things. The *friend zone.* .

I turned away from her in aversion. I didn't even want to look at her. I just wanted to close my eyes and write this off as a bad dream. "But I will always be here for you. I swear," she commented as I strutted over to my porch to sit in gloom. I continued to stare in the opposite direction of her.

"Sad" would be a way to put it so childishly as she went back to her car.   Even though childish was the way I was definitely acting.

Yet, "sad" was nothing of the sort. That would be like something flimsy, something one would have been able to cast off with a happy reflection or the smile of a friend.

This was different. This was a falling feeling that sat inside of me like the germ seed of depression, just waiting for the right conditions to grow...to send out roots to choke the hope out of my heart.

I didn't even want to look at the shell...wherever it was...for my bitterness would have probably shattered it into pieces that very moment.

CHAPTER SIXTEEN

"I'm over it, Dickie...I just can't take it anymore. I don't know what else to do. She was there...I showed her the shell I found. As miraculous as I thought it was...it was as if she didn't care."

As I was talking to Dickie at his work, he felt every piece of pain I was having. It was like trying to start over all again.

Except you didn't know where to begin. You thought you'd be able to pick up where you left off...but it just doesn't work that way.

"What can I do to help?" asked my gracious friend. I shook my head sideways, took his hand and replied, "You've done enough, Valentine. Believe me...your contrition is appreciated."

I knew he wouldn't stop there. He was always too good to me. But then he mentioned another good friend of ours...Harry the Heat. He was sinking to an all-time low.

The consequences of coke abuse overwhelmed Harry like a ton of gravel, pinning him to the dirt like yesterday's news. The drugs took over his mind, drove his body to unconscionable acts of depravity, doing anything to attain his next sniff.

It decomposed him slowly like a walking corpse, meat on bones, ready to be nailed into a coffin and swallowed by darkness.

He just wasn't the same anymore. It was if he was already dead, though he breathed and shouted obscenities.

He was skeletal…his once snug and fashionable clothes looking like they were thrift store cast-offs.

Dickie and I figured it was just a matter of time before he overdosed or somebody from somewhere did him in to rehab.

I knew when that would happen, the part of me that still loves the man he was will mourn all over again. I would visit his grave with the flowers and tell my future children how their uncle used to be.

I would try hard to forget every detail of the ghoul he became and how he broke our hearts into ever smaller pieces.

What was even sadder was Georgie's lack of care. To him, Harry was making the family money. That of course, was top of the agenda.

It was his mission to see his nephew rise to the top for sure…but it was never for his best interest. Perhaps it was our mission to save him…he was just hard to get a hold of.

That very week, Dickie had a mission of his own. Once he realized how let down I was about Rachel, he took matters into his own hands…just in case Amanda didn't for him. He said what he said to her…but he felt, being the good friend he was, he had to do more.

He spotted her outside of Stockton University, the same way he barged in on Amanda. "Rachel!" he yelled as she made her way to her car.

She came over and gave him a big hug, asking him how he was doing. He didn't say much, just simply smiled as he reached into his pocket for something valuable.

"I wanted to give you this." He handed her the double of the same picture of Rachel and I which was kept in my drawer at my desk at the apartment in Philly.

"It's literally the only picture of you two that exists. He has the double at home."

She couldn't believe it. She hadn't seen herself that young in years. It was like taking a trip down memory lane to see the miracles of the past.

And the both of us...the way we looked with the beach in the back, the sun setting, and the seagulls flying...it was a priceless thing to see for anybody. It almost looked professionally done.

"Why did you keep it all these years, Dickie?" she asked. She kept the picture close to her, overwhelmed by the magic of her youth.

"Because, his happiness is important to me. And that was the last time I saw him smile that way." He left her on that note. It was a lot to think about.

These were the days she wondered if her mind was an engine or an exhaust. Was she the master of what she thought or were her ideas the result of deep thinking she was loosely aware of?

There was a third possibility of course, which is that her feelings conquered all. Feelings are like temperatures. Attraction is warm, curiosity is warmer, and anger is boiling. Hate can torch, but it can also freeze. Love...well, that's a temperature best left under neutral.

Rachel wasn't quite sure where she found her feelings on this day after Dickie saw her...but she was destined to soon find out, she figured.

It was a long day for her but Rachel was fighting to find time at the end of it to relax once she got to the house. She had a lot on her mind but wanted to put it aside for the night and watch her television shows with Edward that she kept OnDemand.

Just as she came in and put her belongings on the kitchen table, it wasn't long until she noticed the mail, piled up in the center of it. Immediately, she scattered through the bills and random offer throwaways before she found exactly what she was looking for...a letter from the University of Madrid in Spain. It was a shining cream-colored envelope, addressed to her in the finest manner.

With a smile bursting out from her face, she wasted no time to tear the envelope apart while searching the house from Edward to show him. "Hunnie!!!!" she yelled.

He came down the stairs after changing out of his work clothes. "How are you, love?" he asked, coming in her direction while she was opening the mail.

She then paused in her walk while she held the open letter as if it were the holy grail of all mail. Her eyes widened and the smile she had grew shinier. "I got accepted to Spain, oh my God...EDWARD, LOOK!!!" flashing the letter around like a winning ticket.

Edward grinned, hugging and kissing her, telling her, "Wow, congratulations baby!!" She was so ecstatic, she could barely stand. She was jumping up and down like a school girl. "I have also have good news to tell you, Rachel," he continued. He put his arms on her shoulders.

While she was imagining what could have been sexier than hearing about going overseas, she looked at Edward directly in the eye pending his news.

"I got accepted to take on the Chicago job."

Unreal. Her world shattered. She didn't know what to say now. It came out jumbling with mumbles. "But...what? I thought...Edward, I mean..."

"No no, Rachel...listen...this is so perfect. I was thinking, you go to Spain and I'll go to Chicago. We can visit each other. Maybe once a month or so. I told you we can make it work. Don't worry, dear."

All while he injected this proposition, he kept his smile. For Rachel, she had a look on as if a family member had just died.

"You can't be serious. You won't come with me?" she asked, now throwing the letter on the table. It didn't make sense. He was on board with her dream before...now he had a different itinerary...one that seemed merely for himself and not them.

Yet, it all worked out when he thought of the way it would go down. In his mind, he had the ultimate plan. They would both still be together, yet fulfilling separate dreams. "What? This way we are both happy, Rachel."

"You wouldn't be happy with me?"

"Baby girl...what do you mean?

"Edward!! How is that ever going to work? We will be worlds apart. That is no way to stay together. How are you okay with this?"

190

He tried to parlay that he wasn't okay in her absence...he just wanted to create the best solution. In his selfish banter, he kept trying to make sense of it. She was no longer excited about her offer.

"Couples do it all the time, Rachel. My one friend from Brazil, his girlfriend lives in Asia."

"But, Edward...I'm going to be your wife. This isn't how I planned it. This is no way to start a marriage. Not whatsoever"

She was flustered. She walked back and forth around the living room and kitchen, trying to find miscellaneous tasks to occupy her mind with, away from the melodrama.

Edward persisted. "Baby, it will be fine. We both have opportunities we don't want to pass up on. Now, trust me...in about three or four months, you're gonna see I was right about this."

"Listen, Edward...I don't want to be away from you that long. Please...just stay with me...in Spain. You said a long time ago that you would." She begged and pleaded.

This was something she always envisioned. She figured if he really cared, he would go for it. She gave him the ultimatum.

But he countered. "We will get used to it, Rachel." There was no getting through to him. "Or hey, you can come to Chicago with me. I can't give this up, babe. There's a lot of money at stake."

That was it. She ran out of things to say. She was exhausted. It was as if he already made his mind up many of moons ago, before she even mentioned Spain.

Once it came time to call it a night, she sat silent on the edge of the bed with her hands tightly folded while Edward washed up. He kept trying to talk to her but she fired back with one word answers and "mm'hm" or "yeah". Yet, who could blame her?

With a million things to think about during the day, this just made it a million and one. Her hands were now sweating from the friction of holding them together.

Would she give up the job in Spain and follow him to Chicago for this multi-million dollar project? Would she stick with stability instead of creativity?

Just as she opened her perspiring hands, out came the *junonia* sitting in her palms with the old necklace rope, dangling down. She must've snuck down and scooped it up while I wasn't looking a few days prior. I guess...she didn't want to see it break my lawn...perhaps.

CHAPTER SEVENTEEN

"Dickie, I cannot fucking take it. Steve is the ultimate pain in the ass. This job is just not worth it anymore. They're on me every day about sales going down," I was telling my great friend as we were finishing upstairs construction at the place on an early Sunday eve.

My mind became a constant poison, filled with venom. High deluges from this sea of depression, not knowing how to swim amongst them. I was hoping Valentine had some good words to give me or could pave a path in the right direction, as always.

"Just keep fighting the good fight, daddy-o," he told me. I'm sure it was easy for him to put it into one simple line…but I needed more at the time.

The stress spread through my mind like ink on paper. I took in a deep, ragged breath before placing my hands, enclosed together, onto all the tools, cleaning up. "Did you want to stay for dinner?" I asked him. "I wish I could, B…I got that fuckin' pro bono I'm working on. It's gonna keep me up all night just doing this last bit of research. I better get started." I could tell he had some stress of his own, almost equally as perturbed as me.

"Yeah, I guess…I have some stuff to work on too. No worries, Dickie. Another time." Between the misery at the job, the past eight weekends working on the house, mishaps with Rachel, coping with the loss of my dad alongside my mom's worries…it was hard trying to figure anything out at all.

I felt completely helpless. All alone, like the black crow dying in the middle of the forest while all other creatures watched, not knowing how to truly help it.

"I'll see you over the week," I told Dickie as he left. I went ahead and decided to stay the night at the shore.

It was dreary as could be for a cold end-of-April night. Finally feeling good about the construction that was getting done at my new home, I found some time to do what I did best: peacefully work on my memoirs while enjoying a little music playing in the background. I had everything from Frank Sinatra to The Weeknd on my playlists.

The weathermen were calling for rain shortly after eleven o'clock but I decided to take my chances by sitting on the back deck I just finished building, right outside the study. The flaming wood in the furnace was crackling loud enough, if there were anyone outside, they'd hear its pop.

During this time, I kept getting distracted by text messages from Rachel. On the surface, I wanted to pay no mind and keep writing but of course, something deep down inside of me wanted to read every word and respond in less than a second.

However, I knew what it was at this point. There was no denying it. Slowly but shortly I was pushing myself further into the *friend zone*. The more I fed into her stories about her days with the art purveyor and collector fiancé, the further I got away from building upon more than what I saw this was worth…everything.

So, I went back to the pen and notes along with the laptop while reclining in the patio chair I rested in. Punching the keys on the keyboard and doodling notes on my scratchpad, it felt like I was on a roll with what I was putting down. It was one of those sessions where I was spitting verbal flames…you know, where you feel the pages are hot and on fire.

Shifting my glasses up and down to make sure I was reading things right, I took another look at what I was jotting down. I was starting to make no sense with my writing. Simply jumble. Incomplete sentences and unexplainable paragraphs encompassed the current chapter I was trying to perfect.

It was official. She was in my mind now. She completely overwhelmed my thoughts. My focus was fading. I stood up for a few minutes and paced around back inside the study. Going over to the leather bounds to pour myself another 7-n-7, I kept looking outside as the wind gusted in through the open glass door. I was glancing out into the ocean.

"Sixteen years…where'd they go?" I asked myself as I scooped some ice out of the bucket that rested by the liquor bottles and cigar humidor. As tempting as it was to go over and read the texts on my phone that sat on the chair, I kept holding back. Why torture myself and get into meaningless banter with her? It wasn't going anywhere anymore. She was in love with a man and it surely was not me, not even a little.

The whole thing was getting annoying. These bothering ways were looming into the night as I continued to contemplate if I should examine her texts. Going against my inhibitions with clouded judgment, I picked up the darn phone to open the messages.

"What are you doing?" and "How is your night?" followed by a smiley emoji with sunglasses on. Either way, she was three sheets to the wind, I could tell. This was not her typical behavior.

I texted back and said, "Thinking of you, of course," and put the phone back down. The rains were picking up. I saved my work, closed my laptop and put my notes on top of it. I then placed everything in one of the drawers at my desk. Enough was enough for the late evening. Writer's block now began to consume the best of me.

Shutting the glass doors, I stood still for about ten minutes and watched the weather outside. The sky became dark and low with ominous black clouds. The wind picked up, howling, crying, warning, baying like a wolf into the moon. The first bang of lightning ignited the air and within seconds, the rolling boom of the thunder rang overhead.

The drops of rain fell as if from buckets, cascading like a waterfall from the clouds. It pounded on the porch as if it were demanding entrance.

KNOCK! KNOCK!

It wasn't the rain, nor the wind. It sounded like the door was being beaten down by police. I couldn't imagine who would have wanted to stop by this late. Of course, only one individual came to mind. It was more than obvious.

"Hey," I yelled from the staircase, stepping down into the living room. "No need to knock. Come in." Good Lord, what was going to walk into my house? At this very moment, I had no idea whatsoever. I didn't want her to come by. I didn't want to talk. I didn't want to deal with her drunk bullshit.

The knocks persisted. "COME IN, WOULD YOU??" My thoughts differed from what I actually gave verbal. *Just go away, Rachel. Dish your problems out on another ex-boyfriend.* The last thing I wanted to hear about was this jerk-off losing a Monet while they fought over what grade of rhubarb was entrenched in their pinot noir. No time for any of it...until I opened the door. My temperament changed completely...instantly!

Rachel stepped inside and I strolled towards the ingress, aware of the power in the air the second she marched through. It was like a sizzle in the air. I hadn't remember feeling this way in forever. Fireworks were going off from her sparkle.

The way she came in from the storm sent combustions into my blood hotter than a thousand hells. Hair frizzled, makeup running down her face, long-sleeve skin-tight white shirt and ruffled crib skirt tampered and soaked. I wanted it all, of course.

I had every intention of punishing this beautiful bombshell until I'd made her numb. The acceleration of my heart-rate had nothing to do with fear and everything to do with what my body really desired.

I looked away as if the outside world held my attention...but after all this time she read me like a book, eyes on my chest, my breathing rate duly noted. With a

197

gentle finger, she moved towards me and reoriented my face so that she held the gaze I didn't want to give, stealing the passion from my eyes in a way that only magnified the spark. There was no smile on her lips, only the hot intensity of her stare that we both knew was the start of an inferno that was yet to come.

I let the Weeknd album on my Spotify app stay playing into my sound bar by the rest of the Bluetooth entertainment system.

Just as my favorite track "Till Dawn" came on, this girl completely lost herself in me. No warnings, no words…just our lips locking.

I tell myself that I'll take you for the last time…
I'll be over you eventually.
Time after time, you seem to push me off…
I understand what we have become.

Before the door even had the chance to close, Rachel wrapped her arms around my neck, still unable to remove her mouth from mine. One inhale of her enchanting yet deadly scent sent a shock into my veins. It was paralyzing.

My right hand dropped to her hip, pulling up the skirt that hung loose just above both her knees. I picked her up by those luscious thighs as we tumbled to the couch immediately, toppling tables and the chachkies on top, to the floor on our way. It was a mess already.

Her eyes looked back, searching mine. I smiled and kissed her likewise as she knew I would. With my lips, I felt her mouth stretching wider than ever, fighting between grinning and kissing. Sixteen years of lust bottled up into a moment so intense, so pure and truly real in every single sense.

You wash your neck when you leave,
Now I know your routine,
I was in love with your mystery...
Now I just take what I can get from you,
I'm not embarrassed to be what you want me to be.

All of a sudden, she halted my journey. "Get away from me!" she yelled. Standing up from the couch, she walked towards my staircase and away from the blaze of glory we were creating.

Rachel was all suspense at this point, everything was one extreme or another. I wasn't sure if it was her slight tipsiness at the time or the artful vixen she had enhanced in becoming. Either way, I was enjoying it way too much. "I hate you...I hate you, Brad!" She was passionately angry, zealously happy and then inconsolably sad walking around.

It was going to be a roller-coaster night, not knowing the next weave of the track or the direction it would take. What else was there to do but take the seat and strap in?

She took a black bowl of mints I had on a table near the staircase and tossed them all over the place before smashing the dish on the floor. I still didn't care. The only thing that mattered to me was touching her more...kissing her mouth, her stomach, her breasts. I had to go for the kill here. I tried to be gentle with her clothing, not to rip the lace…but it was hard.   I ended up tearing them to shreds…even the skirt. I did that one with my teeth. Shoes flew off.

She came up to smack me in the mouth when I did this, but it was certainly followed by many tongue kisses aplenty.   I had her down to her bra and panties already, pressing and forcing her up against the wall.   She was loving it as much as she tried to fight it.

"You are fuckin' trouble…you do this so well, my gosh…you and your ways," she whispered.   I kept chortling, kissing her neck while her mouth remained open. She was echoing wails from one side of the house to the next. "Don't act like you're surprised, my little mistress," I responded.   During this, I stuck two fingers in her mouth while she slurped on them, one of her greatest talents that I had never forgotten from the early days. She still sucked like a vampire.

Meanwhile, she went ahead and grabbed my dick while my pants stayed on. I reciprocated much the same, taking my fingers from her mouth only to go down and to travel around the margins of her vagina on the surface of her panties. She was breathless, I was rock solid already. I couldn't believe what was happening.

"Ahh…I can't do this…I can't," she huffed.   I simply smiled and took off my shirt, throwing it behind me wherever it would land.   She tried turning around and walking towards the door. While she had her back towards me, I grabbed both hands and forced her behind in front of me so her ass met my cock.

I wanted to lose my pants so badly. I reached around front of her with my two fingers, sliding over her smooth hips, into the underwear and on down to her clit, vibrating it until she was panting. She flipped her hair, looked back at me with her mouth open and placed her arm around me backwards while I continued to gesture. I could feel how wet she was already. It was soaked.

I shoved my finger inside. God, she was tighter than she was back in the day. Either this guy had a small cock or he wasn't fucking her right…it was like she had been living in a convent.

I couldn't resist but smack her ass twice while I was doing this. It kept looking at me in the most delicious way. I couldn't let it escape

She then stopped me once more. Forcing my hand away, Rachel walked towards the couch in my living room. Afraid she'd step on the shattered remains of the miscellaneous debris on the floor, I scurried over right behind her.

"I can't go through with this…I'm telling you Brad, I can't," said Rachel. I grabbed her by the wrist and pulled her in my direction while she slowly continued walking. Our faces were an inch from one another's. I replied, "Then what the fuck ya doin' here already?" so softly and seductively.

She grabbed the pillows from my couch and threw them at my coffee table, knocking down whatever was up. I even saw the television wobble a bit from the vibrations. It looked like a warzone in my house, but a combat worth fighting I must say.

"I'm not talking about you," she said. I grinned. All of a sudden, we heard the sixty inch television fall onto the coffee table, shattering to pieces right before us.

"I've been so bad. What are you gonna do about it?" she said to me with that girlish tone, that innocent smile and that charming lure.

Once again, I back handed her on her ass until I saw it jiggle red. She kept her mouth open, flipping her hair at me. Such a devil.

I wanted to make her feel this one. I wasn't going to be gentle by any means. This was the high stake medal round right here.

I picked her up and threw her over my shoulder as she wiggled from head to toe. Slowly yet carefully, I walked up the stairs as I felt her bite my back and smack my rear-end concurrently.

Cause unlike you I got nothing to hide...
I don't pretend to have any shame.
I got a box we could put all your lies in...
Until the end of days.

I let her down to her feet gently as she smacked me once more in the mouth, obtaining her balance. I pressed her up on the wall immediately after. I wasn't letting her go anywhere!

She emitted a tiny gasp once I noted the familiar sealing over in my eyes, seeing inside her. It's like I had just enchanted her, ensnaring her with my erotic facial expressions.

I sensed her squirming with passion while the scent of the cologne drifted in through her nostrils, a musk I notice she is quickly becoming addicted to.

A tingling sensation disrupted her ruse and the tables turned. She was now caught in my web. This game of desire was intoxicating.

You know that I will be a call away...
The call you'll make when you're all alone.
And I know that I will always be the one,
You repent when you are done.

"You are the only healthy drug there is, engulf my senses and steal me away," she panted, jumping into my arms once more while trying to give me a hickie, digging her fingernails into my back, already panting.

"You're a little shit, you know that Rae?" I went on, not far from three sheets to the wind myself during this time. She hopped off, grabbing my chin for another quick make-out session. Biting my lip and still digging her claws into me, attempting to draw blood, the pain was pleasurable in every way.

I leaned back to grab the champagne bottle on the bar. She let go and pushed me away, walking away backwards towards my desk.

I then popped the cork, sending it into the air, flying above her head while she screamed in fear, laughing in joy all at the same time. It was adorable.

The cork knocked a few of my books from the shelf down. After the fizz settled, I took a swig before I went over and poured champagne down her mouth and all over her body. It was going everywhere, making a complete mess near my desk and on my paperwork.

She took more to the mouth and then spit it back at me like a rolling sea wave. Ohh, boy…she was wild. Once the bottle was empty, I threw it behind me and let my pants fall to the floor. It was time to show her what she hadn't seen in so long. We needed to *get something straight between us.*

Once and for all, I put a cease to Rachel's inner fight, ultimately ending that battle…between the mind, and the body.

She had a look on, as if it had been ages since she'd gotten to suck cock. At the same time, I hadn't craved receiving it in a way more than I did at this moment. The paroxysm of pain in my chest made it seem as if my heart would burst inside.

She went down with a flourish, sucking hard and fast, relishing it and sliding in and out of her mouth. I saw her get wetter by the second. She ignored the tender want and slipped more into this thrill.

The touch was possessive. She was staking claim and I knew it. "Suck on to that thing good," I coaxed as I held her hair and got lost in the rapture before me.

She was hungry. I let her move with her wicked ways. It was clearly witchcraft. My body responded to a new level of ecstasy. My nerve endings stood to attention, fully aware of the presence of magic.

I had come a long way in the last sixteen years being able to hold my explosion. There were some victorious nights. However, even after all this time…Rachel still had her own style of making it difficult for me to contain my boom. It must've been what she did with her tongue while she went up and down.

So, I lifted her head after a few minutes, gave her a kiss on the lips and picked her up only to throw her on my desk, flat on her back. Pens went flying, post-it notes scrambled and paper clips kept flinging. Thank God my laptop and memoirs were out of sight and out of mind.

Her legs were wide open. The panties and bra were gone. Those sweet toned stems and that immense perfectly-sculpted and shaped ass were right in front of me, all for the taking. "Touch me, taste me...I won't move a muscle. I want to obey to your tongue," she spoke as my lips moved closer to her thighs.

The softest of moans escaped her as another cheeky grin set upon my face. "Oh, yes please." A tremble ran through her but she fought to not let it be known. A single finger I let path along her slit while finding her deliciously wet, teased us both like no other.

Casually, I hit her clit, testing how loud I can get her before I shove my face in. I leaned forward, getting into a comfortable spot. My hands circled around her legs as I pulled her closer towards me.

I then let my mouth engulf her pussy, shoving my face deeply between the folds. Her hands didn't know what to grab expect for my head. She cried out but shut her mouth quickly. Another shake was felt as she allowed me to devour her.

Our minds were lost and her body was mine. In and out, deeper I let the tongue go. "Don't stop...fuck me more with that it as if it's your cock," she gasped. I lifted her legs higher, arching her back a bit, finding more of her to please. I kept lingering amid those sweet perfect pussy lips.

"Oh fuck. Oh God, oh God oh God, ohhhhhhhh," she cried. She wasn't holding back. I kept attacking until that eruption came close. I wanted her head to spin and her legs to crush me in a hungry, needing way.

My tongue kept flickering as the mixes of her juices and my salvia dripped all over my face, her pussy, and my desk.

"Ohhh, you own meeeeeee!!" she yelled long and softly, right before she shook like a blender. Her pleas turned into moans of desperation.

Watching her breathe heavily and practically lay paralyzed neck-down for a minute made me feel I did my initial job.

I then picked her up after I released my lips from her. She came up with my pull, shoving her tongue right into my mouth. "I wanna taste my pussy," she said, puckering and licking. "You're a crazy girl." She was far from the sweet Georgia gal I had on the beach at twenty-two years old.

I turned her around and bent her over on my desk as the lamp fell off, unplugged, leaving us in the dark.

Well here comes the sun...
And you're in my arms.
And my denial keeps me on the edge,
Of the chance...
That you'll stay through the night.

"Yes, shove it in me, Brad," Rachel said, tilting her head back to me, getting ready for it to go down. Prior to

206

her trying to finish saying that, I plunged into her pussy and went all the way in, balls deep from behind.

She tried to grab onto the table but there was nothing to hold anymore. Everything was scattered onto the floor. Her fingers crawled the wood as I groaned and held still for a moment, enjoying the feeling of her wet pussy surrounding my cock. Then, I pulled out slightly and smashed back into her.

"Jesus Christ, you are so tight," I said through a gritted jaw. "Oh, fuck me...fuck me," she replied. I imagine it hurt being stretched so much but she knew it was going to all elate soon.

I gripped harder onto her hips and started to pull her back onto my cock in time to my thrusts. "Just like that." Her body soaked with layers of sweat, beading all over the table and floor. Her nipples were so hard when I reached over to get a handful of her tits.

I kept beating that ass up, not just with my pounding but with my hand as well. I wanted her to be bruised all over.

She then pushed me off and commanded me to lay down on the floor. I scattered whatever wreckage rested in front of me out of the way and replied to her, "Your wish is my command."

Taking no pity on herself, she squatted right down onto my bulging hard-on. She immediately began pumping her hips, fucking herself on me...but it wasn't enough. She kept speeding up.

I pushed a finger up into her asshole just to see how it would go. Her back rounded and her pussy spasmed as another orgasm slammed through her. But she didn't want to stop riding…nor me cease from jamming away.

I added a second finger, pumping in and out, harder, faster, going with the tempo of her ride. She felt another climax rise, but before she could go over the edge, she pulled away and slid up her body, leaving her pussy clenching on air, her head twisting in pure adrenaline and bliss. Her eyes even rolled to the back of her head.

I was extremely close myself at this juncture. I put her flat on her back again, stretched out on the floor. I loved this position. It allowed me to see all of her.

"You are mine," I grunted out, pumping back into her. The length and level of my arousal brutal. "MINE," I swore, over and over. I pushed her forward, yanking her legs back.

Keeping my hands gripping her waist, I slowly moved them down to cupping that juicy ass. I didn't slow the movement at all. I kept giving full, hard pushes. The intensity in her face was unmatched. Her body was smooth and wet, her breasts were bouncing…and I was seconds away from putting my load in her.

She was about go again, she had warned me. "I'm going to cum," I told her, closing my eyes. She felt the cock get bigger and squeezed herself around me, whispering, "Put your load in me. I want to feel you shoot deep down." I moaned hearing this and triggered something in me. I gave a few more fucks before pushing all the way in her. A deep groan carried over as Rachel certainly felt the hot cum shoot inside.

Her entire body jerked from the force of our simultaneous climaxes. Her hold onto my hair was painful as she continued to moan. I felt all of me go inside of her. Her hips moved rhythmically, my cock stayed throbbing.

She relished the pulse of my cum, telling me she loved feeling it in her. I kept it in just a little longer, slowly making my way out. Still shaking, Rachel took my cock in her hand, cleaning me of the juices with her fingers. She then proceeded to lick her hands. "I love it." I then began lying next to her, parallel on the floor.

I stared down at her once more, finding the sated pleasure still etched over her beautiful features. Bottom lip swollen from biting, black hair moist with sweat and clinging to her temples, body so red she looked like she was in the sun...Rachel really did wear debauchery well.

It wasn't much longer until she drifted off into peaceful slumber. I was so numb, I could barely move myself. This moment was too precious.

I kept streaming in and out of consciousness into the rest of the night while I kept her in my arms. I didn't want ask questions. Excitement, confusion, satisfaction, exhaustion and elation were all built up into one sleepless emotion for me.

I looked outside the glass doors of the study after one of the final quick moments of rest I had gotten in those wee hours. As my eyes fully opened, I saw the storm had passed for awhile. Everything was still wet outside but the skies were clear.

Twilight melted away while majestic daybreak made its path. Red and orange glow seeped over the horizon as if the light itself was being poured from a molten sun. Powerful rays flooded over the landscape, lighting every crash of the waves that shined from each ripple.

CHAPTER EIGHTEEN

Epic. Hell of a fuckin' night. I couldn't believe it. Once the sun fully rose that morning, I fell back asleep for a little. When I woke up the next time around, I noticed that Rachel had already left my house.

Nobody would have believed me, no matter how many ways I could have told them. But, it happened. I wanted it to be known...at least with the fellas.

I called for an emergency breakfast at Maria's. This was too juicy to keep secret by any means. My joy was overpowering me.

"We banged our fuckin' brains out," I told Dickie and Harry. The two of them just stared at me, open-mouthed. Their brains formulated no thoughts other than to register that they were shocked. Dickie closed his mouth, then looked at his toes before glancing back up to catch her eye. "How the fuck?" he asked.

"You've gotta be kiddin' me!" they both yelled. I grinned and remained coy. I didn't want to give the gritty details, for words surely wouldn't have been able to depict how great the night actually was.

"That is insane. I am meeting Amanda tonight for dinner," said Dickie. I then commanded, "Don't fuckin' say anything to her, Dick, ya hear me?" Valentine promised that he would keep his mouth shut.

"So, have you talked to her or what? Isn't she engaged?" he then asked, chomping on his breakfast before him. I shook my head 'no' sideways. Heat then couldn't help himself. He had that snare on, as if I were doing the wrong thing. "So, what the fuck? You gonna start dating her again?" he asked.

I didn't even respond do him. There was no need. I didn't have time for that kind of talk. He looked coked up to the tenth degree.

He then changed the topic and addressed to me that I had bigger things to worry about at the time than Rachel Weston. I told him he was crazy.

"Uncle Georgie called. What's going on at work, kid? Stevie is telling him your first quarter numbers were substantially lower than they were last year. Everything okay?" he asked me.

While I was trying to figure out why Harry cared so much about my job, I started to care less. About the job, about what he was saying…and certainly anything else in my surroundings.

I just wanted to hear from her again. I needed to know what last night was…if it were real or not. I kept waiting…waiting…waiting.

There is a kind of waiting that feels like gentle onshore breezes kissing salty stones. It isn't warm but there is a sense of calm, of nature, of things expected.

Then there is the kind that feels like the head of a medieval mace is loose in my guts and my head had taken a beating with a hefty plank of wood. As I waited to see if Rachel responded to any of my calls or texts, I thought I was going to combust each time I tortured myself in looking…because there were no replies.

I stared so hard my mind almost conjured some to please me. Yet, I knew it was crazy. I had to stay in reality, for my sake, and to not depart into the false hopes that demanded my attention at all the worst moments.

It took me all day to reach Rachel but she finally answered. After six text messages and three phone call attempts, she agreed to see me in one simple typed command, "let's talk."

Coffee was much needed. I had to have answers. She left me high and dry the night prior. No note, no goodbye, and no contact throughout the day...it was almost like there was no hope. Was this a one-time deal? Or was she looking for more? Answers were sparse, I was searching.

We met at one of our old spots in Brigantine...the *Casale di Java*. I arrived a bit early to get one coffee deep before we would enjoy one together.

I sat outside so that she would see me when she pulled up to the shop. I was by a metal table right in front of the café window.

She said it all with her actions once she arrived. No kiss, half a hug, and barely asking how I was. She had showed up for coffee...but wasn't there for me. Her mind was made up on something else. But, she didn't look happy in the least bit.

Her eyes looked frozen over like the surface of a winter puddle, robbing them of their usual warmth. She was in there, I knew it...but it was like she just took a huge step back from life. I wasn't quite sure what to say when she came up to my table.

I kept it simple. "So how are you?" I asked. She wasn't conversing much back. "I am fine," with stares into the sky.

"How was your day?" I proceeded. Still, no true purge of emotion, just "fine" and "good". A bit of what I expected and a lot of what I dreaded. I continued. There had to have been something she was going to utter back to. No worries, I though, I had a million questions locked and loaded. I could have played this game.

"So, about last night?"

"I'm leaving for Chicago."

All of a sudden, I had nothing to say. I thought my insides were going to burst, every single one of them. That tingly feeling ran through every nerve ending of my body. She took the stage from here. This was the last response I expected. "Edward took a position out there. I declined the offer from Spain. It's what is best for us."

"You can't be fuckin' serious. Rachel...what are you doing? You declined on your dream??"

She was out of her mind. The guy was being selfish. After all her plans about getting away and becoming an art teacher in Europe...this was preposterous!

"I mean, yeah...I wanted to go. But this is what is going to work for us."

"Wrong. It is what it going to work for him, Rachel. Don't let him play mind games with you."

"It's not a game. This is real."

"Then what was last night? That wasn't real? Nothing we ever shared is real you're telling me?"

"I'm not saying that. Last night was great...but I'm already engaged to Edward. I just can't, Brad...I can't."

214

As much as I tried to convince her that he wasn't out for her best interests, she didn't listen. All she heard was a future with a man he had already said 'yes' too. She was leaving me behind. She then hit me with the two scariest words that were the last ones I planned on hearing at this time. "I'm sorry."

Rachel stood up. She put her sunglasses back on and headed back to her car. There she went again, shattering me up and leaving the pieces for me to collect...for the second time in my life. It was like déjà vu of 1999. It felt too surreal. However, this time I wasn't wrong.

"Listen, I can't let you go," I told her. She stopped herself in her tracks and turned around, looking at me for a good reason why.

"I let you walk away from me one time before in my life without saying anything. But, not now...not this time...I won't make the same mistake twice. If you go to Chicago, you'll be miserable. He says he wants you to be happy...but he won't go to Spain for you? Your lifelong dream of getting to Europe that he was on board with since you met him...now he's backing out? All for his own benefit? He calls himself a man of his word?"

There wasn't any getting through. Again, her mind was made up this time around. "Brad, it's over! Spain is over! Any other offer is over!" she yelled.

"No, Rachel. I'm offering you this...all of me. If you want to walk away and live your life in Chicago...then by all means, go for it. But second chances don't come often in this lifetime, you know that."

Now, I had her. She looked around, shaking her head sideways. She knew I was right. She knew if she left, it would be the worst thing she ever did to herself.

"I am so sorry for what happened years ago with your sister and the fact I was absent the night you needed me. I told you I'd spend the rest of my life apologizing once I tried contacting you in the years that followed. Yeah I was a jerk in the beginning and I was too coward to say anything right away…but it's haunted me for so long. All of it. And I will continue to devote myself to you, like I always intended."

"Brad…" she went without anything to say after. Just incomplete sentences from half-finished thoughts. Her mind was going a mile a minute.

"Rachel, I would have gone to Spain for you, I would go to any country….any moon, any planet!!! That's how much I care. That's how much I love you." I was saying my words slower, softer and closer.

I kept inching in her direction. Walking, striding…slowly, gently. Time was drifting slowly. My world was right before me. Nothing else mattered. I had to win her back, this moment.

"Can you picture him actually being there for you in Chicago, fulfilling your every need and want? Can you picture him being there for your kids and actually letting you decide what you want to do with them when they day comes? Can you picture him there in 20 years? 30 years? 40 years? Or can you…deep down in your heart…your soul…your every being, actually picture me doing all the above and more?"

"No matter what has happened. No matter what's been done. No matter what is to come…I will always love you. I swear it!"

She began crying. I leaned and took her sunglasses off to help remove the tears from her face. And just as I opened my mouth to make my next point, she leaned in and kissed me. It was the longest and most passionate kiss we had in awhile, more so than the night prior. I didn't want it to end. Her taste, again…so sweet.

"Oh, Brad…oh, what was I thinking? You are amazing. I am sorry I ever doubted you and made you wait so long!! I love you forever, baby!!"

Were we ever strangers? I'm not sure we were. That day I first saw her was something even then, though I didn't know what.

The power of love, like an orange glow bursting over a dark distance. It was lit for our hearts only, something to carry us through this life. That very minute…it was the dawn of the person I am today, the person I was destined to be.

God was on my side the whole way. I would have given up anything in the world to win her back. I could never wish to go back to even a day before that.

That very night, she told Edward she wouldn't be joining him on his voyage to Chicago. She even left him the engagement ring he gave her.

The crazy part about it all…he didn't even show one bit of resistance. I didn't care…nor did she. We had every good feeling we needed. It was there all along.

CHAPTER NINETEEN

Early at work, Dickie had touched base with me, calling my cell to let me know Harry wanted him in on a business venture. He was telling me that he declined the offer. "I'm a lawyer," he said. "Not a gangster."

Harry was becoming an odd duck in his old age. It was certainly getting to the best of him. I wasn't sure at the time if it was "mysterious job" with the company, his accelerated cocaine habit, or the pressure from Uncle Georgie in becoming the number one. Little did I know...and little by little, I stopped caring. I could only help those that wanted to be helped. Harry wasn't showing Dickie or myself any of that need.

I could barely deal with the office anymore anyway. The morning was as old as the coffee on my desk. I tapped its murky surface to break the thickening skin and watched the new gap grow. The frigid brown drink dripped from my finger, the ripples spread toward the rim in ever larger circles.

Instead of having available, my usual freshly brewed hazelnut was this instant muck, served warm in polystyrene...more like depression served without a smile. It suited the company at the time though, it matched the beige walls and the melamine desks. It was as welcoming as the unguarded strip lights and the worn blue carpet. The only thing left alive was the ticking clock. I think the rest of us died some time ago. I didn't want to be here anymore.

All day long, I sat at my desk while the paperwork kept piling higher and higher. Save the trees, huh? I don't think the office managers here had ever heard of that.

The clock ticked on the wall and I swore it was slowing down. Sitting there in my office alone made me flatter than a week old glass of coca cola.

Every time I didn't have to think about the task at hand...I was already writing, writing my memoirs and writing my hands off until it made me numb.

I wouldn't be alone either, the whole story was coming. With that tale, that chapter, those crazy paragraphs, crazy words and sentences...I knew I was alive, real, and reality was awesome.

By the end of the work day I was quite word-drunk, I should have cut back and focused again on selling...but who was counting? And why would I care? I had been top performer years on end...what else did I have to prove?

Rachel was on my radar and I couldn't stop thinking or writing about her. That was, of course, until Steve came barging in and disrupted my stream of consciousness.

Boom! He started ranting. Once he went, it was hard to stop him from ceasing. "Numbers are going down, month by month...Brad, what the fuck is going on here? You are projecting to have the worst year yet!!!" Steve screamed, throwing pies and charts on my desk that I didn't even want to try and begin to understand.

As soon as he started to dive into more information, I told him I had an important call coming into my cell, a potential client. At that point, he stormed out of my office like a child would.

Meanwhile, I had no important client trying to get through. It wasn't just the fact that I wanted Steve out of my office, but I wanted to be alone on the phone. The one calling was the only that mattered...Rachel. I had missed a few texts from her earlier...so this ring was a must to immediately tend to.

"Hello, gorgeous."

"Hi, baby! I miss you."

"How is your day, Rae."

"Better now that I'm talking with you, I must say."

Man, her accent still got the best of me, even all this time later. I couldn't help it...it was just so innocent. Something about it made me long for more.

"What are you doin' tonight, B?"

"Probably not too much...how about yourself?"

"My mom is having her 60th birthday party down here at the Carriage House in Galloway. It would be really important to me if you came down. I want to see you...I need to see you!"

My heart melted. Our energy vibrated in such a unique way, each the perfect complement of the other...even on the phone. I was not simply "in love", I was well and truly smitten. "I will be there, darling," I told her. She giggled, thanked me and hung up the phone after telling me the time and place.

I was excited now. I kept at my writing and looked forward to the night ahead. Rachel and Amanda were getting things together for Rachel's mother's birthday party at the Carriage House when she called me.

It was an awkward day for them. They were being funny. They both had something they wanted to tell one another, but they were unable to do it. For the first time, these two found it impossible to communicate. It was odd considering you could never shut one or the other up.

The silence was a poison to them, for in that void of sound the shallowness of their conversation was laid bare. What used to be an intellectual banter of their men and comedic moments was utterly vapid.

I wasn't sure if the ill will at the time was around Rachel and I being together again. Amanda was not my number one fan. However, I knew Dickie had spoken with her recently and all was well, at least it seemed so.

They sat on their phones indulging in moments upon recycled, re-hashed, twittered Instagramming Facebook posts and toggles. They each had a secret to reveal to one another but they were holding their cards close to their chest respectively.

And so without another word, Amanda put the last bit of streamers up in the banquet room and told Rachel she would be back later when the party would start.

It was an eventful day for the media. The news had lit up the papers, television, Facebook, and anywhere else that it could. Harry and two others in my company were arrested that day on money laundering and mail fraud. The mystery of his absence was solved.

Apparently the position Harry held at the company was one that allowed him to set up phony billings to various companies that weren't truly receiving our software or services.

He was doing it on a small pricing scale but in an exponential number in volume of clients, big enough for the entire family to make a lot of money in a kickback to an account setup for them to withdraw.

Inevitably, Georgie gave me a call later on into the day. He wanted me to meet him under the Walt Whitman Bridge right as the rain started coming down. It was rare that he asked me to meet up these days, so I was a bit on edge. I didn't know how to feel.

Years ago, I figured my chances of making it out of a meeting with George were ninety-nine to one. However, now that he was practically a boss and asked to meet away from potential witnesses, I gave myself 50-50.

There he stood by his car with his umbrella canopying him, practically minutes before I arrived. He was up and at it, jittering around like a bug in the kitchen. "What the fuck is going on?" I asked. "It's bad, Brad...the shit is bad!! Harry got sloppy with the drugs, fucked his entire method up at work."

While he lacked to spare me the obvious, I took a glance at the dark skies hovering over the Delaware River and the crowds of rush hour cars whipping by on the bridge at jumbo jet speed. "I need you to testify that Harry had nothing to do with this. We need to blame it on the two others there," he demanded. "Georgie, you have gotta be kiddin' me."

"Do I look like I'm smiling? They're lookin' to give him fifteen fuckin' years!! How am I supposed to live with that? I need ya Brad."

I was having déjà vu. He had a big favor to ask of me, once again. Of course, it was at a time I didn't have.

That night was Rachel's mom's birthday party. I wasn't going to let anything get in my way, especially Griz.

"No, George...I won't do it," I explained. Laughing, Georgie replied in the most condescending way, "Real funny, Brad. I'm gonna have Stevie call you tomorrow with what to go over."

He wasn't going to push me around anymore. Enough was enough. "Maybe you didn't hear me...I said FUCK NO!!!" I exclaimed, unleashing years of anger and frustration towards the man.

He grew silent. His eyes widened and glistened. "You kiddin' me?" asked Griz. "The last cocksucka to turn their back to me...I threw acid all over his face."

I could tell that he was trying to get to me. He thought he could still push me around. At this point, I simply had enough. "I swallowed my pride when you and your irresponsible fuck of a nephew put me in a position of danger sixteen years back and cost me the love of my life once. A guy I thought was my friend and wanted to see me away from this life, a guy who I had to hide out with because you told me to. Don't think I'm gonna listen to you twice."

He grew angry. He responded in a softer tone than before, thinking that by being coy it was going to get to me. He was wrong.

"Fundamentally we are in agreement that my nephew is a *miserab* fuckin' mess. But don't you talk to me like you grew a pair of balls overnight. Do you know that I will..." Georgie rambled before I interrupted him. I went ahead to say, "Before what? Huh, George? You gonna fuckin' kill me? I've known you all my life. Do what ya

223

gotta do, because to be frank…I don't give a shit anymore. You never cared about me. You're all about you and Harry…that's it. I'm your pawn to your big fortunes, a gofer for all of it. I just wish he wasn't under your spell too…because your ego is all that you truly are."

He clenched his fist, a vein popped out of his forehead. There wasn't a doubt in my mind he wanted to swing his arm at me. It was in the way he looked at me. I've seen him use that mien before on others.

"Now I gotta turn my back on ya. Whatever happens next…I have no control of. This is as far as we go, Big B," he whispered, walking away…more than likely for the last time. It didn't matter to me. Georgie wasn't out for my best interest anymore. He didn't care for me…or about me, nor did I for him.

The only thing that mattered to me was getting over to Rachel's mom's birthday party. I wasn't going to let the illicit Mancini Family make me break a promise to the same angel twice in a lifetime.

I was already late. She was texting me like crazy. "OMG…where are you?" and "Get here now, please!!" were the types of messages I was receiving. I couldn't let her down. I was doing everything I could despite the rain that was pouring like a million fists on my windshield from Philly over to the suburbs.

In the grip of silent panic, my wild eyes, pupils dilated, heart racing, and brain on fire felt like a cluster bomb exploding in my cranium, turning my thoughts into a mental soup of conflicting instructions.

I prayed over and over to get there without any mayhem. To detour the storm, pierce through the God-awful traffic and to ultimately fall into a happy Rachel...which history can prove that her unhappiness could crush me. I was going a hundred miles an hour...both on the road and in my head.

From all angles I felt it, building like an unstoppable snowball in the pit of my stomach. I couldn't concentrate on anything else. Next, my heart started to beat harder and faster, adrenaline levels skyrocketing, and my balls trying and crawl up inside my body.

It took some time but I made it. There I pulled up to valet outside the old Carriage House banquet hall, twenty miles from the city. I texted Rachel that I arrived. But there, she already was waiting for me at the front door. She was soaking wet from the storm...and oh boy, she was going to unleash a storm of her own on me. I could feel it. Here it came. Why wait any longer? She was going to give it to me, all the buildup and every bit of wrath that I deserved.

Or was she? You see, there is something so heavenly about a kiss in the rain, a tender moment that just cannot wait. Dying to see one another. One barely letting the other get out of the car and trot over to the stairs of the banquet hall because the excitement is just that pure.

It's that burst of love that is expressed, not caring if the water soaks through to chill the skin. It is a connection that shows the strength of the feeling, the mutual need. It is a rebellion against the elements. Nature can bring the rain

225

but our inner sunshine comes through just the same. That's certainly what happened when Rachel came out, jumping into my arms so unexpectedly.

"I thought I'd be in trouble arriving at this time," I said once I finally got the chance to breathe. She smiled as she continued to sit in my arms, whispering, "I'm pregnant."

I tried to speak…but nothing came out. I couldn't believe it. Not for a second. "Surprise," she went on, smiling like she did. "And I know it's yours. Edward and I didn't do anything for months. I'm exactly five weeks along going back to the exact night I came to your place."

Any thought or preamble to how this night was going to was gone. My stress from Georgie, the car ride over in the traffic and in the weather…diminished. All I cared about was looking into Rachel's eyes that very moment, envisioning what our children would look like…picturing what we had in store with both of our lives together.

"Did you tell anyone inside?" she asked. She shook her head sideways, telling me, "I took the test while I was here…picked it up on the way. Wanted you to know first. I love you so much, baby."

So shall it stay put, a smile eternally stained upon my lips while a tear of joy slipped down my face. My delight, my love, my laughter, my cheer.

All would reach the ears of those who have forgotten the warmth of such harmonies. I couldn't wat for us share it all. To play life's song, the swelling symphony that can mend any broken heart. No one would be left unsmiling tonight.

"You're going to be an amazing mother! This is the greatest news I've ever gotten in my life," I reminded her. She kissed me again. It was so hard to try and keep kissing back with the mile-wide smirk I couldn't take off my face.

We continued to stay out in the rain for another minute kissing, yet eager to deliver the pending news to her family. We wanted to shout it so loud, bursting through the entrance doors when we walked in.

CHAPTER TWENTY

That summer of 2015 turned out to be the best season at the shore of my life, even better than the college years.

Every weekend Rachel and I came down, the weather was immaculate. The kind that felt like the perfect kiss of the sun without the fiery heat of noon time in August. The skies were enough pristine, the white clouds showed you how beautiful the day was. The renovation was coming together at the house and everything seemed to be working out just the way I planned it back in February.

Most importantly, the love I had for Rachel was growing exponentially by the day. It was so full of grandeur, the experience was more than we ever imagined it would become.

The fact that we were back in each other's lives still felt like a dream to me. There was a state of grace that happened every beat of the moment...a feeling I thought was lost or locked away. It elated my mind and helped me in a way to enhance the place easily. Working the day away was a breeze with her on my mind or in my sights.

By one afternoon on an early June day, I had just finished converting what was my study into the new baby room. It contained a small crib, neatly made, two straight-backed chairs, a diaper changing station, a bureau without any mirror...and a small table. There were drapery curtains at the sliding glass doors, greeting the humbling view.

All day the sun had been pouring down upon the roof, and the little room was like an oven for heat. Letting the screens welcome a gentle breeze, it was time to take a break. I inhaled and exhaled the incoming salty wind as I took a gander outside...for it was now time to do something big.

Firing away! I knew I was capable at completing it...I was just nervous as to how she was going to react. I was shaking, head to toe. Barely being able to setup, I had to keep calming my nerves by sitting down and taking deep breaths. This wasn't an everyday thing.

Off I went, constructing a masterpiece downstairs from the front door to the porch up and outside the baby's room, former study. I wrote different poems, all having to do with the beach, our favorite place. They all alluded to great question I had in store for her once she saw my face at the end of the journey.

The front door held the first note, planted on its screen. I awaited. Gazing from the window, I saw Rachel's head tilt sideways as she made her way up the stairs within about an hour after I set it all up. She looked at it in inquisition, then fashioned a smile once she got through the words.

The tide rises, the tide falls...
The twilight darkens, the seagull calls.
Amongst the sands damp and brown...
We travel happily, aligning the town.

The note then instructed her to walk inside and make her way towards the stairs. "Oh, goodness," I heard her whisper as she came into the house, slowly and quietly, noticing the path in front of her. I left an array of shells in a trail from the welcome mat to the staircase. Mostly random ones I gathered that morning upon the water's crest, I made sure that she knew to follow its lead.

By the first banister welcoming the staircase to the second floor, I wrote the second poem that detailed her to make her way up the stairs.

Come walk with me
Along the sea
Where dusk sits on the land

And search with me
For shells are free,
And treasures hide in sand.

Hearing her giggle, I was trying my hardest to contain myself. Step after step she took, it was difficult. I was so excited, I felt like a child. I wanted to yell for her already. This was going to be amazing once she got to the baby's room.

Alone I stood by the screen door, holding our future…all that represented our love in one tiny box. It was like a small prevenience that burned with glittery dazzle and held all the secret of what was to come upon the wisdom in its gleaming domain.

The anticipation was a nervous kind of energy. It tingled through me like electrical sparks on the way to the ground, gathering in my toes.

Before I knew it, she made it up the staircase and was right by the door of the room. She read the last poem before she came inside.

Lie next to me, you will see...
As we read each other's mind.
When your heart beats, mine repeats
and both benefit in kind.

Time stands still,
or so it seems...
in our hammock strung
between two dreams.

Side by side, we hear the tide,
and not a word is spoken.
Love came in through a door
we didn't know was open...

On bended knee, I spilled out of my mouth the four most important words in the utmost question to any great love.

"Rachel, will you marry me?"

Nothing stopped her. She was entranced, excited...more alive than she had ever thought possible. All the mundane worries of the day had been muted and all that existed was this moment. No worrying about the past, no anxiety about the future. In one adrenaline fueled warrior-yell she leaped into the hammock of arms with nothing but air beneath her feet; eyes wide, grin wider. "Yes, oh my goodness, yes!!"

She didn't even look at the ring, she just kept looking in my eyes and kissing me. "When? When? When?" she asked.

"I don't want to wait until the baby is born. I'd marry you yesterday if I could, Rachel."

"Oh my gosh…yes, yes, YES!!!! I don't want to spend another day without being your wife."

I told her I felt the same…and always did. I wish I could have married her years ago at this point. A house, kids, a dog…all in that timeframe. But, this is where we stood…and I was certainly grateful by all means, nonetheless.

"Let's just hope I don't show too much in my dress."

"You're going to be beautiful, even if you were at your full nine months walking down the aisle."

She smiled and kissed me once more. We then began quickly on planning the biggest and best wedding we could have in a two month time. I didn't care…I was ready as I'd ever be.

It wasn't a day that we endured, but one we savored…as much as we could. The union of our two hearts beating as one, each that would sacrifice for the other's happiness and wellbeing.

Many would agree that it was an August afternoon so majestic, everything seemed to have worked in tune with our love. We had it on the 28th day of the month. It was also the exact sixteen year mark of our first encounter.

Dickie and Amanda appreciated it just as much as we did, for it was a milestone for them as well.

At the end of each seated aisle of the beach's rows, scented candles hung from conch shell holders. They were filled with scents of jasmine and rain.

Spread down the aisle were white rose pedals on a blue runway, as far as the eyes could see, slightly moist so they wouldn't crack when we stepped on them. We had the bridesmaids and groomsmen dressed in beach attire. On either side of the center canopy, they stood parallel to one another. I couldn't have asked for a greater crew.

However, the clock was ticking. It was surely past noon and still no sight of my bride. The questions that ran through my brain could fill a trivia game. I was so nervous, I turned to the aging Johnny Horsecock, one of my groomsmen, for advice.

Sweating from every pore on my head, I pondered, "Do you think she really forgot? Do you honestly think she wouldn't show up?" Johnny giggled as Dickie stepped a few feet in my direction, adjusting the arrangement on his shirt. "Don't you doubt her, Brad...she will be here."

The minutes weren't growing any more rapidly. As a matter of fact, it was slowing down to molasses speed. I couldn't even comprehend the rhythm of it all. I was too worried about where Rachel was. Looking around the entire beach, I searched for answers.

It was now fifteen minutes past. Amanda looked over at us all standing, holding her arms in the air and almost dropping her bouquet. This was all so scary. I didn't know who to turn to in the crowd. My mother, her mother, her cousins…who was going to help me? Who had even a clue?

Then, the ocean roared. Just when I thought of running out into the center and creaming for the hills, down she came with Mr. Weston from afar, bringing her down for the last time before he gave her away to this crazy kid.

This lucky guy who made it happen with a mere chance…fate at its finest. Nobody ever saw it coming…not ever. She had made it…thank goodness…all felt right again.

Rachel's father hugged me after he put her into my arms, saying "I'm proud of you" walking away, smiling and patting me on the shoulder. That was his way of welcoming me into the family.

Standing next to my love felt overwhelming. "Excuse my tardiness," Rachel whispered to me elegantly with a grin. It didn't bother me one bit. "You don't ever have to be sorry," I confirmed.

I was so relieved she still wanted to marry me, she could've been an hour late and I would have been totally fine with it.

It was a time to pause, look back, and smile at all the moments that led to this one. And was a time to look ahead at all the moments that were still to come. Our love wasn't only happily ever after, it was the experience of writing our story. It's not one moment — not even just this one today. It was every moment. Even the small ones.

I assured her during our vows the same things I told her on a daily basis. It was a promise I meant, through and through….over and over, and one I'd repeat whenever she requested. Fortunately for me, she reciprocated the same feelings.

You are my reason to live.
All I own, I would give...
Just to have you adore me.

In her embrace, my world stopped still on its axis. There was no time, no wind, no rain. My mind was at peace. That's the way our love worked. Pure. Unselfish. Undemanding. Free. This was the love we waited for, prayed for.

I inwardly thanked God while kissing and hugging her all the more tighter. A love like this was to be cherished for life. Finally, we were where we always envisioned being.

It felt like the grand arrival when the renovation was finally complete that fall. Everything I planned on doing at that time was done...making this a state-of-the-art, two-story beachfront many gawked over when they'd walk by and take a glance at it. A new kind of house...a new beginning.

Though no one can go back in time and alter the past, anyone can start from where they are in the present and make a brand new future.

This was it. This was the start of something exhilarating. I started it all with writing a letter to my dearest the first day after we considered the place "fully renovated".

Rae,

Returning home is the holy grail of my life...being here with you is the one true thing I have ever wished for. This place...the memories, the changes, the growth, and all that is ahead.

I want to be the person you recall, at any time. I want to warm your soul. You are the love of my life....the wind to my sails, the beacon to my bay.

Let love guide our way as we live for the moments that take our breath away.

Every day with you is breathtaking!!

Welcome back, my sweetheart!

I love you,
Brad

  The good times carried into that holiday season...our first one together, married, and in our home at the shore to close out what had been an awesome year. Christmas Eve was the first night I lit the fireplace in the living room.
  What an enchanting time. Our real tree lit up by the window, a bowl egg nog in the kitchen made to

perfection, Perry Como and Bing on the hi-fi. There was no holiday quite like it.

I let the sounds of yuletide tunes fill the room as we awaited Midnight Mass with Dickie and Amanda later. As much as I was against giving gifts the night before, Rachel anticipated giving me one.

"No, no…can't break tradition. Growing up, all gifts has to be open on Christmas morning. We didn't do 'open one' rule on this night," I told her.

"Awww, babe…c'mon. I was really excited about this one. This I found and had to get you."

"No, Rae…I won't do it."

She then lit her face up with the one look that got me every time; the puppy dog scowl. She did it in a way like no other did it before. Before she even fully opened those enchanting hazel eyes, I gave in as if I had no courage to being with. She was so sweet.

"Okay, okay…just one!!" I commanded.

She handed me a six by nine inch shaped wrapped box, about an inch thick. "Must be another how-to book," I joked as she gave another one of her "looks".

I continued to open until I had it in full sights. Throwing the paper and tape on the floor, I stared at this gift for a minute or two…for it was a brilliant and radiant gift.

A leather-bound notebook with a LeGrand fountain pen. "My God…this must have costed you an arm and a leg!!" I exclaimed. She snickered in telling me, "Now your priceless words can be scribbled in a priceless notebook."

"You are the best, Rae…I love you."

"I love you too, B"

237

Just as we kissed, I reached over the pile by the tree to pull a gift out for her to open. However, before I snatched something up, I had to address one more concern. It was a worry that had been apart of me for awhile. I wanted one more present from her.

"Before you open yours, there's one more gift you need to give me, Rae." I stood up and walked over to the television. Behind it, I hid a letter.

"I need you to promise me you'll consider this," I said as I handed her an offer from the Florence Academy of Art in Italy. They wanted her to apply for a career teaching abroad. It had come in the mail that week.

She didn't know what to say. She was happy yet sad. She was excited yet melancholy. A million questions were pouring into her brain as she sat and stared at the letter for a minute straight, holding her belly. "What about the baby now?" she asked.

"We can't have a life in Italy with a newborn. And the place...you just got done making this a castle you always dreamed of. All the work, all this year...what are we gonna do? Just pick up and leave."

I stayed silent as I let her continue spilling her emotions.

"And what about our jobs? We both are in very good roles, we are just supposed to give that up? What are we to do?"

I then chimed in. "None of this means anything...without you and our baby. I want you live your dream. Overseas...you always wanted to be in Italy. Well, this isn't just teaching in Barcelona before you're considered for Florence...THIS IS THE REAL DEAL!!"

She stayed silent as the wood in the fire crackled. I wanted her to know that she needed to do this for me. She needed to be all she could have been and shined like the star I knew she was.

"I'm not going to let you pass again on your dream. This is it, baby. You need to at least apply...just do it for me."

She smiled, kissed me again and promised me she was going to go for it. "You are the best, you really are," she kept repeating.

Late that night after they were both done working, Dickie and Amanda were getting together to chat at a café nearby the hospital. They planned on getting to midnight mass together with us...but they were cutting it close. It was almost candle-lighting time. They weren't going to make it for the first song.

Yet, this gathering prior wasn't necessarily to celebrate the birth of Christ. There were bigger things in play at the time in the minds of these two. Ultimately, Dickie had to know where they stood. There had been some tension between them since they first enhanced the relationship. They weren't being themselves anymore, especially Amanda.

"I just want with you what Brad and Rachel have. I want us to figure this out Amanda, you have been distant," confessed Dickie, unable to pick his coffee mug up at all. Yet, he still forced a smile staring at his favorite girl while she did nothing but look away.

She was haunted. In the space that should have been filled with Dickie's love, there was a void so black, no light could ever penetrate. It was a wound that would never heal no matter how much salve would be poured on. "Richard…I have something to tell you. This is something that I haven't even told to Rachel. Nobody knows this." He could sense the discomfort in the paleness of her face. It kept whitening with every breath she took.

He asked her to go on. "When that accident happened sixteen years ago with Lauren…something changed in me. I was injured from the hips down."

"Yeah, I know…and look, you turned out perfect down there," replied Dickie, chuckling and attempting to get a laugh out of her.

"Stop…this is serious. Something went wrong," she replied, stern in the face as ever. Dickie urged her to tell him what it was. He couldn't wait any longer…he had already been waiting so very long to get to the bottom of her feelings.

Choking on her words every time she attempted to spit it out, when it finally came out of her mouth, it sounded more terrible than either had anticipated. "I'm unable to have children."

Taking a deep, long breath, Dickie simply smiled afterward. "Look, there are plenty of other ways to handle it these days. There's further investigation, there is adoption, there are a million ways."

She interrupted him, holding both of his hands across the table, convincing enough to the point where it was as if she planned the entire conversation prior to the meeting. "I'm sorry. That's not what I want to do. This isn't gonna change. It's just not gonna happen. I will never be a mother, no matter what." Then, she began to cry.

"I still want to be with you, Amanda...I truly do. Don't let this come between us." A tear then passed down Dickie's face. He couldn't stop them from coming down.

"Haven't you always wanted kids? You told me your dream was to have a family."

"That was before I reconnected with you....before..." Dickie was detailing before he was interrupted by Amanda. She couldn't keep going.

"Still...your future always had kids in it. That is something major you would be giving up for me. I can't live with that, Richard...I can't. You'll wake up one day, hating me...full of regret. So this needs to be end between us, okay?

Dickie didn't know what to do. The pale glow from his face let anybody who saw him know that he was in pain from the inside out. Amanda was adamant on ending their relationship, right then and there. "I just cannot do this to you. I am so, so sorry!"

She stood up, balling her eyes out and storming out of the café. Dickie stood up and ran after her, only until she made it out the door. After that, he stood still. He watched her jet into her car, peel out of the restaurant parking lot and screech down the street.

The snow continued falling and the Christmas music began playing. However, inside Dickie's world...it was nothing but sad songs and rain storms scattering.

I received a text that he wasn't coming to Midnight Mass. Amanda never showed up either. It was an emotional night that heated to its boil in a short duration.

Dickie didn't like the feeling of having no power, of having no good ideas to counter Amanda's storm. He hated the feeling as if he were about to throw up all over the sidewalk. He hated the feeling of being now obsolete to a girl he adored.

CHAPTER TWENTY-ONE

It was Christmas Day. Both Rachel and I were equally as enquiring as to why we didn't see our friends, Dickie and Amanda for midnight mass. Neither of them were answering their phones…it was a bit concerning.

As much as we tried contacting them, it was to no avail. However, we weren't going to let it ruin the day. There was so much to be grateful for. It was the season of Yule tide spirits.

As soon as I put on the Clancy Brothers Christmas playlist and made hot cocoa for us both by a lit fire, Rachel gave me my gift in the best five words I could hear her say, "I will apply for Italy."

I was so proud of her, I immediately went over and kissed her lips. I told her that not only would I be there to support her with her job, I'd be the best father I could be. If we had to do it overseas, it would be more exciting than anything.

"After the baby, of course," she reminded me. The capstone to our love, the soon-to-be symbol our combined creations. The baby was going to be everything I dreamed of, I knew it then.

Just as we were about to dig into the rest of the gifts under the tree, we heard a knock at the door. I stood up and went over to see who it was…Amanda!!

She came in, face flushed red and looking like she was up all night. She cried as if her brain was being torn apart from the inside out. Passionate agony flowed out of her every pore. From Amanda's mouth came a scream from so raw that it even made me wet with tears once I learned why she was sad.

It was tragic to hear she'd never become a mother. I was certainly sad to learn that she and Dickie wouldn't be taking it to the next level. I always thought they were just as right for one another...close, if not comparable to Rachel and I.

For that, I was sure there was still potential in our days to come. However, the demons inside her she'd be chasing would be that of a lifetime. She would be unable to ever say "I'm proud of my son or daughter".

Rachel came and consulted her like the good friend she was. It was still hard to bear. I had never seen Amanda like this before.

She grabbed onto a chair so that her violent shaking wouldn't cause her to fall. From her eyes came a thicker flow of tears than she had cried for losing Lauren years back.

"I'll never have kids. I'll never be happy either. I let down the only man who would ever love me," she told us.

Amanda was mentally disheveled having to hide her broken insides for so long. We all wanted the happy version of her, the one with the instant smile and the delightful things to say...even if she hadn't liked me for so long.

However, we would adapt. Even if over the years her loneliness would grow. Dickie could be broken and expect her love and patience, he could show his scars and she would always help. Yet if Amanda was sad for more than a few hours, a day even, his impatience grew. Then she would stop herself, swallow down that bitter pill and continue, giving him the impression that a little "tough love" had been all she needed.

Yet now Amanda found herself unable mask the hurt, unable to just switch on her happy side and act as if nothing wrong had ever happened... and that is where their problems began.

And just like that, 2015 came to a close. I was barely able to believe it was already the end of December, but that meant time for sparkling cocktails and delicious appetizers.

I needed it. Especially after Steve Smith sent me a certified letter from J.R. Montague the final week of the year, telling me he was putting me on a performance plan. This meant I had thirty days to get my act together at the office and start the year with a splash of sales. However, I just wasn't caring anymore. It wasn't time for all that.

It was a time to reflect, and one to look forward...a night spent only with the finest. Year's end is neither an end nor a beginning but a going on, with all the wisdom that experience can instill in us

Thinking back to where I was this night only a year previous blew my mind. So much was different. My entire life took a 180. At the end of 2014, I was top salesman at my company chasing any tail that walked in front of me.

The energy in the air was inviting when we got to The Playground Club in Atlantic City to celebrate. There was everyone and anyone around us in attendance. We weren't going to be out late considering Rachel's stomach was the size of a boulder and she was unable to drink. But that was okay...I was just glad to be with her.

I took a deep, frozen breath as my lungs swelled with air in the cold of the night. Overhead, the sparse clouds exonerated interchangeably, opening curtains to let out the young darkness.

It was an exciting time, counting down...getting ready for what was to come. There were so many things ahead to be excited about.

I couldn't wait to see if Rachel would get accepted to an overseas career. With the baby due first week of February, there was a lot of great things we had to look forward to.

The great things didn't show well in the eyes of Dickie when he showed up at the club. He walked past the crowd and through the many guests to come over and say hello to us both at our table.

"There he is!" I yelled, coming over to give him a hug. I could tell he didn't want to stay long...he was wearing a scowl I only saw on him seldom. Dickie took me aside. He had some big things to tell me.

"I got a job...Los Angeles. My dream position. I'm going to be representing Hollywood actors and producers. I go in the spring.

I couldn't believe it. As happy as I was for him and showing it in the many hugs I gave, I was sad knowing he'd be gone soon. There was a moment in our lives where we were apart for more than a month at a time. Now that he'd be on the west coast, who knew what was in store?

"Congratulations, brother!" I said. We'd been friends so long. Every year, we grew closer. I thought back to our childhood at that very moment, all the great times we had…we'd never forget.

It was that kind of friendship that bloomed in the center of your heart - that kind of friendship that grew from the seed basking in the warm soil to a vast tree with many ups and downs.

We certainly had many…but not enough to disguise the enormity or the grandeur of such a tree, the sheer brilliance and beauty of it.

I loved Dickie. I was proud of him. All of sudden, he changed the tempo. He shifted gears on me. He told me some not-so-great news after we jovially discussed his new venture.

"Harry's trial ended. He got twenty years. The judge handed it to him this past week like it was nothing," he told me.

To say I didn't see it coming would've been a lie. Harry made the bed he slept in. I felt bad for him yet he knew what he was getting into lately with the mess he had. I could only have so much sympathy for the guy.

"Look out for Georgie. I'm hearing things," continued Valentine. "Word on the street is that he is coming after you now that Harry has this hefty sentence. He is blaming it on your lack of testimony."

I knew George would be upset. The fact he would potentially be coming after me was ludicrous. It was as if I made Harry do what he did, like the kid didn't have his own decision making power.

Looking around the club, I knew the guy was sneaky and could end up being anywhere at any time. He operated in a smooth stealth-like manner at all times. I wasn't worried. However, all that mattered to me was the safety of my wife and our unborn child.

"I'm just hearing you need to watch your back, that's all. I wouldn't take what he says lightly." Dickie informed me that whatever I needed, he was there for me. I told him it wasn't necessary though. I wasn't going to run…nor would I hide.

I was alert, ready for whatever came my way. I didn't want to let Georgie scare me…but I knew he was crazy. He would definitely kill my family and I if he truly wanted to.

CHAPTER TWENTY-TWO

2016 was off to an interesting start. Part of the process of beginning anew, or changing directions is to know where you want to go. What sounded simplistic and easy was the most difficult of choices I had to make with clarity one day.

It was a Friday morning. The weathermen were calling for snow later. I knew I had to get to work...just didn't want to get stuck in a blizzard being an hour and fifteen minutes away. So, I was reluctant to leave. It was a day meant to be spent at home. Plus, I was hating my job more than ever.

Rachel and I were having a chat while I was preparing to hit the road. We were discussing the future and possible life overseas...and some of the other options we had if she didn't get the teaching job and if we stayed where we were.

All while this was happening, I was experiencing some difficulty with my laptop, trying to get it working on the kitchen table. For the past few days, it would turn on and off randomly. It was driving me crazy, making me pull the hair out of my head.

The infamous "blue screen of death" had frustrated many a user, as it brought the computer to a halt that day, displaying an error message that was utterly indecipherable to most. It could have been a number of issues — maybe it was buggy software, or perhaps it was the system running out of memory.

I wasn't upset…after all, it was a piece of company equipment.   My biggest concern was my story, the memoirs, everything I had been writing for more than a year.

Just as I realized I jotted notes down on paper as well, I started to notice those were misplaced as well. They weren't in my desk or anywhere in the room that used to be my study.

They weren't in the bedroom, any of the closets or any of the boxes I had placed miscellaneous things. This was a terrible way to start the work day.   I scrambled around as if I were a pirate looking for his missing box of treasure.

In the grip of silent panic, my eyes were wild, my heart was racing, and my brain was on fire. I looked under every couch, table and chair for my notes.   They were nowhere to be found. Where did I put them? How could I have been so careless?   Where could they have possibly gone?

I could feel it, building like an unstoppable snowball in the pit of my stomach. I couldn't concentrate on anything else that I'm doing. Rachel started to grow worried as she walked over to aid me in my state of anxiety. But this was stress she certainly didn't need in her state.

I couldn't believe it. My heart was starting to beat harder and faster, adrenaline levels rose and I was unable to finish getting ready before I left.

My memoirs were officially gone. I searched high and low for the notes but to no avail. I felt lost. The only thing that was there after searching for so long was now vanished, vaporized. It slowly seeped in how much of a fool I had been, living in my own dream world. I floated away from the fake reality until I was just an absent star in the skies.

"I'll keep looking for your notes, babe," Rachel told me. I thanked her, kissed her, grabbed my briefcase and made it out.

You'd think the road would be empty at eight in the morning on a Friday heading to the city. Everyone should be asleep, right? They aren't though. My car joined a pile of others, mostly other office workers like myself with "vital" paper to push for twelve or more hours. It made me late.

To make it all worse, there was no sound when I arrived to the J.R. Montague building...yet everyone was moving.

They were walking...but not talking. My secretary paced back and forth by the front desk as I slowly made my way in her direction to sign in and enter the building. She had a confused look on.

I stood still at first, unable to comprehend the note she slid to me. "Permission to enter denied." That was all she wrote.

Within the next sixty seconds, the phone rang at her desk. She didn't say anything when she picked it up...she just handed it to me. "Hello?" I went, now a bit concerned.

"Your credit cards are cancelled and the car is now repossessed by the company."

I almost popped out of my skin. I wasn't sure who the voice was. Whatever this person thought they were doing calling me, trying to add to my list of nightmares was beyond me. "Because I was late?" I asked.

The person then hung up. I was still in shock, holding the phone in my and a few seconds before I hung up. I tried asking the girl at the desk what was going but she didn't have a clue. More unfamiliar faces kept running around the building. It was definitely a sight to see.

Laptop at home: washed to shit. Cell phone: off…company car: gone…expense account and company credit cards: ceasing to exist. I had nothing. For whatever reason that was unbeknownst to me, I figured it had to get sorted out and I would get the answers later.

Perhaps I was fired. Perhaps there was a crazy tax audit going on. Perhaps I would be back the next day. Regardless, I went out the front door with nothing in my arms now, looking for a cab to bring me to the train station and to get back to the shore with the little money I had in my possession.

I fully expected to be escorted out by security and dumped on the street by the way things were mysteriously looking around the building! That would have added to the suspense of the morning. Or even worse…getting a third eye from Georgie from out of nowhere. He would gut me in an instant.

The train was anything but luxury when I got on it, the seats dulled by the grime of thirty years. It sure was no ride in the Cadillac.

The pressure was building, but I knew I had to stay calm. What was next? Was this it? Was Georgie really after me like Dickie told me? Were my days at J.R. Montague truly over?

This was stress that I certainly did not during these delicate days of awaiting my child to be born. Even though I hated it at that office anyway, it would have been nice to know where I stood.

I could feel finally the locomotive move. The train trundled from the depot as the snowstorm began. Everyone awake. Everyone asleep. Eyes blurry, reactions slow, tiredness running through the entire rail. It took forever, it seemed, for the old engine to roar into life and get moving.

When it did, a funny feeling came...not excitement, though at first it appeared that way. Ahead was unknown...and all I could do was pray for things to be better where I was heading for I didn't know what was on the other end of the day.

It began to snow even more outside as this expressing fear sat quietly inside, eroding me as a person. What started as a contortion of my stomach became a feeling of being smothered by an invisible hand.

A swirling storm of screaming silver. There was nothing friendly about it. It fell thick enough to blind any traveler by foot or vehicle. The gale whipped each flake, so pretty on its own, into a projectile that hurt unguarded skin.

The sky above had none of the light that noon-time should have, so thick are the black clouds. And the sound, like one wind-chime taking the force of these almost hurricane force winds roaring with the sounds of the train.

And then halt! There stopped our motion. What was going on? I looked around for who had the answers...but all passengers had the same questions.

The lights were flickering as train conductors ran back and forth between the cars to try and fix the situation. This wretched storm. I had to get home. I had to figure out what was going on.

I had no cell phone, little money, and barely any time before I went absolutely crazy. The job was something I could have gotten over. But this enigma of what Griz wanted to do was aching as the uncertainty built. I then began thinking of where I could have obtained a gun, just for protection.

The lights on the train then immediately went out. Darkness. It surrounded everything. It ate up everything in its path. It gave us no mercy.

Normally, I could have handled. I certainly was never afraid of the dark. But, this time was different. This was like being in hell.

This was the darkness that robbed you of your best sense and replaced it with a numbing fear. In this darkness I sat, muscles cramped and unable to move. I only knew my eyes are still there because I could feel myself blink, still instinctively moisturizing the organs I had no current use for. I couldn't hear much either. Just random chatter, babies screaming, and people coughing and hacking.

All of a sudden, the lights came back on. When they did, I saw a man lurking down the center aisle. He was clothed in a black saffron-like robe and strutting slowly in my direction.

There is nothing creepier to me than a person with emotions that don't match the situation. They consistently look happy when others are in pain. They are unable to truly look sad when others have a trauma to relate. Those people are feeling an inner surge of pleasure when others hurt.

It worried me the closer he came to my seat. This was it. This was the final moment. It was either Georgie or one of his guys, coming to whack me. Enough was enough. I was an outsider in his eyes…I had to go.

He came closer…and closer…and closer. He pulled out his hand from his pocket. I closed my eyes. My final moments were here.

"My watch is broken, sir…do you have the time?" this gentleman asked. When I opened my eyelids, he was showing me the timepiece on his wrist. I chuckled, looked at mine…and replied, "12:30." I was surprised that my Rolex was even working after the morning I had. I figured that would break too considering how everything around me was disappearing. The mysterious man walked away and smiled.

This was brutal. I was barely able to contain myself. I tried taking deep breaths and calming my nerves. I had to get home. "Get it together, Brad," I was saying. I had to cease this fear.

My paranoia was certainly at an all-time high. This had to end. It had to be this night. I needed to get some satisfaction.

CHAPTER TWENTY-THREE

The wind howled by 2:30, piling up snow in drifts, blinding the night with ice-white dust. I walked bent-over against the cold, protecting my eyes with my arms when I got out of the cab from the train station that took me home. Trees, posts, and sheds loomed into my vision, then vanished, swallowed in white.

The blizzard kept blasting away in my path, walking to the door. It was time to see the wife…the only thing mattered.

Although it seemed as if I was out of a job now, it was certainly nice knowing I'd be home to help my pregnant love with whatever she needed tending to. Each day. It gave me more happiness than any sale I had ever made in my sixteen year career at J.R. Montague.

Yet there was still some stone-cold suffering despite being unemployed. Before I tried to figure out a way to tell Rachel about what happened, my mind was consumed by other things.

One of my two biggest upsets now came with the mystery of where my writings could have gone. It just didn't make sense how it all vanished.

The amount of time I spent working on them was enough to build a city from scratch, enough to travel the world over and over.

I always told myself I'd feel better if I put my memories on paper, so I did. But I always knew deep down inside me, neither the ink in my pen or the taps of my

257

laptop keyboard were strong enough to handle the words I wrote. They were intense, full of light beaming onto some the darkest of secrets of my vault. I just hoped the next set I would capture held potential to turn out even better than the initial.

The other worry was, of course, where I stood with Georgie. Whatever his plan was for me held all the enigma I could handle. I lived in fear wherever I went. Not that the biggest concern was that of my particular safety…but more importantly, that of my wife and our child she was carrying.

He was a man of many capabilities. Now that I had turned my back to him, all of those things were possibilities for me. Knowing this, the anxiety sat below my smile, my actions, and through all of my silly jokes. It was there like over-caffienation but without the option not to drink a cup. I knew I had to tell Rachel it was time we got away for a few days until this mess with Georgie blew over.

Zooming inside and upstairs to the bedroom, I was as mobile as I could be when I came into the room, noticed Rachel writing a letter on the bed. She was lovely.

"Where have you been? I tried calling you all day," she said. I also saw her glued to the television for a minute as if they just announced 9/11 again on Breaking News. I came over and gave her a kiss. "It has been an insane kind of day. I don't even know where to start."

Rachel replied, "J.R. Montague's lawyer called you. He has been looking to talk to you. Brad, what is going on?" I then said to her, "Exactly what I am trying to figure out," as I grabbed the house phone.

"George was arrested this morning. So were six more from your old company, I think Steve included. They're looking to put them all on trial and give similar to what Harry received for the mail fraud case. They're going down hard."

It was on the news she was watching. "What? They got Georgie? Are you kidding me?" yelled my inquisitive self, now glued to the brief along with her.

There it showed the big bust, right at the building I worked at for so long...live on TV. It appeared that Georgie and Steve along with even more from the office were all indicted on charges of theft by deception and money laundering. Thank God I was fired.

Nonetheless, somebody inside J.R. Montague blew the whistle and brought a cease to the entire operation and stopped anyone else who was involved with Harry on it.

It now made sense why I wasn't allowed in the building. The Feds were raiding the place, shredding it to pieces like paper.

I had to call this guy. I had to see if they were coming after me too. This constant worry needed to end immediately.

"Brad Mulligan, this is Lou Daza, legal representative from J.R. Montague," the man said. I took a huge gulp, a deep breath, and prayed to God that he had something good for me.

"I wanted to make you aware that you were not listed on the indictment today. Your boss Mr. Smith had already listed you on performance review in December...practically shielding you from any wrongdoing

259

considering he would have fired you the end of this month. But if you do have any information that you would like to share about him or George Mancini, you can let me know."

I smiled cheek to cheek. I couldn't believe it. Who would have known that Steve being a jerk off would have saved my butt from jail? "I got nothing, Lou," I told him, hanging up the phone. I gave Rachel the good news and had a quick celebration, hugging her.

Unbelievable. It was a load off my mind. The house of cards Georgie had been living in for so long finally crumbled. He was certainly gone for now.

Was this the complete end? Who knew? All I was sure of was that I felt safer than I had the past few weeks. There I laid down, sinking into the bed, sighing in relief. Finally, I didn't have to hide behind a mask, not of happiness, not of coping...I could be myself. It was the release valve I needed for sure.

"What are you up to here, baby?" I asked Rachel, rubbing her back as she got back to her writing. It was finally time to tell her all the details of the day. From the office madness, the snow storm, the darkening train ride, the mysterious man, all of it...I just wanted to talk to her for hours.

"I just thought since you're such an amazing writer, I'd see what I was capable of with my own," she told me. I was so happy to hear that she was inspired with my writing. It made me smile.

While I tried seeing what she was writing, Rachel then dropped her pen and stared straight at the wall. "Is everything okay?" I asked.

All of a sudden, her mood changed. She stopped writing and began taking very deep breaths, closing her eyes and exhaling slowly, holding her stomach.

She kept mentioning she felt woozy and was in a good deal of pain. The contractions intensified and were happening about every five minutes instead of the days and weeks prior where they were spread out in long durations. "I think my water broke!!" she gasped as she held her belly, now screaming. I jumped up, feeling anxious and excited all in one emotion.

Gathering all I could in sight in preparation for the hospital, I was trying to simultaneously calm Rachel down as I was helping her up from the bed.

Down the stairs and through the door, I sped-walked her out of the house and gently put her in the back seat of her car. I was out like a flash once I popped into the driver's seat.

The hospital was four miles away but it took nearly thirty minutes because there was construction on all the roads we took.

Rachel felt every bump in the road. I kept telling her to try and distract herself by taking deep breaths and closing her eyes. She was starting to yell louder. The time was coming. This baby was greeting us today whether we planned it or not.

Once we arrived, they admitted us into a delivery room, with a stunning view outside. Her family arrived shortly after we did; her mom, my mom, Dickie, Amanda, etc.

Several hours passed. She walked, squatted, and lunged around the room in a daze. The pain levels were becoming unbearable for her. She couldn't form words, her vision became blurry and she began to doubt if she'd even be conscious soon. So, she gave in and they provided her with the epidural.

I was emotional wreck. Poor Rachel was confined to a bed. Suddenly the room was filled with close to fifteen nurses and doctors and they were hoisting her into different positions…onto her back, one side, then the other, onto my hands and knees, while their eyes were glued to the monitors.

I remember her at one point looking at her mom, unable to speak, with complete terror coursing through my body. She held her hands and kissed her forehead, whispering that everything would be okay. I came over to do the same. I couldn't wait to meet my new baby.

Her mom then left the room. Rachel had been in labor for close to six hours and was ready to be done. Our doctor instructed me to "grab a leg!" while the nurse took her other one.

The pain was more powerful than anything poor Rachel had ever imagined. It was more than obvious. Nothing could have been this brutal, not whips or chains. The room was only its bed and four walls, the nurses melting into the light, rooting her on to bring life into the world.

I thought to myself, "Is there anything more isolating than intense pain?" I could see it in her eyes and actions the way she was breathing and pushing while many instructed her to keep doing so.

Yet in those moments that came, Junonia was born. Into the world, she said hello to all with her initial cries. It was as if only sunshine existed in the world, as if all the earth was ushered into harmony.

We both looked into those new eyes, a new consciousness, perfect and reaching out for love. In that instant, Rachel and I were well aware that we would do anything to protect our child.

Our love was as vast as the universe yet solid as rock. She was a mother and would always be the best while I would strive to be the greatest of fathers.

Newborn cries filled the room as I burst into tears of relief and joy. I turned my glossy eyes to my wife and in a voice that was almost broken, I told her, "We have a beautiful daughter."

I held her in my arms after cutting her cord, feeling like nothing less than the happiest man in the world. She was gorgeous, precious...everything that was pure and innocent.

In that moment, Junonia intensified her cry to the sweetest tears I'd ever hear, allowing all the pain of moments before to melt away. This little girl was only seconds old and her tiny ways begins to root, mouth wide, instincts strong.

Through Rachel's exhaustion, she smiled...and then quickly lets her eyes shut after. But, she wasn't opening them. It was rather odd. I even went up to her while I held the baby, seeing what was going on.

Something was wrong. She couldn't hear nor see. She wasn't responding to anybody in the room. Her hearts rate blood pressure went down to zero on the monitor. The nurses were instructing for the head doctor to come into the room. I began to panic. "We have an emergency!" yelled the nurse.

I didn't know all that meant or entailed. I kept at it with questions but IV's and more random people were coming into the room. Nobody acknowledged that I was even there anymore. Junonia was taken from me.

It became complete chaos of running around and yelling everywhere. I was forced outside by many who dragged me out while I resisted. "What's going on?" I screamed, tearing up. Still no replies. It was frightening to those who witnessed it.

Rachel wasn't moving. The scene was quite unbelievable, shocking really. My mind was sent reeling, unable to comprehend or process the images. I looked away, then looked back to see if this was still happening. "I love you, baby!!" I shouted before I as removed from the scene.

I waited outside her room for about thirty minutes, pacing back and forth in the same ten foot line. My nerves were worn to the quick. Within my building anxiety, I constructed elaborate justifications for why everything would turn out alright, but still the nagging voice in the back of my mind spoke of nothing but doom ahead.

I then began jumping all over the place in different directions. I could see Dickie, Amanda, my mom, and Rachel's family sitting in the waiting room from afar...but I was anything but still. I was a mess.

In a flash, the nurse came outside exactly at that thirty minute mark. Everybody in the room stood up, but she came to me first...quietly, slowly, and without recourse to anyone else. The face she wore was one that spelled disaster in every direction you saw it.

"Mr. Mulligan...I'm sorry. We lost her. Rachel had an amniotic fluid embolism, which escaped the uterus when her water broke and entered her bloodstream. It went to her heart, which caused her cardiac arrest. She also had internal bleeding. Nothing we could stop as much as we tried," said the nurse. I laughed at first, thinking it was a joke. For whatever reason this young lady thought it would be funny to say such lies was beyond me. "You're fucking with me? My wife is dead?" I asked, still smiling as if this were all malarkey, a bad dream. "There is no way this is true."

"I am afraid so," she replied. I couldn't move. I didn't believe her. I almost wanted to throw the poor girl out the hospital window. This couldn't be...no, no...this was all just so wrong. "She can't die...she promised me a life together forever."

She kept shaking her head sideways. As much as I tried to hold it in, the pain came out like an uproar from my throat in the form of a silent scream.

"She said it to me...she said it...said this was forever." I was panicking, breathing heavy, holding my chest as if it were going to burst.

265

The beads of water started falling down out of my eyes, one after another, without a sign of stopping as I slid my back down the hospital wall onto the ground.

"NOOOOOOO!!!!!! NOOOOOO!!! NOOOO!!!!! THIS ISN'T FAIR!!!!!! AHHHHHH, WHAT THE FUCKKKK!!!"

I remained there for about ten seconds until I turned around, got on my knees and punched the wall three times and would have gone for more if the nurse and other staff members didn't come over and hold me back.

The world turned into a blur, and so did all the sounds. The touch. The smell. My balance. Everything was gone. Everything darkened into nothingness as I passed into the oblivion practically becoming unconscious.

Rachel was dead. I couldn't even say it at the time. How was I supposed to go on? What the fuck was next? I saw Dickie, Amanda, and family members come after me but I ran away. Far, far away. I honestly wanted to jump out of the window and fall onto the street. I wanted to die too.

CHAPTER TWENTY-FOUR

The next week or so is all complete haziness when I reflect back. I wasn't quite sure how I made it through. I still can't tell you how.

I could barely think, let alone be present and fully mindful for the worst day of my life. How was I supposed to sit there for all of the dreary talk and misery? How was I supposed to pretend to give a fuck about anything else and act like a happy widowed father? How was I supposed to say goodbye to my best friend?

I had no faith. I had nothing. God took everything from me, my one and only. A light had been extinguished forever in my heart. There was no person or thing I could have imagined saving me from the fall into the deep dark abyss that stood before me.

But I dealt with it. That morning, I pulled up right at the last moment I could have stretched it to, alone out front of the same church where I said goodbye to my father almost a year prior. The sun brightened intensifying before I exited the limousine. The illustrious color of the winter day under its glare was offensively lively and cheerful. It was as if the skies conspired to show me how the world would go on without her.

At that moment, I felt it shouldn't have. Everything should have been as grey and foggy as my emotions, cold and damp with silent air. But the sky was still blue and the cruel world kept spinning.

I pushed open the front door, skipped the holy water, and walked down the center aisle of the church like a silhouette of myself, wishing I was as insubstantial as the shadows so that my insides may not have felt so mangled. Everyone stared at me in awe, especially her side of the family. As I took the pew in the front left along where Dickie, Amanda and Rachel's parents sat, the long held back tears began to fall slowly from both eyes. However, I made no noises, just quiet sniffles. I sat in my silent grief and awaited the start of the service while the others tried to comfort me and relieve my pain. But I budged none and continued to be as icy as can be.

Once it began, the mass was slower than a country bus, taking just as many detours. Everyone had a memory to share, a favorite hymn to sing. Whoever arranged this thing must have agreed to anything. I didn't know if it was her mom or Amanda, but I wanted nothing to do with either one at the time. I wanted this to end.

I looked over at the pew across from us where my mother held my newborn, silent as falling snow like she had been since her birth. My mom's attempts to smile and comfort me from afar did no justice as I turned my head immediately back towards the mahogany coffin and the two candles on each side of it, center alter.

Closing my eyes while the priest continued talking, I tried to envision our days together, Rachel and I…what was left of happiness: simply the memories. It was so hard considering my weakened status. It was hard to do anything at all.

Every time I tried paying attention, I became more saddened by seeing what was around me. The place was all black clothes and white waxy faces, every one of them with puffed red eyes. The fragrance of frankincense was making me light-headed, enough to vomit everywhere in front of me and around.

That's why when the viewing and mass had finally ended, I took a few deep breaths being glad to stand again. The funeral director came over to escort us all back to the limousines. He wore empathy like his overcoat, just for work. It wasn't that he was a cold person, quite the opposite, but he had to find a way not to be drained by constant grief. Stepping into the daily world of the bereaved, I'm sure wiped him out emotionally. He'd seen more bodies returned to the earth, more souls returned to the Lord, than most people saw sunsets. Today was no different.

As we all gathered from the despondent church towards the windswept graveyard his face was a perfect picture of controlled sadness.

I was envious of him. I wanted to feel that way. I wanted this pain to be gone. I couldn't stand missing her anymore. Why couldn't she just be here?

Yet, I also knew at the same time that this was what I had left of her…the ache of her absence. There was no other choice but to cope. During the drive over to the cemetery, my mom kept nudging for me to hold my little girl, but I kept refusing the gesture. "She needs to be with you right now. She never cries, she can make you happy, Brad," my mom whispered. I shook my head sideways.

Judging from their looks, I could tell Dickie, Amanda, and Rachel's family thought I was crazy refusing to hold my daughter at the time but I began to care less and less. Getting this day over with was simply top of mind.

Along the wide central pathway, the convoy of black limousines was already stationary. There was a crowd of Rachel's family who probably didn't want to see my face. I was the guy who broke her heart sixteen years back, the guy she left her long-term fiancé for, and the guy she had a daughter with and died before meeting…now leaving them with the second and last child of theirs to bury in their lifetime.

Nonetheless, I remained inaudible in my walks. To trot over and hover above her burial site at the graveyard, I had to skirt around a pile of brown frosted leaves, the innumerable flashing fragments that shined in the brilliant wintry light. Ahead the path glistens like white quartz, yet ice crystals on weary concrete is all it is. All this beauty over everything dead. And here I am to add to it with a bunch of pink roses in my hand over my beloved.

I paused as my breath was rising in visible puffs. The many who circled around her casket while the pastor awaited the final moments with the bible in his hand made my chin tremor. Amanda and Dickie came over and held one of my hands each. This time, I didn't fight them.

My body was crumpling, the way I didn't want it to. I wanted to be strong for this day. It was getting harder and harder. Amanda stared straight ahead, out at the trees. Her face was perfectly still and serious. I could see how hard she tried holding it together for everyone, but the bloodshot lines that surrounded the blue of her eyes told me she had teared just as much. She turned her face to look at me, smile and reassure she was there for me as we walked over to the front of the casket.

There will always be a part of me still at Rachel's burial, listening to the hymn, "The Lord is my Shepard." It's the part that refuses to let her go, that piece of me that needed our bond to extend past our mortal life together.

It was at that very moment where I broke down not only in tears, but cries loud enough to wake the dead around me. I was motionless after my attempt to jump into the ground with her. Many knelt beside my sagging hunched-over self, as many as could fit in calming me.

My trembling overwhelmed my breathing as they lowered her casket. I just wanted to die and be with her, right there. But somehow and for some reason, God kept me alive.

We all left shortly after.

Rage boiled deep in my system for the rest of that day, as hot as lava. It churned within, hungry for destruction. It was too much for me to handle. The pressure of this raging sea of anger was forcing me to say things I didn't mean, or to express thoughts I had suppressed for awhile.

I knew I had to get out of everyone's way before I exploded in my manic state. Amanda kept trying to help, but I wanted her to be gone. Even Dickie and my mom. As great as they were, I desired nothing to do with any of them at the time. They were all at my house, pitching in.

Countless amounts of guests popping by sporadically. The gestures were benevolent. It was a great time, just the wrong me.

Especially after opening the day's mail and finding Rachel's full acceptance letter to the job at the Florence University in Italy, I was crushed. They would have taken her in...her dream career was awaiting her.

So many possibilities ahead...all now just flushed down the drain. Nothing left. There I sat, unable to fathom any of it.

All were trying to be supportive. Not saying that my mom wasn't great...she was that listening ear, the one who would wrap me in her love just with her soft face and kind words. She was my number one supporter, my hero.

If I had grown to be half as good as her I would have been proud. Everyone needed a ma like mine, a never depleting repository of love and good feeling combined with a lifetime of experience.

But she was killing me, annoying by all means. She just didn't understand. I wanted to be neglected, completely alone. Amanda was doing the same thing.

Dickie asked me to come into the other room for a moment as I sat in muteness in the living room. Sluggishly, I trotted over to kitchen, following him while huffing and puffing.

"Are you going to be okay when I leave for California in a few months? I'll be going out a few times in-between just to set some things up. You can always call me while I'm away. I just can't stop thinking of how terrible this is. I'm here for you forever, brother."

"Thanks for fuckin' reminding me, Dickie." I was losing it. With Dickie leaving for California, I didn't know what I was going to do. This was terrible...my last true confidant, GONE! It was bad enough losing Harry to the jail cell, but now I had another one going halfway across the country.

The pending tantrum I was about to unleash began with me turning from quiet and regular to a panting gasp. I sucked at the air like it had suddenly become thick and was now almost too difficult to draw in.

I became deaf to the soothing words of all around me. I wanted to smash whatever I could lay my hands on. When I finally exploded, it just ended up being me screaming instead of breaking things.

"I NEED TO BE BY MYSELF!! I WILL HANDLE MY KID!!! RIGHT NOW, EVERYONE NEEDS TO LEAVE ME TO MY LONESOME!!!" I yelled, flipping out on all three of them, bolting out of the kitchen and back into the living room.

The entire house became silent. It was is if mass had just begun. My mom placed my daughter down slowly in her crib and walked backwards slowly. The other stood up in awkward silence and followed my mom out. I didn't say goodbye nor look in their direction. I just sat there...for hours. The clock's hands ticking noises didn't even faze me.

For the first time in my life, I was completely alone...and wanted it that way. I laid in our bed and kept looking around. Among a huddled heap of jeans and coats, I remained unaccompanied and utterly terrified in the midst of what remained of Rachel's possessions. Their manifestation in the darkness consumed my frail form. It made everything worse.

Still, I wanted nobody there…nobody to soothe my fears, nor to tell me her stories. I just wanted it to be me, slowly dying inside.

All of a sudden, things got even eviler. There it sat on our bedroom dresser next to our bed. The last letter she wrote to me. It had my name on it, just the way she left it before we went to the hospital. It was eerie to see…but necessary to look at. I went ahead and opened it up.

My darling Brad,

I love you from the deepest part of my heart. Whenever I am with you I feel the warmth and love that gives me the strength to carry on. You complete me and I am nothing without you. Simply with your touch and love, I feel complete happiness, which cannot be compared, to anything.

That is why I never plan on taking the job in Italy, even if it is offered to me. I applied just for you…but it's not what I want…it isn't home. Our home is here at the shore. No matter what happens. I knew once I saw you again this year, I had to have you as my husband. My only regret is that it took so long to fall back into your arms. For that, I am sorry.

I hope that I am caring enough that you agree to spend the rest of your life with me. Whenever you touch me my soul smiles and desires your love more. I will do anything to make you the happiest person on earth because you are my sweetheart. I wish to be with you always.

I know our daughter is going to be the symbol of our love and we will do everything we can to protect and care for her, together...as long as we both are able to. I can't wait until we meet her.

Your one and only,

Rae

She would've never went. This entire time, she wasn't going to go for her dream job because of me. The welcome letter was meaningless.

All she wanted was me. And I, her. I couldn't stop the tears now at this point. Sweat was beating down from my forehead.

Enough was enough. I threw the letter in anger, stood up from being on the bed, ran down the stairs and dashed out of the house. I bolted out the front door only to look around while my breath became visible every inhale I took. The January air was none too friendly, chilly to the core of the bone.

It was over. I didn't want to live. I was finished with all of it. Continuing running outside, I looked at the ocean once more. "There it'll be…that's where I will kill myself," I whispered alone.

Tears kept slipping down my face. The fifteen degree weather didn't help. It was freezing me. The town was so empty. I was alone.

Forever without help in the vast world I was apart of. She left me. The ship sank, and I was the only survivor of that horrible night. Depression, raw despair…followed me everywhere.

It was still there. I had choices, but they were not logical. Then again, what is? Science? Lies. I still had the scars. External and internal.

All I wanted to do was run away. Run away from the blue abyss that locked them down, and yet, I couldn't. It drew me towards it, day by day. Closer and closer, inch by inch.

It was an idiotic choice, but hey…I'm pretty idiotic for not doing it sooner. I rose to my feet. I walked through the wet sand and towards the sub-zero chilling wintry ocean…my grave.

There was no one there to stop me. I stepped foot into the freezing waves. I hesitated briefly, then continued on. Going…going…going…it was like nails going through my skin but it certainly felt necessary.

I had held my breath in water before. This was like having a gun to my head and being told not to let my heart beat. And just like the heart must go on my lungs will inhale whether it is air or salt water.

In the moment that the coolness rushed in, I knew I am already dead. In moments, I would float like the sea weed, nothing more than flesh and bones ready to decay in the currents.

Water up to my knees…

Then up to my waist...

Then up to my chin…

Then submerging me completely. My lungs were on fire.

It was then I heard more crying. This time, not my own. It was coming all the way from the house. Cries of sorrow, echoing down to the watery grave I was welcoming.

Numb to my feet, I swam back out in a flash, tripping and falling as I got to the sand. She never cried. That kid was always silent. What could have gone wrong? My mom wasn't supposed to come over until nine. Was she early?

Crawling on the sand, I inched my way back to the softer grains. So frozen. So sore. So sandy. Breathy gasps resonated through the beach. Junonia was crying. I had to get to my baby. I began crying myself, getting back on my feet with enough energy to hop back inside. Salty tears mingled with the ocean's strike made it hard to stand. The oncoming tempest I dreaded for sure.

My poor daughter. She was alone, scared and devastated. My heart felt butchered, as if her love was taken away bit by bit, even in these early days of her life. Her shitty father going in to take the coward's way out.

What was I doing? Was I crazy? It was time to be a man...a real dad. I got to the staircase and tripped twice before I regained the strength to open my front door.

Just as I ran in and up to her bedroom, I grabbed my phone and dialed for my mom. I cried along with the baby as if the ferocity between us might bring Rachel back; as if by the sheer force of my grief, the news would be undone. She could not be gone. But she was.

I went over to Junonia and picked her up out of her crib. It didn't even sound like she was pausing long enough to breathe. Surely she'd have to either stop or pass out soon. But the screaming ceased once she was in my hold long enough.

She must have felt calm instantly at my stroke. I rubbed the tears away from both of us with my fingers and started rocking back and forth.

The simple touch sent a wave of butterflies coursing through her veins, their fluttering wings easing the dread that had settled inside her. She saved my life.

Dickie, Amanda, and my mom came barging into the door and immediately over to where I sat on the floor, scooping Junonia from my arms while my tears persisted. I couldn't bare another moment. I felt like I was in my own personal hell. "I let my daughter down," I was telling them in a babbling fashion.

Dickie tried to hold me back, to calm me, even as his own tears fell thick and fast. In my hysteria, I was too strong, too wild. After whirling about, unable to look through my puffy eyes at the photographs on the wall, I tumbled down onto the floor, screaming to my daughter how much I loved her.

I watched her mother go so quickly. It dissolved me in the kind of despair that can take one's mind prisoner and never give it back.

My mom was telling Dickie how the paramedics were arriving as they spoke. "DON'T TAKE ME FROM MY DAUGHTER!!!!" I commanded to them. "DON'T DO IT!!!!" I had lost my mind.

They both continued to try and calm me. The paramedics frustrated themselves in escorting me out in the most civil way they could towards the ambulance vehicle. However, I kept sinking down to my knees in the middle of my steps. I could barely walk. I could barely talk.

The thoughts were accelerating inside my head. I wanted them to slow down so I can breathe but they wouldn't. Gasping, panting. My heart was hammering inside my chest like it belonged to a rabbit running for its skin.

I felt so sick. So far away...blackness...creeping blackness...I ended up on the ground in a ball, the fetal position. Where is my daughter, the stairs are too steep, everything around me is spinning...blackness...gone...

CHAPTER TWENTY-FIVE

My grandma always made it a point to tell me during my younger years that when something precious is left in the sand...it can certainly drift to sea. But with enough time and patience, that treasure can eventually return ashore once again, tenfold of its beauty.

I always thought she was talking about contraband from the gangsters of the Roaring Twenties and what they'd leave on the coast from the bootlegging ships. Perhaps even sea glass...or a message in a bottle, holding all the secret of a foreign world.

Here, she meant throughout time in general. In our daily ways. The decisions we make affect us for a lifetime. The things we let go...if they're dear enough to us, we find a way to help them return when they're ready. Or a way to seek them out and fight to bring them back, even if those things resist at first.

It was so hard to lose Rachel the first time when we were in our twenties. To watch her walk out of my life abruptly put knots in my stomach that afternoon on the beach and for the sixteen years to follow it before I saw her again.

Then trying to win her back took each ounce of strength inside of me. It wasn't easy but it was worth every battle. Every lonely night, every tear on my pillow. Every prayer I made and every chance I took. All the fight I put into it, I don't regret a second.

Then to have her for myself, once and for all. To look forward to the beginning of our lives and all that we were going to share together…it was a set up for paradise. I had so many plans for the future. The next fifty years were going to be as glowing as the sun we'd watch rise often, as well as its setting. At least, this was all the way I envisioned it in my head for the majority of that last year.

Which made what happened, a darker deeper emotion than anyone could imagine. My only request at the exact moment of her passing was that it was me dying instead of her. I wanted to bear her pain. I wanted to handle it all for her and let her live just as beautifully as she did every day.

Saying goodbye for the final time the day of her funeral was one of the worst feelings. I wouldn't wish it on anybody.

Because this time I was truly helpless. This time I couldn't charm. I wouldn't be able to chase her, to woe her, to convince her that she is everything to me. To show her that no matter what, where I'd been, and where I was going next, I wanted to spend every waking moment with her. There was no time left for any of that.

In those last moments of her life, those last beats of her precious heart that echoed ecstatically as she was giving to new life…I reassured that the promise we made, I would always keep. That what we had was incredible, unparalleled to any other romance that ever existed. Passionate, exotic, mysterious, full of burning rings of fire to jump in and out of. She kept me on the edge of my seat, at the same time making me a better man.

My other assertion was that ever since I met her, she was the first thing I thought about waking up as well as the last thing before I'd go to rest. Even in the years of her absence in my life, she was still top of mind. It would always remain that way, especially now.

It was four months into the New Year 2016. I was finally out of the hospital from the monitoring of my heart attacks, completing physical therapy, and getting my life back on track...returning to my house. Sitting there on my back porch as the mid-April gusts kicked in, I reminisced on that ravishing night one year prior when Rachel showed up at my house, out of the blue. The night our daughter was conceived.

The night we escaped from reality and swathed into each other, the lamenting lust that had been building up all that time prior. Magical.

Meanwhile to break my day dream, out to the deck walked Dickie and Amanda along with my mom bringing back to me, my three-month-old little princess. She had just woken up from a nap but was so quiet and behaved per usual. My little darling. She saved my life in more ways than one, particularly that January night. I had missed her the past few days. They had brought her to see me while I was gone. However, making the transition back home it was hard to have her with me in the beginning of the week.

"Grandma loves her little June-bug, doesn't she?" my mom whispered to the baby, holding her ever so gently. "Ahh, don't call her that. Her name is too beautiful to shorten it," I quickly replied, of course chuckling at the same time because it was kind of cute.

Then there was all this racket. This crazy girl could not stop moving. "Here are two days' worth of diapers, wipes and formula. There are instructions I have written for you if you get lost during her sleep and eating schedule, but of course you know to call me. I am only twenty minutes from here," the neurotic nurse Amanda so keenly guided me as she placed a million bags in my study/Junonia's bedroom, pacing back and forth, inside and out of the place.

Yet, I was grateful for her. She worked at the hospital I ended up at and made sure I had top notch care. Without her, I may not have recovered so quickly.

"I think I got it, Mand. But I know even if I don't call you...you'll be blowing my phone up ten times a day anyway to make sure your niece is okay. I know it's not little old me that's the concern," I teasingly told her as she lightly smacked me in the arm. "Shut up," she answered, smiling and then going to converse with my mom who was still holding the baby.

Dickie came over to me as I rose from my chair to give me the longest hug I needed. "Good to see you, brother," he whispered. I was going to miss the guy but couldn't be upset as he was about to graze upon greener pastures for sure. "You're the man. Nobody ever like you," I replied.

Into my arms then came my little love, dear as ever. My mom hated handing her over but I'm sure she was also concurrently relieved after the past few days of her and Amanda together. "Were you able to get any writing done?" my mom asked. "Here and there between the job search," I said. "I am so over this writers' block. There are no excuses, I HAVE to get back and try re-finish these memoirs soon. If only I could remember what I put in the first copy."

She reminded me that great things took time. "Heal first. Live for your daughter. Do well. You're a man of many talents, Bradley," quietly and sincerely Mom advised as she kissed me goodbye. "I will be back at the end of the week after I help with the shelter back home." Dickie gave my mom his final hug. "See you soon again," he told her. She wished him luck with his L.A. endeavors.

Nothing else mattered. It was all about Junonia and my writing now. Fortunately, I had good people around me to help. Without them, I would have lost my mind recently and God only knew what else. To say I was blessed is simply just a piece of my good doings.

"I have to go into the hospital for a twelve hour shift. Talk to you soon," said goofy Amanda as she ran over to kiss me on the cheek. "Believe me, you've done enough. But I know I will be seeing you later," I prompted. She giggled again as she kissed her favorite niece goodbye.

Then the final look between her and Dickie took place. He took her aside and thanked her for everything. "I know we had our close calls...but it was great knowing you and getting to know you again this time around. As we've seen, you never know what can happen later in life," retorted Valentine before she exited. He reached his hand out for a shake but she grinned and came to kiss him on the cheek. "Good luck out there, cowboy," she told him as she tried her hardest to hold back that last tear that fell down her face, giving him a wink.

It was sad seeing us all take different paths, especially knowing what could have been of Dickie and Amanda. Maybe one day in the future. They both needed to explore themselves as well.

Once we were alone and I was able to sit back down with the baby, Dickie pulled a chair over and scooched right next to me to detail me on his mini trip out to Cali in the beginning of the month.

"I already met a girl out there...can you believe that?" he alerted. I was shocked. Dickie settling down was the next craziest thing to me doing it. "Get the fuck out of here," I laughed, as I was quickly reminded not to curse in front of the baby. He assured me that he wasn't playing games. "It's the real deal I think."

We always talked about the next steps in our lives. High school, college, post-college, adulthood. Everything had its time. I was initially upset with Dickie leaving when I first heard he was going to fulfill his California dream, but I knew it's where he belonged. My happiness was truly incumbent on his.

"Well, Richard Valentine. I'm speechless. You get out of here and go to this poor girl that actually decided to date you, would ya? Fulfill that part of yourself in her," I went on. Of course, I was teasing him about the girl being poor. Honestly, I was happy for him. He deserved the world, this guy.

"You going to be okay without me," asked Dickie. I nodded up and down reassuring him that it was all a day at a time. I apologized again for my initial reaction to his move earlier in the year.

Dickie leaned over, put his hand on my shoulder and said to me, "We have no way of knowing the future. We have to take each moment as it comes. Just know…that if all else is false, everything we are taught and each lesson we learn…keep in mind that the ones we love, they come into our lives for a reason and a season. I know this isn't how you had things planned out…but it's happened and you're resilient enough to rise above it. You will find love again and rest assured…your heart will once again have its home. Have faith, Big Poppa!!"

He was right. For a period of time after Rachel passed away, I never thought I would regain that loving feeling again. I wanted out of this world because I thought that would be the only way to recede the heartache.

That was until the first time I held Junonia without crying my eyes out, saddened by the loss of her mother. When I finally sat there…and stared closely at those beautiful, breathtaking and illuminating eyes for the first time assiduously, I knew…all was right.

"Look for love? You kiddin' me?" I had retorted staring straight at him, smiling ear to ear for the first time in months. "My heart is with this beautiful brown-eyed gem. She is just like her mother. She is elegant, free and everything I know. Love…I've already found it, Dickie. Right here."

My old friend smiled as he stood up slowly and nodded his head at me. "That's the answer I was looking for. Because I now have another surprise for you," he replied.

Oh, I couldn't wait to hear this one. Surprises from Dickie were always special. Again, you never knew what he had up his sleeve. "Your memoirs," he began. It was then I reacted, "They're gone. I can't find them."

Smirking heavily and shaking his head sideways, my good friend answered quickly, "They aren't gone. I know where they are." I begged and pleaded for him to tell me where. In awe was not the word.

"The girl I met in Cali. She's also a producer for Universal Studios. She took a few looks at your story the past few months and thought it was amazing. Her and her team will be calling you next week for an offer. They want to turn it into a movie. I mean, they're looking to pay big BIG bucks," he detailed.

Just when I thought this guy was out of ways of shocking me completely, he had did it again. I was speechless. My mouth was wide open. I was so numb, I thought I was going to drop my daughter. Well, not really…but still.

"How the hell did you get a hold of them?" I asked. To my knowledge, my notes were gone and the file was deleted from my laptop.

"Rachel wanted to surprise you. She gave them to me when I first told her about the job. She went in and got your laptop, printed out the story, saved the file to a hard drive…then went ahead to erase them from your computer."

Right as I was about to ask him why she went through the kind of trouble in doing that, he responded, "She wanted you to be so shocked and swept off your feet, that you would have nothing to say. Just like you are now...speechless."

After he gave me two pats on the back, Dickie made his way off the patio, into the house to grab his coat and leave out the front, reassuring me that he would text me when he landed in Los Angeles. "I guess I have a little more to include into the story now," I said, winking at him. "We'll be talking," he replied.

I still couldn't believe it. Even in the midst of her absence, my angel is still working overtime for me. Between her and an amazing friend like Dickie, I felt blessed.

With this new venture ahead, things were finally looking brighter. For the first time in a long time. This was going to amazing...a movie, wow!

Once I was outside alone with my daughter, I looked ahead in blissful silence, at last, while the ocean crashed continuously down. For the first time in a long time, a tear of joy ran down my face.

It always remained beautiful out there, the same tranquil waves her mother and I would gaze at together for that short week in our youth, as well as the past year we had.

Nothing equated to the crisp smell of the salty zephyrs blowing over from the crest of the whitecaps rolling. It was all so nostalgic while I reflected some more, yet I was now confident that new memories were ahead. Certainly with another gorgeous girl, right in front of me.

Like I've said before, life comes down to few special moments…particularly the ones that take our breath away.

Every minute I spent with Rachel was amazing. Felt like the first time…every time we were near each other. I still get butterflies harking on that inaugural night at the Beach Bar, August 28th, 1999.

The only thing I still ruminate on is that I wish I had met her sooner in life and didn't let so much time pass in-between us being with one another again.

Reminiscing on our stints and thinking back while I wear her shell on my neck, I'd give all the riches in the world to have those sixteen years I lost just to be at her side. To kiss her, touch her, feel her, hold her.

Yet I was taught a valuable lesson during all the madness…life isn't always completely fair. It's not always going to be the way we envision it. That's just how it is. Our plans, they change.

Knowing this, I have been able to grow since she's been gone. Because each moment in the day, I am reminded right away, she left me something gorgeous…something so precious, I still can't fully fathom it all quite yet.

Even this very minute in time, I am still learning new things...about love, about being a father, and about living to lead.

I've let the sadness drift out to the sea only to allow happiness to float back on my sand whenever I stare at my daughter.

This is what Rachel would want. I am where she would see me being…immersed in life. Junonia is as flawless as the shell she is named after and exuding the best qualities given by the greatest mother of whom I can't wait to tell her all about. For that, I am the luckiest man there is.

THE END

Proof

Made in the USA
Charleston, SC
24 March 2016